ALSO BY AYELET WALDMAN

FICTION

Love and Treasure

Red Hook Road

Love and Other Impossible Pursuits

Daughter's Keeper

NONFICTION

A Really Good Day: How Microdosing Made a Mega Difference in My Mood, My Marriage, and My Life

Bad Mother: A Chronicle of Maternal Crimes, Minor Calamities, and Occasional Moments of Grace

EDITED BY AYELET WALDMAN

Fight of the Century: Writers Reflect on 100 Years of Landmark ACLU Cases

Kingdom of Olives and Ash: Writers Confront the Occupation

Inside This Place, Not of It: Narratives from Women's Prisons

A PERFECT HAND

A PERFECT HAND

AYELET WALDMAN

ALFRED A. KNOPF NEW YORK 2026

A BORZOI BOOK

FIRST HARDCOVER EDITION PUBLISHED BY ALFRED A. KNOPF 2026

Published by Alfred A. Knopf, a division of Penguin Random House LLC,
1745 Broadway, New York, NY 10019.

Knopf, Borzoi Books, and the colophon are registered trademarks of
Penguin Random House LLC.

Library of Congress Cataloging-in-Publication Data
Names: Waldman, Ayelet, author.
Title: A perfect hand : a novel / Ayelet Waldman.
Description: First hardcover edition. | New York : Alfred A. Knopf, 2026. |
A Borzoi book — Title page verso. |
Identifiers: LCCN 2025005765 | ISBN 9781101875346 (hardcover) |
ISBN 9781101875353 (ebook) | ISBN 9781524712990 (open market)
Subjects: LCGFT: Romance fiction. | Novels. Classification: LCC PS3573.A42124 P47 2026 |
DDC 813/.54—dc23/eng/20250210
LC record available at https://lccn.loc.gov/2025005765

penguinrandomhouse.com | aaknopf.com

Printed in the United States of America
1st Printing

The authorized representative in the EU for product safety and compliance is Penguin Random House Ireland, Morrison Chambers, 32 Nassau Street, Dublin D02 YH68, Ireland, https://eu-contact.penguin.ie.

To Sophie,
whose idea it was

A PERFECT HAND

ONE

The heroine of our story was neither the daughter of a bankrupted gentleman, nor of a dissolute younger son. She had no wellborn ancestor to make her interesting to the discerning reader, nor was she brought up in such penurious circumstances as to be an object of the tenderhearted compassion of a sentimental one. Miss Alice Lockey was the eldest of three daughters and two sons of a tenant farmer on the estate of Bevil Marlecombe, tenth Earl Alderwick, in ——shire. Her father worked the same twelve and a half acres as his father before him, and as his father's father, and as all the Lockeys inked in their dozen generations on the flyleaf of the family Bible. Prior to her marriage, Alice's mother had been happily employed at Marlecombe Park, rising to the rank of upper housemaid, and had encouraged her daughter to follow her example and pursue a career in service, but only until marriage. The daughter's aspirations exceeded the mother's, however, and at the time of our telling, Alice had, by dint of hard work, innate intelligence, a skillful hand with the needle, and a sense of style and color in clothing unusual for a girl of her birth, raised herself to the lofty status of lady's maid to Lady Jemima Alderwick, eldest daughter of Lord and Lady Alderwick. Alice had thus far resisted the temptations of matrimony, preferring to enjoy the fruits of her own labor, or at least that part of it her father returned to her when it was paid to him by the steward at the end of each quarter.

Alice possessed a stature so fine-formed, a bearing so dignified, and features so fair that those prejudiced in favor of the superiority of birth and breeding might have resented these qualities as inappropriate to her station. She had thus learned to dress simply, to maintain a self-effacing expression, and as much as possible to hide her light under the proverbial bushel.

I have described a charming young woman, but no matter her qualities, both physical and of character, I fear my gentle reader might wonder whether a servant, no matter how exemplary, is not beneath her notice and concern. In response, I ask, do not the travails of ladies and lords eventually become wearying to the devotee of novels such as this one? How often can we trouble ourselves with the comings and goings of tiresome young creatures whose sole occupations are taking incessant turns about the room and producing heaps of embroidered silk cushions and painted fire screens? Let us for once immerse ourselves in the narrative of a vigorous young woman, an exemplary servant in a house that boasted no fewer than twenty-two members of this invisible class. A young woman who rose before six, worked without rest the day long, and slept only once her lady was safe abed. For does not such a young woman, despite days full of menial tasks and concerns, nonetheless deserve the joys and agonies of romance? Does she not experience ambition, delight, and sadness, all subjects captivating to you, dear Reader?

Let us begin our story not during Alice's first days at Marlecombe as an under-housemaid, when she learned how to whiten the manor's front step with lime donkey-stone, to carry coal in a heavy scuttle from the basement heap up to the rooms in which the family did their living, to polish grates and beat carpets, and to engage in all the tasks too myriad and dull to take up even one more moment of our time. Let us instead skip to the fifteenth day of the final month of the year of our lord 1879, as the peal of the dressing gong reverberated through Marlecombe Park, and the dozen guests of Lord Alderwick and Lady Alderwick returned to their rooms to dress for dinner. We find Lady Jemima in fine fettle in her room, Alice patiently listening to a tirade of the sort all too typical of her lady.

"Mr. Smythe-Roberts was just about to seat himself next to me on the settee when that insipid Miss Mountjoy positively slithered by me and took the seat herself. I nearly flew at her!"

Alice helped Lady Jemima out of her gown, sniffed her camisole for odors, and checked her petticoats and drawers for stains. The results of her inspection unsatisfactory, she assisted the young lady into a clean pair of drawers, and bundled up the discolored and malodorous undergarments for the laundress. Then she loosened Lady Jemima's corset, and unwound her blond tresses from their simple chignon. Alice took up a jar of pomade of her own concoction—a mixture of palm oil and castor oil, scented with a generous dash of rose water—and smoothed Lady Jemima's hair into place.

"A Eugénie coiffure, this evening?" Alice queried.

Lady Jemima considered. "But with a Grecian plait. And a bow."

"Both?"

"Yes, and ribbons."

"Too much, my lady."

Lady Jemima looked about to object, then shrugged her shoulders. "Just make it look original. You know I must be original, Alice. Always." That Lady Jemima called her abigail by her first name was unusual, and had at first troubled Alice. Once raised to the level of lady's maid Alice had assumed that she would graduate to be known by her surname, as the other personal servants were. But Lady Jemima was used to calling her Alice, and so Alice she remained.

"Yes, ma'am."

Alice, upon assuming her role as Lady Jemima's maid, had sacrificed a month of half-days to a course of study at the London salon of Monsieur Jean-Luc Autié, and she now expertly rolled the young lady's hair into a bandeau coiffure, complete with four smooth loops arranged in a bow at the nape of her neck. She pinned a braided rat she had made from hair harvested from Lady Jemima's brushes and combs around the bow, and decorated it not with ribbons but with a handful of delicate seed pearls, strategically placed where they would catch the candlelight to best effect. Lady Jemima's face she treated with only the lightest dusting of Saunders's roseate face powder, because the girl was so pretty she needed little embellishment, certainly not the red lip salve to which her mother too often resorted.

After that, she relaced Lady Jemima's corset, assisted her into a cotton corset cover and a new pair of delicate silk stockings, then tied the horsehair bustle pad at her waist before helping her step into a petticoat of fine Lyonnais silk. She dressed her in a shimmering satin gown of a pink so pale it looked nearly white, and helped her to pull on a pair of pink silk gloves that daringly reached up over her elbows. Lady Jemima's hands were well formed and strong, shapely in their way, but not the tapered-fingered, blue-veined, and rosy-nailed ideal. Ironically, but for years of rough labor, Alice herself might have had a perfect hand.

Alice then slipped a pair of gold-embroidered kidskin slippers on Lady Jemima's feet. The slippers were the only element of the ensemble with which Alice was not entirely satisfied. She had spent upwards of an hour scrubbing, powdering, and perfuming them, but the delicate young lady's feet had an overpowering odor that took a tremendous amount of Alice's creativity and industry to suppress, and she worried the slippers might yet stink. Shoes that might last Lady Jemima's far more homely and stout sister an entire season needed to be replaced after no more than two or three wearings, and by then their reek was such that Alice could not sell them on, and would not have saved them for herself even if they shared the same size. She passed them to the housemaids, who were glad enough to receive them, though even they winced at their odor.

More than once, Alice had wondered whether the unpleasant stains and stinks lurking beneath Lady Jemima's fetching façade might not be an apt metaphor for the girl's person. Lady Jemima was pretty, even beautiful, and during her first season had been considered among the finest young ladies presented to the Queen. Even three years after that triumph, with the first blush off the rose, she continued to be sought after. She was lively and gay, charming in company, an excellent horsewoman, an accomplished archer, and, unusually, an expert falconer. She was a young lady whose company was much desired, both among the eight and forty families with whom the Alderwicks regularly dined in the country, and among their much more expansive London society. Lady Jemima's character, however, did less honor to her lineaments than one might have hoped. Indulged by a doting father, raised on a pedestal by a vain and shallow mother concerned with appearance to the detriment of temperament, Lady Jemima was coquettish and selfish, imperious and quarrelsome, and too indolent to nurture any innate intelligence she might have possessed.

The finest quality of Lady Jemima's character was her fondness for and loyalty to our heroine, whom she had raised from the position of housemaid directly to that of lady's maid, despite her mother's exhortations that she employ a German girl as was all the rage at the time, a Parisienne like her own maid, or at the very least a girl experienced in the position.

"No gentlewoman would release a decent maid from her service," Lady Jemima had told her mother before her first season, when she had been (*finally,* she grumbled) granted the service of her own maid. "Any maid with 'experience' will inevitably have been sent away for either incompetence or stealing. I won't employ a ninny or a jewel thief. I refuse!"

"Oh, Jemima!" Lady Alderwick murmured. "Why must you answer every suggestion with an opera?"

This conversation had taken place with Alice standing, hands folded, in Lady Alderwick's sitting room. Rather than look at the ladies, she gazed about the place. She had never before been granted access to this sanctum. It was a wildly over-ornamented excrescence, each wall decorated in a different Chinese wallpaper printed with a riot of exotic plants and birds, pagodas presided over by haloed buddhas, aubergine-faced monkeys squatting on crimson petals, and gold leaf enough to adorn all the stupas of the Orient. Carbuncles of Sèvres porcelain figurines crowded the occasional tables, and vast heaps of garish cushions made sitting on the sofas and chairs an impossibility. The predominant hues were rose, salmon, shell, carnation, mauve, fuchsia—every shade of pink, that favorite color of Madame de Pompadour, once mistress of Louis XV, whom Lady Alderwick believed herself to resemble. This fancy was engendered by an article about the infamous Parisienne that Lady Alderwick had read decades previous in *Le Journal des dames et des modes.* Unfortunately, as Lady Alderwick's French was poor, her vision limited, and her reading rudimentary, she mistook the illustration. It was not in fact of Madame de Pompadour but rather of Madame de Pouderoux, an infamous Parisienne murderess, relieved of her head by the guillotine. Interestingly, the anniversary of that diabolical lady's death was the same as Lady Alderwick's birthday, so perhaps the feeling of commonality was not entirely misplaced.

As mother and daughter debated Alice's future, a blush in a hue matching the room stained Alice's cheeks—not, as one would imagine, because of the torment inspired by the cacophony of dreadful taste, but because she was herself as interested in Lady Jemima's petition as was the young lady in employing her.

Lady Alderwick sighed. "Perhaps Lefebvre might be prevailed upon to give her some instruction." She turned to Alice. "Do you speak any French at all?"

"Some, my lady."

Another sigh. A terrible thought struck the countess. "You can *read,* can you not? Oh, that would be too dreadful, Jemima, to have an abigail who can't read."

"I can read, ma'am."

Better than Lady Alderwick, in fact. Alice had been the most sharp witted scholar in her parish school. Amiable and witty in addition to intelligent, Alice was a great favorite of her teacher, the former governess of a great house who had in her retirement founded a small institution dedicated to the tuition of the girls of the parish. Alice had received an excellent education, even learning a serviceable French, Miss Elliott having taught her scholars the basic grammatical rules of the language, as well as a not inconsiderable vocabulary. Alice had furthered her fluency by studying the leather-bound French grammar that was among the small stack of books her teacher had given her as a parting gift when she took up her position at the Park. Whenever she had the opportunity, Alice listened closely to the conversation between Lady Alderwick and her maid, though Jeanette Lefebvre, having grown up on a pig farm in the southern department of Tarn-et-Garonne, was far more fluent in her native dialect than in the pure French her ignorant lady believed her to speak.

Lady Alderwick had collapsed, as she always did, in the face of Lady Jemima's insistence, and Alice had embraced her new position. Every night before bed, she studied—by the light of the stub of candle permitted her by Mrs. Platt, Marlecombe Park's stern but kindly housekeeper—a small volume called *The Duties of a Lady's Maid: With Directions for Conduct, and Numerous Receipts for the Toilette.*

Alice was proud of the speed and efficiency with which she worked, and that evening, Lady Jemima's toilette took her no more than the allotted half-hour between the dressing gong and the expected appearance of the guests in the drawing room. Because of Alice's competence, Lady Jemima was generally among the first ladies to make an appearance downstairs, which she relished, as it allowed her the unimpeded attention of the men in the party.

While Lady Jemima was in the drawing room preening before the assembly, Alice gathered her work and the dirty laundry, and went down to the servants' wing. Downstairs at Marlecombe Park was unusually capacious and comfortable for a manor house of its size. Even the courtyard leading to the servants' entrance was fine, with potted trees and a small herb garden for when Cook might find resort to the kitchen garden, orchards, or greenhouses inconvenient. The servants' hall was a pleasant room, possessing not only a table with sufficient chairs to seat all the indoor servants, but also two upholstered armchairs salvaged from one of Lady Alderwick's not infrequent refurbishings. As Mr. Dale the butler and Mrs. Platt the housekeeper both had their own armchairs in their rooms, those in the hall were available to any upper servant who might desire their comfort.

Into one of these armchairs Alice now settled, pulling toward her the worn yet serviceable embroidered footstool that had been evicted from its place in Lady Alderwick's morning room immediately upon the death of the dowager. Though not displeased to have received it for the comfort of the servants, Mrs. Platt had been disturbed by the callousness with which Lady Alderwick disposed of the product of hours of her mother-in-law's laborious toil. Mrs. Platt had come up in service to the previous Lady Alderwick, and had been far fonder of her than she was of the present countess. Understanding well Mrs. Platt's feelings for her former lady, Alice wiped the dust from her neat little boots with a handkerchief before resting her feet on the stool and settling back in the chair.

She considered the two tasks before her, one much more

pleasant than the other. She should mend the lace on Lady Jemima's chemise, but though she was skilled, sewing was her least favorite of her many duties. Instead, she took from the pocket in her apron a silver paper knife monogrammed with the initials "JEA" ("E" for "Eugenia") and a book bound in chestnut leather with blue marbled papers. Lady Jemima and her sister, Lady Grace (who, regretfully, possessed little of the quality her name promised), had a spinster aunt who took their education more seriously than they did themselves, and who regularly sent them parcels of books. It was Alice's job to cut the pages of Aunt Bennett's gifts preparatory to the unlikely event that Lady Jemima might decide to spend a morning reading, or the more probable possibility that she desired to be *seen* reading by a suitor with a scholarly bent.

Alice, on the other hand, was a quick and eager reader, and though it certainly took her longer to read the books than simply to cut their pages, so far Lady Jemima had not noticed, or if she had, did not care. Alice was just settling into the pleasures of her novel when she found herself distracted by a commotion happening at the other end of the long dining table. Disputatious Mr. Symes, the under-butler, was as usual mixing it up with someone. He was a decidedly unpleasant character, as discourteous to the other servants as he was unctuous to their masters. Today's victim was one of the visiting lady's maids, who had taken the seat he preferred and earned for that minor error a tongue-lashing that would not have been undeserved had she broken a priceless piece of Venetian glass.

To her defense leapt a young man, another visiting servant. He was not what you would, on first glance, call handsome, his features stronger than what is generally admired. But he was tall and fit, and in that not-quite-plain face blazed a pair of gray eyes ringed with a rare and beautiful deep blue. He told Mr. Symes that, as the young maid had vacated the seat immediately upon being apprised of her error, no further remonstrance was required.

Unsurprisingly to those who knew him, Mr. Symes's response to this most mild of censures was ferocious. He snarled, "Speak to me like that again and I'll be sure your lord knows the blot your impudence makes on his household!"

The young man, seemingly unbothered by the volume of Mr. Symes's fury, merely replied, "Sure I'll not need to speak to you at all so long as you don't abuse anyone else."

The young man spoke with spirit, and even if Alice had not loathed Mr. Symes, she would have appreciated the stranger's confident retort.

"Barefaced pup!" Mr. Symes shouted. "I'll have you dismissed!"

"What is going on here?" boomed Mr. Dale from the doorway. The butler was a small man, but despite (or because of) his deficiency of stature, he possessed an imposing and austere demeanor, and a thunderous voice. "I don't know what the rules of Wynstowe Manor are, Mr. Wynstowe," Mr. Dale continued. (At Marlecombe Park, as at most grand houses, visiting maids and valets were referred to by their family's surnames. This made it simple to recall who belonged to whom and saved having to bother learning the names of the many servants who passed through the house.) "But here at Marlecombe Park, the servants don't shout."

"Please forgive me, Mr. Dale," the stranger said.

"It wasn't him who was shouting," Alice said. "It was Mr. Symes. The young man was as civil as he should be."

Mr. Symes glared at her, but she stared back at him until he lowered his eyes.

Mr. Dale said, "If I was in need of your testimony, Miss Lockey, I would have solicited it." He turned back to the quarreling men. "Mr. Symes, is it not time to prepare for service, or have I misread the clock?"

Mr. Symes rose stiffly to his feet and retreated to the butler's pantry, but not without sending another scowl in Alice's direction.

"And you, Mr. Wynstowe? Has Lord Wynstowe not assigned you any tasks that require your attention?"

"I'm fortunate to be at my leisure till his lordship is done for the night," the young man said. "But I'd be happy to help out in any way needed."

Mr. Dale harrumphed. "Servants' meal is at nine-thirty, Mr. Wynstowe. Until then, I trust you will manage to keep from brawling with anyone else."

"Yes, Mr. Dale. I am indeed sorry, sir."

The genuine quality of the young man's apology softened Mr. Dale, and his scowl faded as the bustle and bang from the kitchen interrupted them. He turned to the footmen who had been quietly observing the fracas. "Come, boys. Cook has readied the soup course."

As the seven liveried men, four of the Park and three hired for the duration of the season, followed him out, the gray-eyed young man crossed over to the hearth and eyed the empty chair next to Alice.

"May I?"

She gave a small nod. He settled himself in the chair and smiled at her, flashing a mouth of milk-white teeth. "You're a kind girl, standing up for me like that."

"It wasn't for your sake. It's only that I despise that man."

"Thanks just the same." After a long moment of quiet, he said, "What's that you're reading?"

Alice turned the book's spine so he could see it.

"'*Emma,* by Miss Jane Austen,'" he read aloud.

"Have you read it?"

"No. Are you enjoying it?"

"I am."

"Have you read Mr. Dickens? *David Copperfield*—that's my favorite. Do you know it?"

"I can only read the books my lady's aunt sends her, and either she doesn't consider Mr. Dickens appropriate for ladies or she doesn't care for him herself."

"Oh, he's wonderful. He writes about all sorts of people. Well-to-do and not. People like us, even."

Personally, I don't share the young man's appreciation for Mr. Dickens—not, as you might assume, because I envy the quantity of his book sales, but because of his verbosity. That this logorrhea entertains the masses, I don't dispute. I do not, however, understand why. Still, I recognize that one like our hero (surely you realize by now that this young man has that role in this volume) would no doubt find much to admire in Mr. Dickens.

The young man continued, "It's kind of your lady to let you read her books. Lord Wynstowe wouldn't. He keeps the pages so clean he'd know if I touched one even with my gloves on, so I must buy my own." He put out his hand. "I'm Charlie Wells. Pleased to meet you."

Alice put her hand in his. His ungloved palm was warm and dry. It was callused, though not as rough as her father's, one of the few other male hands she had had occasion to touch.

"Alice Lockey," she said.

"You're lady's maid to the lady of the house?"

"To her daughter. Have you been long in Lord Wynstowe's service?"

"Not so very long."

Charlie's first position in service was as a small boy in the home of a prominent Mancunian merchant and mill owner, Mr. Arthur Stokes. Like Alice, Charlie was a steady, industrious worker, and year by year had procured himself ever better preferment in the house. Finally, when Mr. Stokes was abandoned by his valet, he invited Charlie to step into the role. Charlie remained in that employ through that man's final illness and death. When he realized the end was near, Mr. Stokes, whose feelings toward his servant had grown ever warmer, had written Charlie so fine an attestation of character that after his death Charlie easily found a position as valet to Nigel Deverell, seventh Viscount Wynstowe.

"Have you worked at Marlecombe Park long?" Charlie asked.

"Since I was fifteen."

"It's an awfully fine house."

Marlecombe Park was indeed an impressive country home. Constructed originally in the fifteenth century, it had been enlarged one hundred years later into a classic Tudor courtyard house, with dozens of tall brick chimneys, gabled roofs, and mullioned windows. The previous Lady Alderwick, the present earl's mother, had used her own fortune to impose her Gothic revival imprimatur on the home, adding crenellations, a decorative tower, and any number of carved stone finials and pinnacles. The house now had an asymmetrical, romantic silhouette that, as was that lady's intention, evoked an ancient, if slightly fantastical, English castle. The current Lady Alderwick had reserved her fervor for the interior of the house, which she had sumptuously if incoherently furnished. The walls of the rooms in which the family did their living were covered in flocked velvet paper all but invisible behind dozens if not hundreds of paintings. Where there was not a painting there was a gigantic gilt-framed mirror so that no one could avoid his or her reflection for very long. Multibranched chandeliers dripped with cut glass and prisms, and the floors were covered with Axminster and Wilton carpets upon which were layered Oriental rugs of every kind. Swagged and fringed curtains bobbing with tassels the size of a man's fist covered the windows, and antimacassars of point de gaze and point d'Angleterre lace were draped on the back of every richly upholstered settee, armchair, and button-tufted sofa.

"Have you had opportunity to see many manor houses?" Alice asked.

"Lord Wynstowe pursues as many invitations as possible during the season."

"I have always wanted to see the country," Alice said. "But Lady Jemima prefers the amusements of her father's estate to others. Perhaps once she's married she will visit more." The prospect of travel was one of the things that most excited Alice about her position as lady's maid. She was unlikely on her own ever to have enough money to visit Brighton, let alone the Continent, long a dream of hers, but she hoped that Lady Jemima would one day take her along on a wedding tour of all the cities and countries she had only read about in books.

At that moment, Billy Beane, a local boy newly hired, came rushing into the hall. "Alice!"

"Miss Lockey!" Mrs. Platt reminded him. The villagers with whom Alice had been raised and the lower house servants who knew her from her days among them often forgot to treat her with the respect her current position demanded. It did not trouble Alice overmuch, but the housekeeper insisted on correct terms of address.

"Sorry! Lady Jemima says come up to her room right away. The ninny Mountjoy—" Mrs. Platt sputtered, but the boy was undeterred. “Ma’am said specifically to tell Alice that ‘the ninny Mountjoy’ stepped on her train and tore the ruffle right off.”

The servants laughed, some with more ribaldry than others. As Alice gathered up her book and mending and left the room, Charlie gazed after her.

From the table, an Irish-inflected voice said, “Stand down, son. That one’s too fine a cailin for the likes of you.”

Mr. Cahill, Lord Alderwick’s valet, was nearer fifty than forty, but as hale and vigorous as a man ten years younger. He had been with the house for more than twenty years, since Lord Alderwick had poached him from the Earl of Listowel. Lord Alderwick had not been so close an acquaintance of the Irish earl’s as to be troubled by the crime of servant theft, and had offered Patrick Cahill a substantial increase in salary to abandon Convamore House and his native County Cork in favor of England and Marlecombe Park. Affable and generous with his time and possessions, appreciative of a joke or a piece of harmless gossip, Mr. Cahill was a great favorite in the servants’ hall, even managing on occasion to cause normally severe Mr. Dale to smile.

“Our Miss Lockey has no time for silliness,” he said to Charlie.

“She seems amiable enough to me,” Charlie said.

“Amiable she is. Foolish she’s not. She won’t be impressed by sugar words.” Cahill’s friendly demeanor turned stern. “Best leave her alone.”

Though sociable by nature, Charlie was far more earnest and thoughtful than he might at first blush have seemed, and he wanted to cause no trouble. He turned his armchair over to one of the visiting lady’s maids and came to the table to take his tea. There he noticed Mr. Cahill staring at a gold pocket watch. Mr. Cahill picked the watch up, took it to his ear, and sighed in frustration.

"Is it broken?" Charlie asked.

"Twice I've taken it to the watchmaker. Twice the maggot-headed eejit said he repaired it. And still it doesn't keep time."

"May I look at it?" Charlie asked.

"What do you know of watchmaking?"

"It was my father's profession."

Mr. Cahill passed the watch to Charlie.

"I'll not promise anything," Charlie said. "My father's head might not have been full of maggots, but it was certainly full of liquor, and there was only so much I could glean from him in the best of times. Do you have methylated spirits?"

As Charlie was laying out a bleached cloth on the table, Alice returned to the servants' hall. Having been chastened by Mr. Cahill, Charlie did not look at her, so she resumed her place in the armchair, but she could not keep her eyes on her book. Instead, she watched Charlie disassemble the watch with delicate fingers, place each part in a bath of methylated spirits, and set it to dry on the cloth. There was something about the focus and confidence that he brought to his task that she found both intriguing and appealing, and she was reminded, oddly, of the village blacksmith, who hammered with sure blows at circles of iron, or of her own mother, whose fingers flew at her knitting, creating beautiful mufflers, socks, and sweaters seemingly without effort. Watching a person perform a difficult task with ease inspires admiration, even awe, no matter the undertaking.

Charlie brushed each cleaned part individually with the delicate sable brush he had asked one of the housemaids to fetch. Once the sundry parts and pieces were perfectly clean, he reassembled the watch, wound it, and handed it to Mr. Cahill, who again held it up to his ear.

By now, all the servants in the hall were watching in breathless silence. Even the scullery maids were peeping in from their broom closet of a room.

Mr. Cahill clapped Charlie on the back.

"Well done, my boy!"

The crowd clapped, and though Mrs. Platt hushed it quickly, she nonetheless gave the young man an approving nod.

Only then did Charlie catch Alice's eye and wink. Her cheeks grew warm and pink, and she turned back to her book, though she found she could hardly make sense of what she was reading.

TWO

That night, as Alice brushed Lady Jemima's hair, the young lady gave a breathless account of the evening's activities abovestairs. After successfully ruining Lady Jemima's gown, Caroline Mountjoy had seated herself at the pianoforte for "hours and hours." She stopped only when the card tables were brought in, and then only because Lady Alderwick and the other old ladies told her that they could not hear themselves think over the clamor.

Alice had to suppress a smile at the thought of how Lady Alderwick would have responded if she had heard herself referred to as one of the "old ladies." At forty-two, though she had birthed four children, three of whom survived infancy, Lady Alderwick considered herself far from the age at which she must cede the attention of the room to her daughters. She was, like Lady Jemima, a coquette, and delighted as much as any debutante in simpering and fluttering her fan. Mademoiselle Lefebvre said it was all she could do to keep her lady from wearing a gown of virgin's blush or petal pink. It was hopeless to argue against the favorite color in general, but Mademoiselle Lefebvre did her best to steer Lady Alderwick toward darker shades, like turkey red and morone, more suitable to a woman of a certain age.

"Plus à la mode, madame!" Mademoiselle Lefebvre would insist. *"Moins déclassé,"* she might have added.

"How did you divert yourself whilst the others were at cards, ma'am?" Alice asked. She knew her lady loathed any game that required her to remain fixed to a chair.

"Fortunately, Mr. Thomas Smythe-Roberts announced that he could not be bothered with any card game in which the stakes were insufficient to cause true excitement, so we spent the evening in conversation. He is so droll! I could barely catch my breath for laughing. He is *nothing* like his older brother."

The Hon. Mr. James Smythe-Roberts, heir to his father, third Viscount Harlowe, had a few years before been the object of excitement, even anticipation, in the Alderwick household. Though it cannot be said that he precisely paid court to Lady Jemima, in her first season he had demanded two dances at three different balls, including at the one hosted for her at Lord Alderwick's Mayfair house. He had come to call three times that April, and there had been great hopes for his continued solicitude. However, in May he called but once, and then never again for the rest of the season. It became known that he was paying his exclusive attentions to the daughter of a wealthy marquis, a young lady rumored to have near £100,000. Lady Jemima could not hope to compete with such bounty. She was herself only the daughter of an earl, and worse, the Alderwick estate was entailed, the entirety to be settled on the heir, seven-year-old Lord Alderwick, known to his intolerant sisters as "wretched Dickie." (At the time of our telling this young gentleman was away at school and absent from the house, and thus irrelevant to our story.) Lady Jemima herself would receive £20,000, a not insubstantial portion, but nothing compared with the girl who went on to become the future viscountess. When the viscount's son had stopped calling, Lady Alderwick had been quite beside herself, though Lady Jemima had pretended not to care. The effort she took with her dress for the couple's wedding breakfast, however, proved that she took the insult very seriously indeed.

Examining herself approvingly in the mirror, Lady Jemima had said, "For the rest of his life, when he looks at that long nose and twisted tooth he will think about me in this Italian silk and regret what he might have had if only he had been less greedy."

Sorry or not, the Hon. Mr. James Smythe-Roberts was not at Marlecombe Park this year for the shooting, despite having been invited. His mother begged pardon for his absence by reference to her son's lady once again being in delicate health. In the three years since their wedding, this twisted-toothed matron had borne her lord no fewer than four children, among them a set of male twins, and had, it seemed, no intention of stopping.

Mr. Thomas Smythe-Roberts, however, was newly returned from a long tour of the Continent and had taken his brother's place alongside his parents Lord and Lady Harlowe at Marlecombe Park, much to Lady Jemima's delight. Since his arrival, she had been full of praise for this younger son, extolling his looks, his fine singing voice, the quality of his mount and of his seat, his humor, his firm jaw, the thickness of his mustache, the color of his teeth, the silk and patterns of his waistcoats, the delicacy with which he removed an oyster from its shell. Alice expected at any moment to be treated to a disquisition on the perfect quantity of hair in Mr. Smythe Roberts's nose.

"Mama is being impossible," Lady Jemima said. "For some reason she has taken against him. How can she not like him? He is so very amusing!"

Alice continued brushing the yellow hair, which crackled with static, until she realized that her young lady was waiting for a response.

"I suppose it's because he's a younger son and won't inherit."

"He will get *something*. I'm sure it will be enough."

"Perhaps enough is not enough for Lady Alderwick."

"She keeps pushing me on Lord Wynstowe!" Lady Jemima gave a shudder.

"You don't like him?" This surprised Alice, for when Lord Wynstowe had first appeared he had made a fine impression upon all the ladies, so handsome was he. Lady Alderwick swore he was the very image of the infamous Sir Edward Bulwer-Lytton, with the same piercing eyes, refined nose, and thick waves of hair. She had danced with that now-deceased scoundrel, she reminded her daughter, not once but twice at her first ball, and him a divorced man! Lady Jemima had little patience with her mother's remembrances of youthful glory and dismissed the comparison, claiming Lord Wynstowe to be far more like a young Lord Leighton, with soulful eyes that set her trembling when first she saw him step from the carriage. But now, handsome as he was, this unfortunate young man seemed to have fallen out of favor.

"Oh, he is abominable! He barely speaks, and when he does it is about something so dull I can't keep from yawning. I must keep my fan so constantly in front of my mouth that I have crushed it! Look!"

She rummaged around on her dressing table until she found

her fan, a pretty thing painted with bunches of peonies. It was indeed crushed, one of the sticks bent. Alice would be hard-pressed to repair it herself. She would have to take it to the milliner and see if something could be done.

"He must be very dull indeed," Alice said.

"He does not join the gentlemen in the smoking room at the end of the evening but goes to bed, just as if he were an ancient dowager. He is a member of Papa's club, but I cannot imagine what he does there. He plays neither cards nor billiards, he has no business to conduct. He even refuses to smoke, yet he takes the most vile-smelling snuff. He stinks constantly of camphor! I heard him telling Caroline Mountjoy that it decongests his head. Imagine having a head that must be decongested! She is well suited to him. I am sure they will be very happy." Lady Jemima hesitated for a moment, looking troubled. "Still, he is very fine looking. And they say he has well over fifty thousand pounds a year."

"So much?" Alice said.

"It is likely to be even more. Papa says he has vast sheep stations in New Zealand, and recently discovered yet another seam of coal on his property."

"That will make him very rich indeed."

Lady Jemima shrugged, twisting away from the brush. "What do I care?"

She got into her bed. Alice took the milk jug from where it was keeping warm by the hearth, poured some into a teacup, grated into it a bit of sugar from a small loaf, and handed it to Lady Jemima. The young lady had not lost the childish habit of having a cup of sweet milk before sleep. She drained the cup and handed it back. Then Alice straightened the blankets, smoothed the counterpane, and doused the lamp.

On her way from the family wing toward the servants'

stairs, she came across Charlie in the bachelors' corridor, just leaving the Prince Regent Room, so named because the Prince of Wales was said to have slept there one night on his way to the Bishop's Palace in Wells. The Prince Regent was a pleasant room, though not the finest in Marlecombe Park. That honor went to the Victoria Suite—always left empty just in case, the servants joked, the Queen popped by for the shooting.

Charlie was looking about himself in confusion.

"May I help you find your way, Mr. Wells?" Alice said.

"I'd be grateful."

She led him through a small baize door and up two flights of stairs to the attics, where a long corridor flanked by numbered doors extended the length of the house.

"Men's bedrooms at the far end," she said.

He set off down the hall, and though it was late and she was tired, Alice found herself suddenly unwilling to take her leave from him.

"Is your room comfortable?" she called after him.

"Sorry?" he asked, turning back.

"Do you have everything you need? Is the bed to your liking?"

"Very comfortable. Better than at home."

"Does Lord Wynstowe not keep good servants' quarters?"

"I'm sure he doesn't have the faintest idea of the state of our rooms, but his housekeeper is a termagant who begrudges any penny spent on servants. A horsehair mattress is a positive luxury to me, to be sure."

Though it was an impressively erudite word—a mark of the degree to which Charlie, despite the limitations of his station, had managed to educate himself—"termagant" might have been too kind a description for the woman. Mrs. Sweet's surname was a cruel joke. She worked the lower servants viciously and paid them poorly. The steward fancied himself above the business of the house, and the butler was under her thumb, so the housekeeper's dominion extended even to the male servants. As valet, Charlie was answerable to the master of the house and none other, so he was less subject to her cruelty, but nonetheless he kept out of her way. To avoid the nights of vicious cold or sweltering heat, depending on the season, suffered by the servants in the attic, he made his bed in a cupboard-sized room near his lord's water closet and bathroom. But there was one feature of the typical Wynstowe servant's life that he could not avoid. The food was a horror. Lord Wynstowe suffered from Cook's limited repertoire and minimal skill, but the servants who subsisted on scraps from his table were poorly off indeed. Their dinners consisted of whatever meat the lord had left on his bones, ends of bread, and plates of vegetables and fish reassembled into barely palatable stews or pies. They never had pudding. Fortunately, Lord Wynstowe, like other single men of his caste, spent the autumn at shooting and hunting parties, and so Charlie could generally rely on being well fed when billeted at houses like Marlecombe Park.

"I am sorry for you," Alice said. "Mrs. Platt is strict, but she's not a cruel woman or a skinflint."

"You're lucky, then."

"I suppose I am. Though can a servant really be considered lucky?"

"Pardon?"

"Reverend Garland tells us that our work is service to God, and we have a Christian duty of humility and obedience to the families in whose houses we are employed. But why? Lady Jemima is not more pious, generous, or kind than Sally the scullery maid. What form of godly plan is it that has Sally up to her chilblained elbows in filthy water and Lady Jemima wearing silk dresses, eating fine cakes, occupied by little more than flying her falcons or flirting with gentlemen? Why is one girl more worthy of God's blessing than the other?"

"My goodness, Miss Lockey, but you are a radical."

She flushed. Though her opinions about the lot of the servant class had been germinating in her for no small time, this was the first time she had expressed them aloud. She was not, to be sure, resentful of her work. For most of her life, her path had been clear to her. She would follow in her mother's footsteps and work in the great house until she was ready to marry, learning to scrub and polish and do all the other skills useful even to a farmer's wife. After a few years, she would choose a husband from among the tenants of Marlecombe Park or of one of the nearby estates. If she was fortunate, she might marry a yeoman farmer. She would have children, as many or as few as nature allowed, and she would grow old and die. Her lot was as unquestionable as the air she breathed, as inevitable as the sunrise. For much of her life, it had not occurred to her to question it.

When Lady Jemima took Alice on as lady's maid, another path had opened for her. She determined to stay in this role as long as Lady Jemima tolerated her; ladies preferred their maids to be young, so her years were numbered. After that, she aspired to become a housekeeper in a smaller establishment. Once she married, she and her husband might open a small shop or inn and thus raise themselves in stature, though of course only so far.

But then, one day, Miss Sarah Bennett, Lady Alderwick's spinster sister, had pressed upon Lady Jemima and Lady Grace a pamphlet by one Mrs. Barbara Bodichon titled *A Brief Summary in Plain Language of the Most Important Laws*

Concerning Women; Together with a Few Observations Thereon. With their habitual scorn for their maiden aunt's offerings, the girls had tossed it aside unread, but Alice had taken it and secreted it in her room.

A few days later, at breakfast, Miss Bennett had asked after the pamphlet. Lady Jemima had laughed at her and said, "Oh, silly old Aunt with your pamphlets and books! Of course we did not read it."

At Miss Bennett's request for its return, Lady Jemima said, "Don't be ridiculous. We long ago threw it away."

Miss Bennett's gentle remonstrations had been greeted with another bout of hilarity and teasing about "spinster ladies" and their "manias."

"Poor Aunt Bennett," Lady Grace said. "If only you had found a man to marry you, you would be so much happier."

Miss Bennett said, "Would I? I have often thought that matrimony is like an electric battery, once you join hands you can't let go, however much it hurts; and, as when embarked on a toboggan slide, you must go to the bitter end, however much it bumps."

"What is an electric battery?" Lady Grace asked.

Upon being told of this exchange by a footman, Alice had worried that she might be disciplined for having taken the discarded pamphlet from the floor. It had, the night previous, kept her up far past her bedtime, introducing her to the many regulations that control the lives of the fairer sex. Among the lines that Alice had whispered aloud to herself in the dark of her garret was this one: "A mere five years ago, a married woman had no legal right to any property; not even her clothes, books, and household goods were her own."

Alice looked down at her night-dress of plain linen on which she had indulged herself by embroidering a garland of vines and flowers. How could it be that so recently, had she married, even this, her intimate robe, would be the possession of some husband, who would control her in all ways?

She continued reading: "Even now, any money which she earns can be robbed from her legally by her husband. Unimaginable suffering and privation is caused by the exercise of this right by drunken and bad men." Alice's family had among its acquaintance any number of drunken and bad men who spent all their earnings on whiskey and left their wives and children to borrow and scrape what food they were able. She had seen women pulling their bonnets low to cover the shame of bruises inflicted by their husbands. If this, then, was the lot of women, why did any of them ever marry? she wondered.

Alice came upon an opportunity to return the pamphlet to its rightful owner while on her way to the dressmaker to retrieve a gown Lady Jemima particularly wanted for that evening. She happened upon Miss Bennett on the path to the village and would not have had the temerity to do more than acknowledge the lady with a curtsy had not Miss Bennett commented that as they were walking in the same direction Alice should accompany her.

While they walked, Miss Bennett asked Alice a series of questions. What education had she received? What did she like to do during her half-days? When she inquired whether Alice enjoyed reading, the young woman screwed up her courage and admitted that she had borrowed Lady Jemima's copy of Mrs. Bodichon's pamphlet and found it very interesting indeed. She had it in her room, she said, and would bring it to the lady as soon as they returned home. Far from being annoyed, Miss Bennett was delighted.

"You must keep it! I am so very glad you read it. It was foolish of me to expect my nieces to. They are especially silly young ladies." At Alice's expression, she continued: "Oh, come, my dear. You are clever enough to know them to be just what they are."

Alice had not dared to acquiesce, though she did agree.

"They and their mother so frequently express the loudest pity for me. 'Poor Aunt Sarah, a tragic spinster.' Could I be blamed for offering a secondhand defense of my circumstance? Upon his death, my father settled on me enough for me to live comfortably if modestly, and it is my great blessing that I need not hand my fortune over to any husband. I believe myself to be more liberated and contented than my sister. What do you think of that?"

"I think I should like to be a lady living quite comfortably in liberation and contentment."

For a moment Alice thought she had gone too far, but a bark of laughter had issued from her companion.

"You are indeed a clever girl."

From then on, when Miss Bennett visited, she would occasionally slip to Alice a pamphlet she thought might be of interest to her. In these writings, Alice learned that there were philosophers and lecturers in the world who did not agree with the dictates and assumptions upon which she had been raised. Some argued that a man's (and indeed a woman's) situation in life should not be immutable, and that the upper classes are, as Alice had just posited to Charlie, no more deserving than the masses. Often Alice lay abed pondering the injustices described in these pamphlets, a world and a God that awarded some with a life of idleness, and others one of unremitting toil. But she had never shared these thoughts with anyone, not even the lady who had provided her such an education.

Charlie looked at her now with even more interest than

he had before, but Alice, pink to her ears, muttered a quick "Good night" and rushed off to her room. She closed her door, leaned back against it, and tried to take a breath, but her corset left her gasping. What if Charlie told his lord of her reformist tendencies? She would lose her place without a reference with which to find another! Disaster. Utter disaster.

"No matter," she whispered, trying to reassure herself. Charlie Wells would be gone soon enough, and with any luck she would never see him again.

Need I tell my reader that that wish was in vain?

THREE

Alice stayed clear of the bachelors' corridor where Lord Wynstowe's valet would most often be found, sat as far as possible from Charlie at meals, and begged off from pudding with the other upper servants in the housekeeper's room after dinner, but she could hide only so long. Eventually, one morning, she pushed open the door to the boot room, her arms laden, to find the object of her avoidance at the worktable, blacking a pair of shoes. He rushed to relieve her of her burden, and they ended up in a ridiculous tug of war, which ended, inevitably, with the contents of Alice's arms knocked to the floor.

"Oh goodness!" she cried in irritation, but Charlie had already knelt down to gather up Lady Jemima's muddy boots, stained slippers, and dusty shoes. He set them on a boot tray and returned to his own work.

For a few minutes, they toiled side by side in silence. Lord Wynstowe believed that, though a small serving of bracing country air was necessary for his good health, too much of a good thing was liable to result in a catarrh, so he went outdoors only to take a short morning walk; thus Charlie had very little mud to scrape, and was finished nearly before Alice started.

"May I take care of the boots for you?" he asked.

"No need."

"Give them to me, please. Otherwise, I'll have no more work to do and will have to go to the servants' hall and be in the company of your odious Mr. Symes. It is within your power to spare me, Miss Lockey. Shouldn't you?"

Alice could not help but smile, and after a moment's deliberation, she handed him Lady Jemima's riding boots.

He wrinkled his nose. "My goodness," he said.

"Do you regret your offer?"

"Not even a little." He began scraping away the horse manure from the soles. "I think you are avoiding me because the other night you spoke freely, and you don't know me well enough to know that I would never reveal your confidences to those who would judge them ill."

She glanced over at the door to make sure no other servant was entering. "I hope that's true, Mr. Wells. It would be as much as my job is worth for anyone to know what I said."

"You can trust me. I've never been one for telling tales."

"All servants gossip."

"Not I."

She did not respond, only scrubbed vigorously at a stain on the sole of a slipper.

After a moment he said, "Your book. Did you finish it?"

"My book?"

"*Emma,* by Miss Jane Austen."

"Oh. Yes, I did."

"Did you enjoy it?"

"Not very much."

"Oh no? Why not? What was it about?"

"A silly young lady who fancies herself a matchmaker and causes no end of mischief."

"The couples she matches don't love each other?"

"She tries to push a lowborn lady on a conceited man, which goes as you might imagine it would."

"Matchmaking is a perilous endeavor. I have seen many a lady push her daughters on Lord Wynstowe. He pays about as much attention as he would to a fly buzzing around his face. He might swat at them occasionally, but mostly he ignores them."

"Does he not want to marry?"

"He has never mentioned such an inclination."

With Lady Jemima's boots now clean and shiny, he took a pair of outdoor shoes from Alice's pile. This time she did not object. Instead, she recited:

" 'It is a truth universally acknowledged, that a single man in possession of a good fortune, must be in want of a wife.' "

"Beg pardon?"

"It's the first line of another of Miss Austen's novels. Gentlemen must marry, mustn't they? In order to father a son and heir?"

"Lord Wynstowe's mother and father are both dead, he has no relative other than a cousin in India, so there's no one to force him to marry or to be concerned if he puts it off."

"Doesn't he tire of his own company?"

"He keeps very busy. He is writing a physiognomic history of the Wynstowe family."

"What is that?"

"Lord Wynstowe believes a person's character can be assessed by the features and contours of his face. You might be surprised to know that he's discovered that the Wynstowes all have uniquely wonderful faces, the most remarkable faces in all of Britain. Perhaps the world. All of which he has evaluated based on the portrait gallery."

"He is a handsome man," Alice allowed. "And your face, Mr. Wells? What does Lord Wynstowe think of it?"

"My face doesn't warrant analysis, Miss Lockey. Yours, on the other hand . . ." He stepped back and squinted at her, waving his hands about. "Your face appears physiognomically superior, though to be perfectly sure I'd best go get my lord's measuring tools. It's so hard to make an assessment without accurate measurements."

"Are you being cheeky?"

"I'm being scientific. You must also let me measure your hands, Miss Lockey, for Lord Wynstowe is also very interested in them, specifically the ratio between the second and fourth digits."

Alice laughed. "Now you're just being silly."

"I'm not! Surely you know that the longer a ring finger is, the more masculine its owner?"

He reached for her hand as if to assess that crucial ratio, but at that moment, the door of the boot room opened and the tiny French maid belonging to Miss Caroline Mountjoy, the one who had earned a tongue-lashing from Mr. Symes, came in carrying a pile of dancing slippers.

"Regarde ça!" she hissed. "All of the roses of the shoes crushed! *Cette fille est un buffle!*"

Charlie raised his eyebrow at Alice.

"A buffalo, I think," Alice said.

"*Oui, oui!* A buffalo! Big and fat and stepping on herself. Also, she is full of hair. Her arms, her legs! *Et sa toison!*" She shuddered.

"With your permission I won't translate that last word," Alice said.

"Best not," Charlie replied.

After helping their employers change for the afternoon, Alice and Charlie, as if they had planned it, ran into each other on the tradesmen's drive at the back of the house. She wore a wool shawl over her dress, but he seemed not to feel the bite of winter in the air.

"You're on your way to the village?" he asked, falling in beside her.

"Yes. You as well?"

"Aye. Do you have an errand for your lady?"

"Do you imagine my lady would otherwise permit me to wander about in the middle of the day?"

"Is she tyrannical?"

Alice laughed, the answer too obvious to bother with. "And you? Why are you going to the village?"

"Lord Wynstowe suffers terribly from piles, and Lord Alderwick recommended a remedy produced by the local apothecary."

"Lord Wynstowe and Lord Alderwick had a conversation about *piles*?"

"They did."

"And to think *we* are meant to be the ruder class."

"Miss Lockey, if you had fifty thousand pounds a year, you, too, could stand before the party and discuss the state of your—"

"Don't!"

He laughed. "I was only going to say your dress. Or hair. Or shoes. All of which are very nicely turned out."

"You are free with the compliments, aren't you?"

"Only when they are deserved."

By now they had walked the length of the long tradesmen's drive and passed through the stone gates to the road leading to Barton, the village closest to Marlecombe Park. They waited a moment as a wagon pulled by two massive shire horses trundled by, their harnesses jingling. Alice twitched her dress to rid it of the dust the mighty beasts kicked up.

"If you're not afraid for your boots," she said, "there is a path from Marlecombe Park to the village. It's a bit muddy, and will cost us a few minutes, but it's pretty, and we won't have to contend with wagons or coaches. Do you have the time?"

Charlie might have answered, "Time in your company is all that I desire," but he had already surprised himself with his forwardness. He was no swell used to making love. On the contrary, he had managed for the entirety of his adult life to resist the advances of any number of housemaids and farm girls. He was no Social Purist saving himself for marriage, but neither was he a cad. Though half the young men of his acquaintance had caused girls to need to let out the seams of their dresses before their wedding day, he had no interest in risking either a trip to the altar or the cruelty of abandoning a girl with child.

Charlie liked this Alice Lockey more than any girl he had met before now, but his tenure at Marlecombe Park would likely be no more than a few days. Lord Wynstowe, uninterested in the typical occupations of a country manor, inevitably wore out his welcome more quickly than most. If the master of the house was himself interested in the topics of conversation on which Lord Wynstowe fancied himself an expert (the aforementioned physiognomy, Dr. John Snow's investigations into the source of the cholera, the precise chemical composition of the London fog and its effect on the lung, and, most important, the condition of Lord Wynstowe's own gut and bowel and the resulting effect on the frequency and quality of his evacuations), and the lady of the house generous with her larder, he and Charlie might be in residence for some weeks. But Charlie could tell by the rising of Lord Wynstowe's anxiety that he felt himself growing unwelcome at Marlecombe Park, and so Charlie feared that soon enough they would be on their way.

The path between Marlecombe Park and Barton was indeed lovely, featuring meadows that even in winter retained a few flowers, the memory of golden pastures, and the nutty, sweet scents of alfalfa and clover. Charlie helped Alice over a stile into a field dotted with bright-purple Michaelmas daisies and red-and-orange helenium. He bent down, gathered a handful of flowers, twisted a blade of grass to bind them into a posy, and, with a flourish and a bow, handed it to Alice. She blushed but tucked it into her waist. They walked on.

Along the way, he asked her to tell him about her life on the estate, and, surprised at her own volubility, she found herself recounting in detail her childhood spent playing in the meadows and woodland, troubling the pigs in their sties and the horses in the pasture, wading the streams, gathering blackberries and gooseberries, being scolded by her mother when she returned with an empty tin and a juice-stained face. She did not tell him of the endless toil of her mother's house. She did not lie, exactly, but no young man desired to know details of scrubbing the privy, hanging laundry, scouring tables, minding younger sisters and brothers. And she herself preferred to talk of the joy of play and of school, of sitting still of a morning listening to Miss Elliott read from *Peter Parley's Tales* or *Rollo in Scotland*.

As Charlie listened, he grew wistful. His own childhood

had been anything but bucolic. As a boy, he played not in meadows but on cobblestone streets, dodging carriage wheels and slipping in horses' muck and other filth even worse to contemplate.

Too soon, they reached the first cottages of the village, and Charlie courteously stepped away from Alice, in order not to present a picture of intimacy that would inspire disapproval and induce gossip. They parted at the door to the milliner's, and Charlie went on to the apothecary.

Alice waited at the polished oak counter, looking about her at the cascade of fabrics, the display cases filled with a profusion of hats, bonnets, and headpieces in an array of vibrant hues, the piles of feathers, ribbons, lace, and silk flowers. She wished she could make herself pretty by these fripperies, but she could afford few. A ribbon or two. A length of lace. Not a bonnet entire. Many of the items in the shop cost more than her wages for a month or even a year.

And yet, when she glanced at herself in one of the large gilded mirrors decorating the shop, she was not displeased at what she saw. She was dressed simply, as usual, but not poorly. Her bonnet she had trimmed with bits and pieces left over from one she had made for Lady Jemima, and it looked very well, setting off as it did her eyes and her hair. She did her best with what she could afford, and that was no small accomplishment. She hoped—no, she knew—that young Charlie Wells had noticed.

She made quick work of her purchases, and stepped out of the store and into the road, only to have to jump out of the way of a passing coach. It was Marlecombe Park's own, and the coachman pulled up the horses and called down to her, "Miss Lockey, climb up on the boot seat! I'll give you a ride up t'the house!"

Alice looked round, hoping to see Charlie, but he was not to be found, and it would not do to be seen loitering in town. She clambered up to the small seat at the back of the coach and held on tightly as the coachman flicked the horses with his whip. From her vista up high, she spied Charlie on his way back to the milliner's shop. He noticed her, too, and raised his hand. She wished that she had waited just a few minutes longer, so that they could have resumed their tête-à-tête. As she watched his figure grow smaller in the distance, Alice took the wilting bouquet from her waist and bent her nose toward it, inhaling the spiced apricot scent of the Michaelmas daisies. She hoped Lord Wynstowe would stay for the rest of the shooting season.

FOUR

At Marlecombe Park the servants' ball was held on Boxing Day, a tradition dating back centuries to the time of Sir Thomas Marlecombe, a knight of modest standing whose courage on the battlefield at the Battle of Crécy earned him the title of Earl of Alderwyck (as it then was styled) along with the estate, the park of which alone covered nearly a thousand acres, with tenant farms and woodland holdings extending the family's influence across five parishes. The servants themselves might have preferred that they be permitted to celebrate on Twelfth Night as was customary in some other country manors, as that would have allowed them time to recover from their grueling Christmas labors, but this was not in keeping with tradition, and so Cook and her kitchen and scullery maids worked through the night cleaning up from the family's dinner and then preparing the feast Lord Alderwick so generously provided for the servants and tenants of the estate, and the tradesmen of the village.

The ball was held not in the ballroom, its crystal chandeliers, large windows, ornate gilding, elaborate plasterwork, and sprung floor ideal for dancing deemed unnecessary for an event that, though important, was not felt to justify that level of luxury. The medieval Great Hall, a large space with a hammer-beam roof and a vast hearth, would do quite well enough. The housemaids decorated the hall with garlands of holly and laurel gathered from the estate woods, so many candles that Mrs. Platt worried that they might set the place ablaze, and paper chains they wove from colored sugar paper and scraps of the wrappings from the family's presents. Tables were laid with a repast of game and mince pies, sides of mutton and beef, slabs of cheese and loaves of bread, bowls of buttered carrots, peas, cabbage, and potatoes, and, in pride of place, a giant roast goose, the contribution of Mr. Fellows, the butcher. The tenants' wives brought tarts of apple, plum, and gooseberry, each competing with the others in the intricacy of their decorative pastry work. Alice's mother's offering was a berry tart from her preserves, crowned with a munificently petaled rose and dusted with castor sugar.

Alice was exclaiming over her mother's handiwork when she spotted Charlie standing in the arched doorway and looking about him as if in awe. She kissed her mother on the cheek and made her way circuitously through the crowd, paying respects as she went as if this mingling were her goal, and Charlie not her ultimate destination. When she reached his side a smile lit up his face.

"All this for the servants!" he exclaimed.

"Do you not have a ball at Wynstowe Manor?"

"Mrs. Sweet would sooner dine at Lord Wynstowe's table than waste such victuals, time, and money on us. On Twelfth Night Cook serves a meal slightly more generous if no better tasting than usual, and the butler sometimes allows us to clear a space for some half-hearted dancing. This . . ." He looked around. "This is *wonderful*!"

"We look forward to it all the year," Alice said.

At that moment Lord and Lady Alderwick made their entrance, Lady Jemima and Lady Grace following in their wake. The servants cheered lustily as Lord Alderwick nodded at the footman, coachman, and blacksmith, who, along with a pub musician on violin, constituted the band. They launched into a sprightly version of Sir Roger de Coverley, and Lord Alderwick held out a gloved hand to Mrs. Platt. He led her onto the dance floor, accompanied by Mr. Dale with Lady Alderwick on his arm. Lady Grace hung back, but Mr. Symes stepped to Lady Jemima, bowed with a flourish, and offered his arm; she had no choice but to take it. Once those couples took their places at the tops of the rows, the servants and townspeople joined them. Charlie turned to Alice.

"If you're willing to show me where to put my feet and to tolerate me stomping on yours, I'd be honored to be your partner."

Lord Alderwick, as evidenced by the hint of a sneer on his lips, disliked to dance, and so weaved, bowed, and circled with a stiffness that might perhaps have been justified had he been pierced tail to skull by one of the family swords that were mounted on the walls of the Great Hall. Lady Jemima suffered Mr. Symes with only the bare minimum of civility, but Lady Alderwick, to her credit, seemed genuinely to enjoy the country dance, perhaps because she so rarely had opportunity to whirl about a dance floor. That their lady was so unusually cheerful was infectious. The music, if inexpertly played, was lively, and every one of the dancers had a terrifically good time.

Alice would have liked to spend the night dancing only

with Charlie, but to do so would have caused gossip. Instead, she spread her attentions as widely as she could tolerate, which was perhaps not as widely as she should have. She claimed to be footsore when Mr. Symes demanded her hand, though was the next minute out with Charlie for the College Hornpipe. She allowed Mr. Dale to steer her through a stately and sedate Duke of Kent's Waltz, resisting the temptation throughout to gaze longingly at Charlie, who was dancing with Mademoiselle Lefebvre. The French girl was enjoying herself in Charlie's arms altogether too much for Alice's taste. Fortunately, the next waltz, the Soldier's Joy, was Alice's, as was the reel afterward.

When it was time for the upper servants to retire and leave the others to enjoy the rest of the night, Alice for the first time regretted her elevation. How she would have loved another hour or two or three of Charlie's touch!

FIVE

Though Lord Wynstowe was not so entirely obtuse that he failed to recognize the distaste with which the young lady for whose sake he had been invited to Marlecombe Park held him, he would nonetheless have been content to enjoy for some weeks longer the excellent dinners and generous breakfasts, the fine wines and quality spirits, the delicate cakes that were served at teatime, the delectable shortbread that filled his biscuit box. To his great disappointment, however, this was not to be.

A few days after the Boxing Day servants' ball, the various valets and lady's maids were gathered in the servants' hall, enjoying pleasantly strong cups of Ceylon tea. For many of the visitors, including Charlie, tea brewed from actual leaves was a rare treat. At home, they had to satisfy themselves with the sweepings at the bottom of the family's tea packages. Some were not even allowed that, and reused the steeped leaves from upstairs. Now they drank their tea and ate Cook's biscuits (ones baked especially for them, not broken ones unsuitable for the family!). Some of the servants were occupied with mending or polishing; others were taking their leisure, reading Lord Alderwick's cast-off newspapers or playing Patience, one of the few card games Mrs. Platt permitted in the servants' hall. Alice and Charlie sat side by side in silence, Alice replacing the worn silk laces of an hourglass corset and Charlie polishing the crystal of Lord Wynstowe's watch.

Had one of the servants looked under the table, they would have seen Charlie's boot resting against Alice's dainty foot in its sturdy shoe. Though the two barely touched, the electric current flowing between them was sufficient to raise a flush on the back of Charlie's neck and cause Alice's breath to come a hair's breadth faster than normal, causing her to feel faint. Fortunately, these signs of their perturbation were indiscernible by their companions, with the exception of Mr. Cahill, who glanced their way with rising concern.

The servants' peace was disturbed when Billy came crashing down the stairs. He tumbled into the scullery, set the silver cake-tray he was carrying down with a clatter, and rushed into the hall.

"Tha'll not believe what's happened up above!" he said.

"Calm yourself, lad," Mr. Cahill said.

"The lady's given Lord Wynstowe his marchin' orders!"

It had to do, Billy said, with Cook's famous raspberry sponge, made with her own jam and Bavarian cream from a recipe she finagled from the chef to the Envoy Extraordinary and Minister Plenipotentiary of the Bavarian Legation, with whom she was rumored to be having a romance.

"When Lord Wynstowe clapped eyes on the sponge, he legged it 'cross the room quicker than a rat up a drainpipe."

"Billy boy, careful now," Mr. Cahill said. "You'll frighten the ladies with talk of rats and suchlike."

But Billy, enjoying his moment in the limelight, continued to recount the scene with great relish.

Lady Alderwick had given Lord Wynstowe "a terrible scowl," growing ever more annoyed as the man scraped his plate clean not once, nor even twice, but a full three times. Finally, she had said to him, "You seem positively famished, Lord Wynstowe. Shall I ask Cook to prepare you a sandwich? Mutton, perhaps? Or she might have some tongue left over from last night's servants' dinner?"

Lord Wynstowe's smile of enjoyment faded.

Lady Alderwick let loose a simpering laugh. "Oh, I jest, sir! I delight in a man who enjoys his food, don't I, Lord Alderwick?" she called to her husband.

Lord Alderwick glanced over, raised a brow, and then returned to his perusal of the view from the drawing-room window. All conversation between Lord Alderwick and Lady Alderwick passed in this way. She called out something at him, generally from across the room; he looked her way in annoyance or boredom, as the occasion warranted; then he returned to whatever occupation she had interrupted. I believe I do not err when I say that the man had not uttered a single word to his wife in twenty years. This suited both tolerably well, Lord Alderwick because he could not abide the mother of his three children, and Lady Alderwick because it was easy enough to interpret silence as agreement.

Among the servants, only Alice anticipated what was to happen next, for Lady Jemima had that morning confided in her maid her plan to rid herself of the annoyance of the gentleman's company. "I simply cannot tolerate him for a moment more," she had said. "And Mama won't stop!" She adopted a fair simulacrum of her mother's treacly simper;

" 'Is not he handsome, Jemima! Does he not have a fine form?' "

"Do not some call him handsome?" Alice asked. She might have asked, "Did you not yourself say that you found him so?"

"I suppose some might do, but he has a very large nose. And his lips!" Lady Jemima shuddered. "They are redder than a girl's and wet with spit. When he eats, he dabbles his fingers in his food and sucks them most abominably. One cannot help but stare at his long red tongue darting in and out; it gives one the most horrible sensation!"

"That does sound most awful."

"And yet Mama treats every moment that I spend in Mr. Smythe-Roberts's company as an impediment to her scheme, no matter that he is so amiable and his birth more than adequate. But I have had a burst of inspiration! I will tell Mama that Lord Wynstowe's mother was the daughter of a merchant who earned his fortune in the opium trade!"

"She was?"

"Of course not. The lady's father was a gentleman, a baronet, who owned perfectly respectable plantations in the West Indies and was very well compensated for the liberation of his slaves. Her family's fortune was properly and worthily earned, and by all accounts Lord Wynstowe's grandfather's character was of the most unshaken integrity. But Mama does not know that. It is not as if she spends her days poring over *Debrett's*. She will believe what I tell her. She always does."

As Lady Jemima anticipated, Lady Alderwick was suitably horrified by this revelation and immediately determined to expel the pretender from their company. Now, in the face of his gluttony, she had the perfect excuse. She said, "We are all so very sorry you must leave us, Lord Wynstowe."

Lord Wynstowe looked befuddled, for he certainly had no such plan.

She continued, cheerfully, "We will regret the loss of your company most painfully." Again she called across the room. "Will we not, Lord Alderwick? Will we not regret the loss of Lord Wynstowe's company?"

Lord Alderwick turned from his window, bowed stiffly to his guest, and turned away once again.

"I shall tell Coachman he must be ready tomorrow to take you to the station. The barouche is entirely at your disposal. Or perhaps we can prevail upon Mr. Smythe-Roberts to take you in his father's phaeton! Would you like that? You do not have one of your own, if I am not mistaken, or do you? Do you keep a phaeton, Lord Wynstowe?"

"I do not."

"Oh, that *is* a shame."

"At Wynstowe Manor I make do with a coach and a landau. I see no need for any other conveyance."

"Then it will be a treat for you! Mr. Smythe-Roberts! Oh, Mr. Smythe-Roberts!"

The young man turned to her with an easy smile on his face. "Madam?"

"Will you do Lord Wynstowe the honor of conveying him to the station in your phaeton?"

"Of course. When would you like to go, my good man?"

Stiffly, Lord Wynstowe got to his feet. "Don't trouble yourself, sir." He bowed to Lady Alderwick. "If you would be so kind, please tell your coachman I shall take the first train tomorrow morning."

"Of course, Lord Wynstowe. And we wish you the most comfortable journey. Do we not, Lord Alderwick? Lord Alderwick! I say, do we not wish Lord Wynstowe a comfortable journey?"

This time, Lord Alderwick did not bother even to turn.

The jangle of the Prince Regent Room bell interrupted Billy's tale.

"Your lord wants you, Mr. Wynstowe," Mrs. Platt said. "You'd best go quick as a flash, before he comes down here to rouse you himself."

By the time Alice had finished dressing her lady and come down to breakfast next morning, Charlie Wells was gone. Gloomily, she sat at the table, stirring milk into her porridge and indulging in resentment at how a servant's life was so utterly out of his or her own hands, dependent on the needs and whims of his or her employer.

"Come now, lassie," Mr. Cahill said quietly. "No point in an admirer who lives so far. As comely as you are, you'll have your pick."

"I don't know what you're talking about," Alice said. She took up her spoon, shoveled a scoop of porridge into her mouth, and swallowed. Either the mouthful was too large or her distress too great, for she ended having a coughing fit that caused her to clap her hands over her mouth and run from the room.

By the time she had collapsed onto her bed, she was in a fit of tears that would have done Lady Jemima proud, but after a few moments, she swallowed her last sob, wiped her face with her flannel, and stood up. As she was adjusting her corset and straightening her dress, she saw on the floor a folded note that in her distress she had failed to notice. It was from Charlie, scrawled quickly on a scrap of wrapping paper.

Dear Miss Lockey . . .

He used the word "Dear"! She supposed she should be shocked by the impropriety, but she was not. On the contrary, she delighted in it.

We travel today to London and will remain there through the week. Is it impossible to imagine that you might contrive a reason to visit London? Could we meet in the Zoological Gardens in Regent's Park on Saturday? Despite knowing that it is unlikely, I will nonetheless wait for you at two in the afternoon by the giraffe house. You can't miss them. They are very tall.

Ever yours. Charlie Wells

P.S. Please bring a small pot of cold cream with you.

Ever hers. She pressed the letter to her bosom. Ever hers.

SIX

Though Alice had initially despaired of coming up with an excuse for an errand so unusual as to take her to London, Lady Jemima provided her one by complaining vociferously about the state of her favorite fan, which she had been forced, she reminded Alice, to "crumple in fury" in response to the tedium of Lord Wynstowe's presence.

"I bought it in London!" Lady Jemima said with fury. "I won't be able to find another like it in the village."

"I would gladly go to London to the fan maker," Alice said. "If I could take my half-day on Saturday instead of Sunday this week, you could have it right away. Would my lady like that?"

"Oh, that's a fine idea," Lady Jemima said. "I'll want you on Sunday anyway, because I thought I would wear my plum silk faille gown that evening and it has one hundred buttons that only you can manage."

Thirty-seven buttons, Alice thought, but of course did not say.

The following Saturday, Alice rushed through her morning

work and then ran up to her room. She put on her best dress, a cast-off of Lady Jemima's. It was of wool in an eye-catching verdigris, with a pinched waist and pleated skirt. Her silklined pelisse was also one of her lady's discards, and complemented rather than matched the gown. Alice had decorated both garments with a set of filigreed buttons of which Lady Jemima had grown tired after less than a season of wear. Alice's bonnet was unadorned, elegant in its simplicity. The only thing she wore that revealed her station was a pair of sturdy black boots.

She had just finished dressing when she heard the unmistakable sound of Lady Jemima's bell. She looked down at herself. Had her lady ever seen her thus attired? Not even for church would she wear such a modish ensemble. The bell pealed again. There was nothing for it, so she snatched up her reticule and the fan she was taking to London for repair and ran out of her room. She was halfway down the corridor before she remembered Charlie's mysterious request, then ran back, took up a pot of cold cream, and hurried down the stairs.

Before Alice had even entered the room, Lady Jemima was saying to her, "I can't find the cross on the chain that Papa bought for me in Italy. I have looked everywhere and she"—she pointed accusingly at Lizzie, the housemaid who was assigned to assist Lady Jemima during Alice's half-days—"is less than useless!"

Upon seeing Alice, Lady Jemima gasped. "Oh my! Aren't you looking well." She did not sound pleased. "Is that my green walking dress?"

"Yes, Lady Jemima. The hem was worn, and you passed it on to me."

Lady Jemima pouted. "It does not look worn."

"As I am of a lesser stature than you, I was able to cut the hem."

Lady Jemima peered closely at the gown. "You have changed out the buttons. Are those the ones from my cornflower-blue gown?"

"Yes, ma'am. You said you didn't care for them."

"I don't remember saying any such thing, and if I did, I was surely mistaken, for they do look fine now."

"I'm so sorry, Lady Jemima. I will remove the buttons and return them to you."

"Pray tell me where you are going, looking so pretty?"

"You asked me to take your fan to the fan maker in London to have it repaired."

Lady Jemima pouted. "It is really too hard that when you go I am left with this nincompoop." She waved an imperious hand at Lizzie. The tears that had filled Lizzie's eyes now spilled over. "Oh, don't cry, Lizzie! It is not your fault you are a simpleton. I am quite sure there is nothing you can do about it."

Lizzie indeed had had no education, but she had taught herself her letters by reading Lord Alderwick's discarded newspapers, and could figure better than anyone downstairs, even Mr. Symes, who insisted that, had his circumstances only been different, he could have been a clerk in a counting house. I leave it to the reader to determine which of these two girls was more a simpleton than the other.

Though Alice's composure did not crack, she was nearly beside herself. It was her very own half-day, to which she was entitled by custom and contract. Charlie Wells would be waiting for her by the giraffe house in the Zoological Gardens, and she loathed the idea of letting him think she had ignored his letter. She might have asked if she could be dismissed, but she would not expose Lizzie to the mood of her petulant lady.

Alice went to Lady Jemima's dressing table, opened the

young lady's jewelry case, and removed the enameled cross from the compartment that was its usual resting place. "Here you are, Lady Jemima." She clasped the necklace round Lady Jemima's long, downy neck. Shall we remark on the fact that it did not once occur to our gentle heroine to twist the chain until the harridan-in-training dropped in a dead faint? What forbearance!

Alice took a handkerchief from her sleeve and passed it to Lizzie to dry her tears. Lizzie whispered, "I can do it. You go on." Alice shook her head, but Lizzie insisted, "I'd only feel awful, you missing your half-day."

Unfortunately, her whisper was not sufficiently quiet, for Lady Jemima sighed heavily. "You know, Alice, there are ladies who give their maids a single half-day a month. You seem to have one every week!"

No more than every other week, Alice thought but did not say, and even then it was as likely as not to be consumed by errands for her lady. "I am so very fortunate to be working for you and not another, m'lady," Alice said. Lizzie mouthed, "Go." Alice, after another moment of indecision, gave the little maid a smile of gratitude.

"Is there anything else, ma'am?" she asked Lady Jemima. "I should be going if I'm to catch the train."

"You will be back in time to dress me for dinner, will you not?"

Alice had hoped to have the evening to herself, but to argue would risk paying the price of the entire afternoon. "Of course, ma'am."

Lady Jemima turned back to assess her reflection, a vision that engendered so much distracting admiration that she failed to notice the two servants leaving the room.

SEVEN

Alice could count on the fingers of one hand the times she had stepped inside of a railway carriage. She had accompanied Lady Jemima on two visits to London, journeyed once with her lady to Bath, and gone up to town once on her own to pick up a bracelet from Hancocks & Co. on Bruton Street. She was thus both excited and fearful as she watched the incoming train wreathe the platform in thick smoke. Lady Jemima had given her money enough only for third class, and she saw when she boarded that the benches were crowded with rough-looking passengers. Fortunately, she found a place next to an elderly lady who, despite her rusty black dress and worn bonnet, looked respectable.

They greeted each other with a murmured "How do you do," and settled in for the journey to London. Alice was in a state of nervous agitation, not only at the near-novel experience of the rail journey, but also at the thought that, for the first time in her life, she was on her way to an assignation with a man, one who was, she realized, all but a stranger. Was this the action of a decent girl, well though simply brought up? What would her mother make of such a thing? Worse, what would Lady Jemima's mother make of it? Were Alice to be discovered, would she lose her place? She only realized that the thought had caused her to gasp when the elderly lady seated next to her patted her on the leg. "Don't fret, love. Though it looks like we're moving quick, me boy says we'll be all right, not to worry."

A young man sitting across the aisle leaned over his companion and said, "Ain't you heard about them poor folks in Winchburgh? Train crashed, and seventeen gone with it!"

"Oh dear," Alice said, looking now with some consternation out the window. They did after all seem to be moving very quickly.

The lady looked down her nose at the young man. "Winchburgh? Where's that?"

"In Scotland."

"Well, *Scotland,*" the lady scoffed.

Alice, determined to calm her nerves, took from her reticule the first volume of *Middlemarch,* by George Eliot, recently received by her from Lady Jemima, who had given up even the pretense of reading the novel after a handful of pages. Dorothea, Lady Jemima had told Aunt Bennett when quizzed, was about as entertaining as a Sunday sermon. "Is it not enough that I must weekly suffer Reverend Garland's endless cascades of pious verbosity? Why would I voluntarily expose myself to such tiresome piety in the pages of a book?" she had said.

Alice did not precisely disagree with Lady Jemima about the heroine of the novel in which she found herself quickly immersed. She recognized that Dorothea's nobility of character was defeated by naïveté, even foolishness. The heroine's entering into a marriage with one so ill-suited as Casaubon was irksome in the extreme, but it was the very unsuitability of the marriage, its unhappiness, that struck Alice as interesting. This was not the first less-than-happy union about which she had read in the novels that came her way through Miss Bennett's largesse. Miss Austen's *Pride and Prejudice* contained two such marriages, that of the cataclysmically inapposite Mr. and Mrs. Bennet and that of fatuous Lydia and unscrupulous Wickham. But the former couple's unhappiness was presented as humorous, and the latter not delved into overmuch. Moreover, the overriding sensation of that novel was of love fulfilled. Alice generally so delighted in the romantic explorations in such novels, ones like Ann Radcliffe's *The Mysteries of Udolpho* or Sir Walter Scott's various books, that one might have thought that *Middlemarch*'s exploration of the particularity of marital disharmony would confuse or even repel her, but instead she found herself curious and compelled to continue. In such immersion, the rest of the journey passed quickly—Alice, though on her way to the most romantic of trysts, nonetheless riveted by a tale of the opposite.

EIGHT

At the station, Alice had to battle her way through the throng of passengers to the Great Hall, where she found that the large clock looming above the crowd read fifteen minutes before one. Aghast, she rushed out of the station and down the road. Cook, who spent many of her own days off in town visiting with her particular friend, had fortunately provided Alice with clear and thorough directions, so she got lost in the labyrinthine London streets a mere half-dozen times. She arrived at the fan maker's in something of a state: her dress damp, her bonnet wilted, and her face beaded with perspiration. She looked so disheveled that the fan maker insisted she sit on a stool to catch her breath. His wife provided sustenance in the form of a cup of tea while her husband made short work of the repair. The fan maker told her that to walk to Regent's Park would take at least an hour, and that only if she moved briskly. He offered to hail her a hansom, but she demurred, as such a luxury was beyond her means. His wife suggested she take the omnibus instead.

"I go on me own all the time, miss. You'll not be bothered by anyone."

Standing out on the curb, Alice considered the contents of her purse. In addition to her return ticket, she had four shillings tuppence. Should she spend it? While she thus dithered, the omnibus pulled to a stop beside her, and the fare collector called out, "Come on, miss! We ain't got the whole day."

Throwing thrift to the winds, Alice leapt aboard.

At the gates to the Zoological Gardens, her typical frugality was once again challenged.

"A shilling?" she asked the clerk in the wrought-iron cage, dismayed. "Is it really so dear?"

He pursed his thin lips, looked down his narrow nose, and said, "If you're not coming in, step aside."

She bit her lip but said, "One, please."

The place was far larger than Alice had anticipated, and the air was redolent with a musk that though pervasive and cloying, was not unpleasant. Her passage by the enclosures of monkeys and birds incited choruses of chittering and squeaking, and she could not help but stop to watch a long-tailed beast with the face of an old woman nibble delicately on a chunk of apple. It held her gaze with solemn eyes, turning away only once it had finished the last bit of core.

She searched for the giraffe cages, growing ever more consternated by the passage of time as she walked the paths until, finally, and much to the horror of the ladies and gentlemen passing, she gathered up her skirts and stepped up onto a bench. In the distance, she saw a long-necked creature with orange spots placidly tearing leaves off a tree. She jumped off the bench and ran in its direction. Once she got within sight of the giraffe house, she took a moment to adjust her bonnet and dab the sweat from her upper lip. Then, the picture of ease, she approached the enclosure by which Charlie stood, anxiously scanning the visitors as they passed. He looked every inch the gentleman in his starched collar and fine woolen pinched-waist frock coat, his velvet waistcoat patterned with charming flowers. When he saw her, his face broke into a wide grin.

"You came!" he said, taking her hand and shaking it fervently. "I didn't know if you would. I feared once you saw the back of me, you'd come to your senses."

Unsure how to reply, she merely shook her head and said, "I'm sorry I was delayed."

"No need to apologize, Alice. Do you mind if I call you Alice? And, please, call me Charlie. You look lovely, Alice. If you'll permit me to say."

"Thank you. This dress was one of Lady Jemima's from a few seasons ago."

"Then we are in masquerade as a lord and his lady, for I'm dressed entirely in Lord Wynstowe's cast-offs."

At that moment, a spotted, horned head appeared over Charlie's shoulder. A pair of thickly lashed eyes blinked languidly. Alice widened her own. Charlie followed her gaze and smiled.

"Is she not beautiful? I've been watching them for the past hour. They are so delicate and gentle. Look." He pointed. "There's her baby."

Alice watched, delighted, as the spindly little creature nuzzled under its mother's belly. "How does it balance on legs so thin?" she asked.

"It is an improbable animal, isn't it? How long can you stay? How much time do we have?"

"Not much, I'm afraid," she said. "I must be on the four-fifteen train, and it will take near an hour to get to the station from here."

"I'll take you to the station, so that we can have that time together as well. Shall we visit the other creatures while we can?"

He proffered his arm and she took it, the first time she had ever walked thus with a man. Then he remembered: "Did you bring the cold cream?"

She took the small pot out of her bag and handed it over. "May I ask why you need it?"

"Lord Wynstowe is under the impression that a certain brand-new remedy for what ails him can only be obtained from a chemist in a very distant part of the city. It was the first excuse I could come up with for why I should be away for the whole of an afternoon. He always insists on procuring the most modern of medicines, ideally ones not yet in common use, so he was only too glad to give me the time. Shall we visit the elephant?"

"Oh yes!" she said. "I saw a drawing of one in a picture book once, and I've been desperate to see one in person."

"Be prepared—it's larger even than the giraffe."

The elephant did not disappoint. Though it was not as tall as the mother giraffe, it was huge, with gently flapping ears and a long, sensitive trunk that reached through the bars of its cage and captured a gentleman's hat, causing much hilarity among the assembly.

For the next hour, Charlie and Alice wandered the pathways from enclosure to enclosure, marveling at the elephant, at the horned sheep, at a tiger who treated them to a wide yawn, which caused Alice to yawn as well, and then to giggle, a sound she had not heard from her own lips since she was a girl.

"Tell me more about you, Alice," Charlie said while they watched an Arabian oryx munch through a bucket of oats. "Tell me one thing about you no one knows."

"You've seen where I live, the village where I grew up. I've prattled on to you about my brothers and sisters. You know far more of my life than I know of yours! It is your turn to tell me a secret others don't know."

He had made his own bed with his question, Charlie thought. Now he must lie in it. Should he make up a pleasant tale, or should he tell the truth, though that would darken the mood?

She must have noticed something in his expression, for she said, "You can take me into your confidence. I will never be shocked."

"I'm not sure that's true, for I spent no small part of my childhood in a workhouse." He looked over at her to see how she would react. Would she draw away?

She was indeed shocked, he saw, but rather than pull her arm from his she held it more firmly and pressed him to continue. He told her what he had told no other, that a series of minor and major calamities brought on by his father's submission to the habit of drink had sent his family, numbering six in all, to the workhouse. He spent three long years, from ages nine to twelve, behind those high walls, before a kindly schoolmaster arranged for his placement in service. It was this man who had drummed into Charlie the importance of speaking in a manner that would not offend a gentleman. "Choose your words carefully," he had said. "Avoid the inflections and vulgar cant of the streets of your birth and you will find opportunity beyond what you might otherwise expect."

"One might say the timing was fortuitous," Charlie now said ruefully. "Though I regretted it terribly."

"Did you not like the job?"

"I liked it very much. For the first time in my life, I earned a wage, and though my days were filled with labor from morning until night, I felt myself a free man."

"So why, then, did you regret it?"

"Because, within a handful of months of my leaving, even as I celebrated my liberty and my prospects, an epidemic of pox took hold of the workhouse."

Charlie's entire family fell ill. He had tried to return to help care for them, but the gates were barred to everyone but the doctor, and even that man came only rarely. Charlie's father, dissipated by a lifetime of bad habits, was the first to die. Charlie's younger sister and brother followed not long after.

"Oh, Charlie. I'm so sorry. And your mother?"

"Unharmed. She had fallen ill with the variola when just a girl, so this time the disease passed her by. My older sister, Mary, was not so lucky."

Mary had lain ill with fever for two weeks, her body covered with weeping pustules. The scabs had eventually fallen away, leaving behind terrible scars.

"Her arms and her legs are marked, but her face bears the worst of it."

"The poor thing. Where are they now, your mother and sister?"

"It took me some time to earn their release, but they reside now in the house of a kind widow in the village of Wynstowe, where I can visit them often. The rent is not too high, and I can keep them tolerably well, though Mary insists on taking in sewing to pay as much of her way as she can. My sister is as proud as she is economical. She would make a fine wife, though it would take a kind man to see past her scars."

"There's many a boy who'd have abandoned a mother and sister to manage as best they could on their own."

"Such a boy would be a cad."

"The world is full of cads."

"Do you believe that? Are there so many villains in the environs of Barton Village?"

"There are some. And I have known maids who leave the house in shame and all alone. You do not see those in Lord Wynstowe's house?"

"Lord Wynstowe hasn't the energy to bestir himself in that direction," Charlie said, then felt ashamed. As trying as was his gentleman, he was at heart moral and upstanding, never cruel. In fact, when the son of the steward of the estate had caused trouble for a daughter of one of the tenants, Lord Wynstowe had not only insisted that the pair be joined in marriage, but had installed them in a cottage and employed the new husband in his coal works. "Lord Wynstowe would never do such a thing," Charlie amended.

Alice said, "They say there are more than a few children in Barton with the air of an Alderwick. I know one young girl who looks more like Lady Jemima than does her own sister."

I know, dear Reader, that you are taken aback. A gentlewoman would never speak so frankly of such things, and it is perhaps in this that we see most clearly the evidence of the inferior circumstances of Alice's birth. And yet must we not acknowledge the truth of what she says? We have all known fallen maids who have lost their places for the offense of posing a risk to a gentleman's good name. Worse, who among us has not excused in the gentlemen of our acquaintance crimes the very mention of which should cause dismay?

"You surprise me, Alice."

Alice said, "You are surprised that Lord Alderwick might behave like so many others, or you are disturbed that I speak of it?"

"I admire your honesty and insight as well as your courage

in naming what you see. I also take pleasure in the comfort with which you confide your opinions in me."

"You are easy to talk to."

"As are you."

As they walked on Alice mused, "I wonder if Lord Alderwick might have behaved in a different manner had he not been compelled to marry Lady Alderwick?"

"He and his lady haven't grown to love one another?"

"Love?" She laughed. "He can't tolerate her company for even a moment, and as far as I've heard, he never could."

"So why, then, did he marry her?"

"Why do any of those endowed with the gifts of rank and wealth marry? For status, for fortune, for property. A baronet seeks the hand of a daughter of an earl, an earl that of a marquis. A man of fortune but no rank marries his daughter off to a man with the latter but not the former; one with rank but no fortune makes the opposite choice. Though the gentry talk of love, they marry for any reason but."

"Then we are lucky."

"How so?"

"We have neither estates nor money. We are free to marry for love."

"Are we?"

"Are we not?"

"Don't poor women marry for protection and security? And don't poor men because they need a wife to care for their homes and bear their children?"

Though we may recognize the influence of Aunt Bennett in Alice's jaundiced point of view, I posit that this is another opinion with which we cannot take issue. When we evaluate our own circumstances, are they so different from what this preternaturally wise young woman describes? If we are fortunate, our unions of convenience or aspiration are planted in soil fertile enough to nurture love's blossoming. But there are many whose marriages are barren fields in which little but resignation takes root.

I must stop with these lectures, however, lest I risk your putting down this volume in impatience. Rest assured, my forbearing reader, this story is one of love. Of connivance and scheming, of setbacks and disappointments, but ultimately, and at its center, one of love.

"My word, Alice Lockey," Charlie said. "You are a cynic. I hope you marry for love. I know I intend to."

You see? It is as I promised.

And with that he squeezed her hand tightly beneath his arm. She fancied she felt the warmth of his body through the layers of wool between them, and suddenly wondered if perhaps she might not have the opportunity to realize his hope.

NINE

Charlie and Alice agreed to meet on her half-day two weeks hence, their last opportunity before Lord Wynstowe removed from London to a house party at Windermere Lake for what Charlie thought might be the rest of the season, unless the viscount was yet again sent packing. Charlie suggested they plan to take a walk along the embankment, an excursion he promised would be entertaining in addition to having the benefit of putting little burden on their pocketbooks.

Upon Alice's return to Marlecombe Park, she had to stay up late into the night removing the filigreed buttons from her dress and pelisse and sewing them back onto Lady Jemima's gown. Her candle guttered out halfway through, and she was forced to finish by the light of the moon. Up until near half-two, she was pressed to disguise her exhaustion the next morning.

"Not this one," Lady Jemima said, pushing aside the cornflower gown Alice proffered. "Caroline was dressed top to toe in Wedgwood blue last night, and Mr. Smythe-Roberts told me she looked like a Jasperware vase. I will wear the sunflower yellow today. He does so like me in yellow."

As Alice was shaking out the gown to return it to its hook, Lady Jemima noticed the buttons. "You put them back?"

"I did, my lady."

"I *gave* them to you, Alice. You insult me by returning them."

"I apologize, my lady. I meant no insult."

"You know what? I am tired of the gown. You may have it," Lady Jemima said, in a gesture intended to make up for her behavior of the night before, for the truth was that, though impulsive, thoughtless, and egotistical, the lady did not intend to be cruel.

Once alone in her room, Alice flung the gown to the floor. It was sometimes impossible to bear the petty humiliations and carelessness of treatment that were the regular feature of a servant's life. Soon enough, however, she shook off her anger. Her place was a good one; her wages were adequate, especially when supplemented by the sale of Lady Jemima's frequent cast-offs; the other servants were by and large amiable; and her lady was relatively easy to manage, if not to like. Take heart! she told herself. Things could be far worse. After all, in only two weeks' time she would be strolling along the Thames in the company of a young man more charming and thoughtful than any of Lady Jemima's suitors.

Never had a fortnight crept by at such a leaden pace. The tasks which she was used to approaching with an admirable briskness and sense of purpose felt tiresome and dull. It was Lady Jemima's monthly unwellness, characterized by five days of irritability and arbitrariness, not to mention the added onus of heaps of soiled flannel bandages, bundles of sheep's wool, and stained underclothes. Dealing with popped buttons was a bore, polishing shoes torture. All was gray and dull.

When it was time to wash Lady Jemima's hair, each of the multiple steps seemed to take forever. Listlessly, Alice beat up the egg and worked it through the blond tresses, startling from her reverie only when her lady shrieked as she rinsed her.

"The water is freezing cold!" Lady Jemima said. "And you have spilled it all down my neck."

"Pardon me, ma'am!" Alice said, mopping up the water and rushing to fetch one of the flannels in the stack she was warming by the hearth.

Lady Jemima allowed herself to be calmed, and the tedious task resumed, with Alice, despite her admonitions to herself to pay attention, still unable to muster the focus required to do her job with anything resembling her usual competence. She cut her finger on the knife she used to shave the Castile soap, and she spilled the vinegar rinse all down her dress.

When two weeks passed and the day finally arrived, Alice woke with as much relief at the end of the interminable wait as anticipation of her assignation. The day was fine—the sun high in the sky and the air unseasonably warm. To Alice's relief, the house party decided to embark on an outing to visit a ruined church. They ordered a picnic from Mrs. Platt and planned to be gone all day, liberating her for even longer than she had hoped.

The unexpected extra hours of freedom allowed Alice to take time with her toilette. She was brushing her hair into its usual simple coil when Mademoiselle Lefebvre knocked on the door and came in without waiting for a reply. The French girl had with her Lady Alderwick's boar-bristled brushes and curling tongs, a selection of her own hair grips, and a small looking glass.

"Assieds-toi," she said. "You are going to meet your *beau, non*? You must be *élégante et chic.* Sit. Your hair is beautiful. And you have so much! I will make you *très belle,* lucky girl."

"I have no beau," Alice insisted.

"Of course not," Mademoiselle Lefebvre said, patting Alice on the cheek.

She styled Alice's hair in a low chignon, with soft tendrils framing her face. When she showed Alice the results in her looking glass, the girl sighed with pleasure.

"Oh, Mademoiselle Lefebvre! I look quite like someone else!"

"You look like Alice. Pretty, pretty Alice!"

Alice arrived in London with plenty of time before her assignation, and as the day was so very fine, walked from the station to the pier, allowing herself a detour to Westminster Abbey, which she had heard of but never visited. Inside the abbey, she stepped into a patch of light shining brightly through a stained-glass window, held up her hands, and watched the kaleidoscope of colors play over her skin.

A young woman's voice interrupted her reverie. "Ooh, look!"

Alice turned to see a fresh-faced young girl clutching the arm of a soldier decked out in his madder-red tunic, a pom-pom bobbing atop his tall shako.

"It's so pretty, isn't it, miss? Don't you find it lovely?"

"I do," Alice said.

The girl leaned over, confidentially. "We're on our wedding trip. We've seen ever so many beautiful things, but this place is the finest." She glanced down at Alice's hand. "You're not married, are you, miss?"

"No."

"Ah, that's hard goin', that is. It's lovely to be married, isn't it, Bertie?"

"Yes" was the stout reply.

"You're sure to find yourself a husband one day, miss. Don't worry," the girl said.

Alice could not help but be charmed by this well-disposed girl. She smiled, bade the young couple farewell, and made her way to Lambeth Pier, stopping only to enjoy the view from the bridge.

As she was still early, Alice sat down on a small iron bench with a view of the clock tower rising over the river. For the next forty minutes, she watched the hands of the clock tick round the clock face. Big Ben chimed quarter past the hour, then half past, then finally two o'clock. She stood up expectantly, scanning the crowds. When the bell rang again, noting the next quarter-hour, she resumed her seat. Just because he had been early last time did not mean he would be so again. A quarter-hour was nothing! At any moment he would reappear.

Alice waited. Quarter-hour, half. Three o'clock, quarter past. The peal of the bell grew steadily more intolerable to her until, finally, at half-four, she stood up and retraced her journey back to the station and home.

TEN

How, Alice wondered as she lay in her narrow bed, the attic room growing colder with every passing hour, was she to know if Charlie had failed to appear because he was unwilling or because he was unable? Would she ever see him again? Lord Wynstowe would not again be invited to Marlecombe Park, of this she was certain, and after Lady Alderwick's insult, he would not invite the Alderwicks to Wynstowe Manor. Was that why Charlie had not come? Because he had realized that the realities of distance and circumstance made connection between them impossible?

As the days passed, Alice's discomposure increased. She felt her want of Charlie every hour, and alternated between certainty that he had been detained by some whim of his lord's and fear that he had seen better of their attachment.

Of Alice's distress Lady Jemima was typically insensible. The young lady was by inclination and habit uninterested in the moods of others, and was now entirely consumed by a single object: Mr. Thomas Smythe-Roberts. She regaled Alice nightly with tales of Mr. Thomas's witticisms, his withering asides about Caroline Mountjoy, and most especially his compliments to herself.

One afternoon, as she divested herself of her dirty walking dress, Lady Jemima confided, "It is not impossible that he might make me an offer soon." She held out a mud-crusted boot for Alice to remove. "Some might think it premature, but we have come to know each other so well these few weeks. I thought he might speak when we were climbing Barton Hill. We walked together the whole way and reached the top before anyone else, and it was ever so romantic. He caught up my hand and said the view was as fine as a painting, but not so fine as my eyes. He does so admire my eyes. He says they are as blue as a naiad's robes." The young lady paused, two double lines marring the pink skin between her brows. "I shall have to ask Papa what a naiad is."

"A water nymph," Alice said without thinking.

Lady Jemima gazed at her with frank astonishment, then gave her head a firm shake. "I don't think that is correct." She turned back to her own concern. "Mr. Smythe-Roberts was most certainly about to propose when, suddenly, the whole group appeared, with you-know-who in the lead. The impertinent girl must have been running up the slope as fast as her fat legs could carry her. Of course, he could say nothing then, but tonight I will wear my white muslin with the Honiton lace. It will put him in mind of a wedding." She frowned. "Do you think Mr. Smythe-Roberts knows Her Majesty wore white to her wedding?"

"I couldn't say, ma'am."

"I am sure he does. He pays close attention to the fashions of the day. He takes *Le Follet*! The white muslin will set me off so well in comparison to the Queen." She lowered her voice to a whisper. "The Queen is positively ugly, do you not think?"

"I couldn't say, ma'am."

"You have *eyes,* do you not?"

"She is the Queen, my lady, and I'm naught but a servant."

"I am sure Mr. Smythe-Roberts will agree with me. He cannot help but be truthful. Some gentlemen lie, but it is not in his nature. It is a matter of character, he says. I do think he has the most manly and earnest character. More than any other man alive."

Alice wondered whether a truly honorable man would describe himself so. She hoped that, if asked, Charlie would say he valued and strove for honesty, but would leave it to others to determine the nature of his character.

Alas for the young lady (though not for our story), Lady Jemima's hopes for an offer that evening were dashed. When Alice returned to the servants' hall, she found Lord Harlowe's valet in a tizzy, demanding the laundress finish pressing the pieces he had submitted to her care, sending the maids in search of soft paper for packing the trunks, and generally communicating his panic and haste for an immediate departure. Lord Harlowe had received an urgent message. The son and heir had taken dangerously ill. Mr. James Smythe-Roberts was being attended round the clock by physicians, but his condition was perilous. Moreover, the physician was concerned that the future viscountess's acute distress could be dangerous, given her delicate condition. Her own mother was at present visiting relations in Ireland, and though she was making every effort to return, he feared the worst if the lady was left any longer on her own. The family must leave immediately for London, their servants to follow with the baggage on the evening train.

Lady Jemima was furious at this delay of her happiness. "I would be less vexed if I knew the disease to be contagious, for if he dies and the little ones follow, it would clear the way for Thomas," she said. When she caught sight of the expression Alice hastened to suppress, she laughed. "Don't look so shocked, Alice. I know you think me terribly naughty, but it is very hard on younger sons. They would be far less likely to wish their brothers and their nephews ill if the estate were divided between them. A radical proposition it may be, but it would be more just, wouldn't it?"

There were, Alice thought, many reforms that would lead to more just circumstances than those in which they found themselves, remedying the plight of younger sons the least of them.

"Would you like still to wear the lace gown, my lady?" she said.

"There is no point to it now. I will save it for the next time I see him."

ELEVEN

That evening, when the servants were gathered round the table for their late dinner, Mr. Dale stood at the head with a small stack of letters and with great solemnity read out the names of the addressees. In his day, he was fond of telling them, a servant received letters only in the most dire of circumstances. Postage was simply too dear, and unless a letter was franked by a member of the House of Lords, its recipient was obliged to discharge the sum. The servants should remember Sir Rowland Hill in their prayers, he instructed, for it was this gentleman who had invented the postage stamp, which made it possible for those downstairs to correspond with the ease of those above.

"Miss Lockey," Mr. Dale announced. "Here is one for you."

Alice was astounded to hear her name. She rarely received letters. If her parents had something to tell her, they would send one of her brothers up to the house with a message. She received letters only at Christmastime, from her teacher, the former Miss Elliott. That kind soul had married not long after Alice left school, and moved with her husband to York. And even there, the frequency of the lady's correspondence had decreased with each child she bore. Given that and the season, she was unlikely to be the correspondent. There was only one other person Alice knew outside of the immediate vicinity, and it was surely too much to hope the letter was from him.

With a hand that, had she not been so levelheaded a girl, might have trembled, she took the letter from Mr. Dale and tucked it away in the pocket of her apron, ignoring Mr. Cahill's raised eyebrow and Mademoiselle Lefebvre's knowing smirk. Challenging herself to give away nothing of her eagerness, she ate her dinner with no appearance of hurry. She even repaired with the other upper servants to Mrs. Platt's sitting room for pudding, and stayed longer than was her habit, pretending to take a particular interest in Mademoiselle Lefebvre's gossip about Lord Alderwick's refusal of his wife's petition to replace the morning-room furnishings, in Mrs. Platt's description of her niece's new baby, and in the upper housemaid's complaints about the state of the gentlemen's rooms. Only when the pealing of the bells demanded it did she take her leave to wait on her lady.

Alice did not even snatch up the letter when Lady Jemima was abed and she back in her room. Instead, she methodically brushed her hair and rolled it up for the night, scrubbed the day's grime from her face and hands, shook out her dress, hung it back on its peg, put on her night-dress, and settled herself in bed. Only then did she open the letter, her anticipation having been its own form of delight. She broke the seal on the envelope and pulled out a page engraved with Lord Wynstowe's name, address, and family crest, marveling at Charlie's audacity. Lady Jemima's desk was stuffed with stacks of writing paper, refreshed every season, but Alice had never had the temerity to ask for a page.

Charlie had carefully lined the blank reverse of the page and filled it with his neat and elegant script.

My Dearest Alice,

I hope that you received my short note of last Sunday. I had no choice but to give it to Mrs. Sweet, and I have little faith that the old dragon put it in the post. In case you did not, let me repeat that I am so very sorry to have failed to meet you Sunday last as per our arrangement. I hope that you yourself were detained, because I fear your justified vexation.

I had every intention of coming, but on Sunday morning, Lord Wynstowe announced that we would leave for Windermere Lake that very evening. I did my best to discourage him. I made up a dozen excuses: the length of time it would take to pack his things with adequate care; the glover's tardiness in delivering the new kidskin gloves he would need for his journey; the immediate necessity of securing his medicinal salve. This last I was confident would convince him, for though he is well built and strong, he is nonetheless a devoted valetudinarian who cannot hear of an illness without becoming convinced that he will become its victim. Incidentally, your cold cream has worked miracles, much to my surprise, meant as it was for Lady Jemima's face and not Lord Wynstowe's. [This next word he had crossed out with a dense black scribble.] *But my pleas fell on deaf ears, and before noon we were railway-bound for Penrith, giving me only a moment to scribble the aforementioned letter of apology which I have now convinced myself that Mrs. Sweet threw directly into a dustbin or tossed into the fire or chewed up and swallowed.*

Lord Wynstowe anticipates a return to Wynstowe Manor no sooner than St. Andrew's Day. We will be traveling once again via London, and I hope to prevail upon him to stay at least for a number of days. Do I have the right to ask you to wait for me until then, dear Alice? In my heart and on my lips, you are "dear Alice," and I do sincerely hope in your heart I find a place as . . .

Your devoted,
Charlie.

P.S. Please write to this address. I have enclosed a page of Penny Reds.

Alice looked in the envelope and marveled at his thoughtfulness. He had provided her with enough postage to write him a dozen letters before they could meet again.

TWELVE

Alice intended to go the very next day to the village to purchase notepaper and a pen, but Lady Jemima was so irritable from the absence of the gentleman she had come to consider her all-but-intended that she kept her maid running from morning until night on that day and many that followed. Alice considered asking Mrs. Platt or Mr. Dale for a few sheets of household paper and an envelope, but she was loath to encourage their curiosity. Though Mr. Dale prided himself on being the soul of discretion, she feared that that courtesy might extend only to the family. In any event, she did not want to give either of the senior servants a reason to question her about the nature of her relationship with Charlie.

It was thus that a second letter arrived even before she had managed to procure the implements of replying to the first. Alice had no choice but to screw up her courage and approach Lady Jemima. Though the young lady was selfish and tetchy, she was not closefisted and would not, Alice hoped, begrudge her maid either paper or pen. She was a gossip, however, and would likely insist upon knowing with whom Alice sought to correspond.

"Do you think I might trouble you for a page of letter paper, and a pen to write with?" Alice asked while she brushed her lady's hair. "Only I owe a letter to Mrs. Mansfield, and I've not had time to buy my own."

"Who is Mrs. Mansfield?"

"The former Miss Elliott. She was my teacher at the village school."

"You mean that tedious old relic Dr. Philpott once insisted on bringing to tea? She actually managed to entrap a husband?"

Lady Jemima rustled around in her writing table and handed Alice a stack of notepaper at least half an inch tall, more pages than Alice could have used even if she were to write to Charlie every week for a year. She waved away Alice's objections, saying, "You know I despise letter writing, and still Mama persists in foisting upon me a mountain of stationery." The young lady also insisted on making Alice a gift of a fine pen and one of the bottles of mauve ink she had received Christmas last, and Alice went away thinking that she was after all lucky in her lady. Lady Jemima was generous, if only when it came to things she did not value overmuch. Alice was as grateful to her as anyone could want a servant to be.

And so the correspondence between the young lovers began, with exchanges of letters so frequent that they were both sometimes hard-pressed to come up with new topics to put down on paper. Alice wrote:

My days are the same one to another. They pass easily, and I am too busy to be bored, but to relive them in these pages would surely bore you. I have tried so very hard to think of something of interest to describe or set forth, to no avail. The only thing I can think of is a silly story from my childhood. I hope it is not tedious for you.

One year, our sow was delivered of six piglets, and my father amused himself by naming one for me. He teased me by talking about how big and fat Alice was growing and about what a good breeder she was. When he finally did slaughter my namesake, he smacked his lips at the table and announced that Alice made for very good sausage. My brother Peter in particular found this very comical, but I left the table in a flood of tears. For all of his teasing, my father is a kind man, and he never afterward named a pig anything other than Mrs. Sausage or Mr. Bacon.

Charlie replied with sympathy for little Alice. He wished he could have been there to scold her brother for hurting her feelings, and suggested that one day she return the insult by naming a dog Lazy Pete.

In composing his own letter, he tried to find anecdotes from his childhood that would amuse rather than incite pity. This effort had the happy effect of bringing to mind pleasant moments lost in the fog of memory brought about by his family's miserable workhouse years. Writing to Alice became a balm he had not before known he longed for. He wrote:

Have you ever been to the circus? Did such entertainments come to a rural village like Barton? Once, when I was a small boy, my father took all of us children to Batty's. The equestrians performed the most astonishing tricks. There was a man who juggled on horseback, and a girl who stood astride two galloping horses at once, a foot on each. I vowed to become a circus equestrian, an ambition that lasted as long as a week, until I saw an organ grinder and decided that I would prefer to spend the days of my life in the company of monkeys.

This reminiscence caused Alice to laugh out loud at the very moment Mademoiselle Lefebvre happened to be walking past her room. The other maid tapped on the door, but entered (as was her wont) before being invited.

"Is it another letter from your beau? *Il est drôle?*"

Alice put a finger to her lips, encouraging the voluble woman to silence. "You mustn't tell anyone I have an admirer, mademoiselle. If they were to know, I might lose my place."

"*Bah!* Who could dismiss a maiden for falling in love?"

"Lady Jemima wouldn't like to hear I was distracted by personal circumstances."

"That girl, she is *impossible*! How do you stand her?"

"She is not so bad as all that. She can be very kind when she chooses."

"Then she is different from her mother, for Lady Alderwick is kind only *par accident.* Read me your letter!"

"It's just foolishness. Stories of when he was a boy."

With a sigh, Mademoiselle Lefebvre lay down on the bed. "I wish I had a beau. But English men, they are *horrible*."

"Mr. Wells isn't horrible. He's lovely."

Mademoiselle Lefebvre leaned up on one elbow. "When will you see him again?"

"I don't know. He will be at Windermere Lake for some time. Mr. Wells says the cook at Wynstowe Manor is very bad, so Lord Wynstowe visits other establishments to fill his belly."

"It's a shame, *non*? That you and your Mr. Wells do not work in the same house. You could see him every day. You could sneak down the corridor to his room!"

"Mademoiselle Lefebvre, the things you say."

Lefebvre tugged at a lock of Alice's hair. *"Ma petite vierge,"* she said fondly, then exclaimed, *"J'ai une idée!* I take the pin for Lord Alderwick's cravat from his dressing room and put it in Mr. Cahill's room! Then we tell Mr. Dale, 'Mr. Cahill is a thief! Search his room!' Then he is dismissed, and I tell her ladyship, 'Oh, his lordship must employ Mr. Wells, he is *le premier valet en Angleterre*!' Most excellent plan, I think."

"We will do no such thing. I will just have to wait. It's not so very long until the London season."

"It could be months! Men don't wait so long. They are like *les chiens*. They must . . ." She made a motion that Alice would have preferred not to understand.

"Mr. Wells will wait," Alice said, sounding more confident than she felt.

His next letter restored the faith which the passing of time had eroded.

Dearest Alice,

(No longer only "Dear"!)

In your letter of yesterday morning, you wrote of your fondness for your former teacher Miss Elliott. I, too, had a teacher whose belief in me changed the trajectory of my life (and the quality of my letters and words). It was my good fortune and his ill that Mr. Alasdair MacGregor found himself an inmate of the institution to which my father's recklessness consigned his family. Mr. MacGregor found occupation in the schoolroom there. For the first time since I was a small boy, I could regularly attend school, as it was provided by the Poor Law without fee. From this thoughtful and patient gentleman I learned my letters and to figure sums. The stories he read to us allowed us for a few minutes or hours to escape the confines of those grim walls. He taught us how to behave among our betters. He even selected me for additional instruction and worked to help purge my language of evidence of my ill-birth. It was he who found for me my first place and wrote for me as fine a reference as any boy has ever received.

I had imagined him as released from that awful place, returning to his native Inverness and resuming life on his father's sheep farm. Alas, he died of the pox, along with my father, brother, and sister, and so many others. I will never forget him. Is Alasdair too unsuitable a name for the son of an Englishman?

Yours alone,
Charlie.

She replied by return post, beginning her letter with that most welcome word. *Dearest Charlie,* and continuing, *I think Alasdair a fine name for a child no matter his birth.* She filled the rest of the page with an account of Lady Jemima's purchase of a new falcon, but both she and Charlie knew that first line to be the only thing of remotest import.

THIRTEEN

Morehouse Castle, the house on Windermere Lake at which Lord Wynstowe was a guest, had proved to be a most inhospitable environment. The rooms were very large, far beyond the capacity of their smoky fireplaces to heat, and so Lord Wynstowe lived in perpetual anxiety that he might catch a chill that would send him to an early grave. This anxiety, though illogical, was not entirely incomprehensible. His father, a devoted hunter, had found himself one day caught with a mount with a thrown shoe, and thus forced to walk near five miles through a torrential downpour. The gentleman had developed pneumonia and was dead within the week. Lord Wynstowe had since then avoided the hunt and the cold, in equal measure. The bitterness of the temperature in the rooms of Morehouse Castle caused him to demand that Charlie sleep on a pallet in his room in order to replace his India-rubber hot-water bottle and build up the fire every hour.

Worse than the cold was the lack of a doctor near to the

castle, or even an apothecary. No fewer than three times in the first two weeks of his visit, Lord Wynstowe had sent Charlie to the town of Kendal, an hour's drive, and he was thus fast wearing out the patience of the castle's coachman. Moreover, the famed German chef his hosts had lured to England from the Kulm Hotel in St. Moritz had proved not to be to Lord Wynstowe's taste. How often could one be expected to enjoy Haselnuss-Semmelknödel? Why was the chef so unschooled in the cuisine of France, which all agreed to be the finest in the world?

"The man could not produce a decent consommé to preserve his mother's life," Lord Wynstowe complained.

Lord Wynstowe also took issue with the dismal amusements of his hosts, who spent their days "clumping around the countryside like a militia on a training exercise," leaving Lord Wynstowe to drift aimlessly about the library or his rooms. It was altogether a miserable visit, and Lord Wynstowe was most unhappy.

"Sir," Charlie said one night as he warmed his shivering lord's bed with a copper pan full of coals. "Might not you be more comfortable in London than here?"

"London? It is home that I long for. Wynstowe Manor is so very well heated, and the air of the country so temperate. And Dr. Fitzpatrick no more than a quarter of an hour away! He should visit me every morning, as I needed. But I have pledged to stay a month in this wretched place, and only a fortnight has passed. I won't survive. Mark my words, Wells. I will die here in the bone-crunching cold."

"Would your friends mind so very much if you were to go?"

"I should think so. They would be forced to make up the numbers for dinner, and how would they do so in this misbegotten hinterland?"

Charlie helped his gentleman into his bed, settling a hot-water bottle to either side and on the belly of the overgrown baby. He removed from the fire the bricks he had been heating all day, wrapped them in layers of flannel, and tucked them at Lord Wynstowe's feet. He heaped a second eiderdown and three woolen blankets into a mound, beneath which Lord Wynstowe trembled, and made sure the man's nightcap fully covered his ears. Then he built the fire up to a blaze. By now drenched in sweat, for the room was an oven, he turned down the lamps, and left Lord Wynstowe to his fitful rest.

Rather than settle on his pallet, Charlie went to the kitchen and knocked on the butler's door.

"Come!" the butler said.

Charlie entered, apologizing for the lateness of the hour. "I hope you can help me resolve a difficulty," he said.

"A difficulty in this house?" the butler said, aghast. He was a stout and ruddy man with a bearing as distinguished as that of a peer of the realm. "Impossible!"

"Rest assured, the difficulty is my gentleman's, not yours. Lord Wynstowe, you see, seeks to return to his home. There is a pressing matter that requires his attention. However, he is concerned that his departure will inconvenience her ladyship, leaving her short a man."

"It would indeed, for Sir Percy Atkinson does not arrive until the end of the month."

"I wonder, is there not a suitable gentleman in the neighborhood who might take Lord Wynstowe's place? Someone whose company the family enjoys?"

The butler hemmed and hawed, then finally said, "The vicar has recently employed a new curate. Normally, such a person would not be invited to anything grander than a small family meal, but he is by all accounts a fine-featured man with excellent manners. Perhaps my lady could be prevailed upon to invite him to dine in Lord Wynstowe's stead. I shall say a few words to her when next I have an opportunity."

"Thank you, sir! That would please my dear gentleman no end. I'll trouble you no longer, then."

Charlie turned to the door but the butler stopped him. "Mr. Wynstowe, I know that in London and other parts of the country the giving of vail money has been discouraged. But, for your information, and the information of your lord, it is still very much the custom here."

Ah. Here we go. The old blackguard had Charlie over a barrel, and he knew it.

Charlie said, "I'm sure Lord Wynstowe would be grateful to know what vails would be considered acceptable in an establishment like this one."

"So generous a gentleman he is!" the butler said. "The amount is entirely up to him, but I suppose, given the length of your stay, the footmen would expect seven shillings apiece."

"Indeed?"

"A shilling or two each to the maids and the stableboys."

"Lord Wynstowe brought no horse and does not ride," Charlie reminded him.

"Then, of course, nothing would be expected of him there. Though the coachman . . ." His voice trailed off.

"The coachman would expect the same as the footmen?"

"Lord Wynstowe made so very frequent use of his services."

"An additional shilling, then. And the senior servants?"

"Any more than one pound sterling would be too much." He tented his fingers and looked down in deep contemplation. "There have been those who saw fit to give as much as two pounds, but they were truly the kindest of gentlemen. Is your lord very kind?"

"He is. So that totals . . ." Charlie did the sums in his head. ". . . six pounds two shillings?"

"So much, Mr. Wynstowe! Your lord is indeed a prince among men."

The next morning found Lord Wynstowe wrapped in an eiderdown and shivering in front of the hearth. When Charlie communicated the butler's assurances that the lady of the house could be encouraged by the butler to accept the curate as an adequate substitute in return for a mere six pounds two shillings, his lord shucked his cocoon and leapt to his feet. "We shall travel directly to Wynstowe Manor," he announced.

This was not the outcome Charlie desired. The journey from the manor to London was too arduous to make feasible an assignation with Alice, even if he could convince Lord Wynstowe to shift his half-day to coincide with hers. He must gently adjust this plan.

As he pulled the night-dress over Lord Wynstowe's head, he mused thoughtfully, "I hope Dr. Fitzpatrick has sufficient experience with the afflictions caused by cold weather to effect an adequate cure to your unfortunate situation."

"Do you suppose he does not?" Lord Wynstowe said, poking his head back up through the mass of snowy linen, worry lining his brow.

"The good doctor has lived his entire life in the temperate clime of Wynstowe. He has little opportunity to treat those afflicted with the diseases of cold weather. But I am sure he will manage."

Charlie helped Lord Wynstowe back into his chair, and began to draw on his stockings. "Oh dear," he said, in tones of great concern.

"What is it?" the viscount said, his voice cracking with anticipated horror.

"I fear I see the beginnings of a chilblain on this toe."

"No!" Lord Wynstowe snatched up his foot and contorted himself, trying to bring his gnarled big toe close to his face. His efforts had limited success, but were nonetheless sufficient to satisfy his fears. "I see it!" he said, probing a spot on the knuckle. "There is a discoloration!"

"I'm sure Dr. Fitzpatrick will be able to treat this serious malady," Charlie said dubiously. "He is, after all, a very accomplished physician, even if inexperienced."

"How do you call a man accomplished if he has no experience in any clime but that of the county in which he was born? Nay, I don't believe Dr. Fitzpatrick can be accomplished. In point of fact, he is the most decidedly unaccomplished physician I have ever known. I shall never again allow him to wait on me at Wynstowe Manor, never, by God! I must away to London immediately. Only there will I find care adequate to my needs." Lord Wynstowe prodded again at his toe and moaned. "Oh, it is so painful! Agony!"

Charlie knew his gentleman to be impressionable, but that he would not only see an invisible spot but imagine excruciating pain was more than he could have hoped for. Nonetheless, Charlie felt a pang of guilt. Poor Fitzpatrick! The doctor was kind and thorough and, if a bit pompous, possessed of infinite patience for Lord Wynstowe's medical whims and whimsies. When next they were at Wynstowe Manor, Charlie decided, he would do everything in his power to rehabilitate the doctor in Lord Wynstowe's good opinion.

How surprising it was, he thought, his newly discovered capacity for subterfuge and scheming. He had, from the moment he knew that such a thing existed, determined, no matter the cost, to be an honest man. Though no one would call his father honorable, the man was not a liar. For the senior

Mr. Wells, this was a matter not of pride but of bluster. Let anyone who disagreed with what he said or objected to his behavior come for him! He cared not. And yet, whatever the motivation, honesty may indeed have been his single merit.

Did the ease with which Charlie manipulated his lord prove him to be the horrible thing his father was not, a dishonest man? For love! Charlie thought. For Alice! He swore that the moment he finally gained possession of the one he adored he would reject all but the most aboveboard paths and words.

On the morrow, Charlie penned a short note to his beloved. He wrote that he would reach London within two days, and he would do what he could to encourage his lord to remain there as long as possible. Alice should write him as soon as she found herself at liberty to visit him there.

Sad Alice! She received this letter not three days after she had gone home to spend her half-day with her family. It would be another two weeks before she would have another day free to meet Charlie in the great city. What if he had left for Wynstowe by then? To add insult to injury, the visit that stole from her the opportunity to see Charlie had been an unpleasant one. It had begun well enough. She arrived in time to accompany her family to church, and though the rector was his usual dull and hectoring self, she took pleasure in the company of her brothers and sisters, their faces scrubbed pink, their Sunday clothes clean and fresh. Each of the girls had a ribbon in her hair, blue for Janet and green for Susan. Her father, resentful of the strictures of his Sunday attire, scratched at the neck of his starched shirt. Her mother wore a woolen cloak in a brown-and-white shepherd's check that Alice had given her on her birthday. It had once belonged to the dowager, and that lady's housekeeper had demanded no fewer than three of Lady Jemima's dresses in exchange. It was hardly a fair trade,

Alice knew, but she wanted the cloak for her mother so very much. Its style was old-fashioned, but Alice had refreshed it, updating it with new ribbons and a clasp she had found at the rag-and-bone shop. That the dowager was dead had given her some pause, but her mother had not minded wearing a dead lady's clothing, so long, she said, as "she ain't passed on while she was wearing it."

Alice's sisters sat on either side of her in the pew, clutching her hands in theirs and occasionally whispering in her ear how much they had missed her. In the pew across from them sat Fred Harris, a yeoman farmer who owned a dozen acres a few miles from the land Alice's father leased. Mr. Harris was near forty, with a reputation as an admirable farmer and an unpleasant man. He had been widowed the year previous, and his three motherless children sat next to him, noses diligently in their prayer books, in stark contrast to Alice's sisters.

When the rector led the congregation in the singing of "My Shepherd Will Supply My Need," Mr. Harris fairly bellowed. Unfortunately, this set Janet and Susan into fits of not entirely unreasonable giggles.

" 'He brings my wand'ring spirit back / When I forsake His ways,' " Mr. Harris trumpeted, glowering at them.

The girls hushed, but Alice did not quail. Such was her character that even a deserved scolding from someone she disliked made her recalcitrant, and in this instance she most certainly did not think that a little girl's giggle was justification for censure, even in church. She glared right back at Mr. Harris. When he was the first to avert his eyes, she was further disgusted. Obnoxious and also weak-willed, the most unpleasant of combinations.

After the service, Alice returned home to find that her mother had prepared a repast fit for a feast day rather than a typical Sunday. There was a roast joint and a fowl, crisp and golden potatoes, sprouts, jugged hare, cabbage stewed in gravy, and a suet pudding served with custard. Whilst observing the preparations for this fine dinner, Alice felt warm appreciation for her mother, who so dearly missed her daughter's presence that she made her a meal fit for a lady of the great house. It was only when a firm knock on the door announced a visitor that she realized hers was not the company for whom the banquet had been prepared.

She opened the door to find none other than Mr. Harris and his children waiting on the threshold. It was all she could do to prevent her face from betraying her dismay.

"Come in," she said, but the man had already led his children into the room, which served the family for sitting, dining, and living.

Alice's father was sunk in his armchair before the hearth, busy with his pipe and the previous evening's *Express,* and looked no happier to see Mr. Harris than she. "Now, ain't this a treat," he said glumly.

Alice went back into the kitchen, crossed her arms, and raised an eyebrow at her mother, who had not the good grace even to blush.

"He's all alone in the world, poor man, raising those motherless nippers."

Mr. Harris's wife had died in childbirth the year previous, along with her baby. Her death had surprised the village, as she had been a robust and capable woman who ran her husband's dairy with the exactitude and firmness of purpose with which the Duke of Wellington led the Seventh Coalition against Napoleon Bonaparte. Her butter was so prized she could price it a few pence higher than other women's and still sell out of her stock on market day. Her success made her arrogant and proud, but that was not the least of her displeasing traits. She complemented her husband's castigating piety with a censorious devotion to bitter gossip, and there were few in the village who had not fallen victim to her malicious tongue. Those who had not thought her too strong to die thought her too unpleasant, for does not the proverb say that only the good amongst us shall die young?

But die she had, and now this lady's widower was in need of a wife.

Mrs. Lockey handed Alice a platter, took one for herself, and hurried out of the kitchen. She stopped in her tracks at the sight of Mr. Harris seated at the head of the table, relegating poor Mr. Lockey to the foot, but quickly recovered.

"Children! Sit," she ordered.

"But, Mam," Susan said, "Mr. Harris is in our dad's chair!"

Mrs. Lockey stuffed a bun into Susan's mouth.

"Let us say grace," Mr. Harris said, as though it were he hosting them in his house and not the other way round. "Bless, O Lord, this food which we are about to receive, and grant that we, who are filled with thy many gifts, may learn to give freely to those in need, through Jesus Christ our Lord."

"Amen," the family murmured, reaching for their forks. The pious man, however, was not done.

"Almighty God, who openest thy hand and fillest all things living with plenteousness, bless, we beseech thee, this food to the use of our bodies, and our bodies to thy service, through Jesus Christ our Lord."

This time they knew better than to stir.

"O Lord Jesus Christ, who when on earth hadst compassion upon those who had nothing to eat, be present with us, we beseech thee, who are gathered together to partake of that which we have received from thy bounty, and grant that, being filled with thy love, we may learn to do thy will and to show forth thy praise; who livest and reignest with the Father and the Holy Spirit, one God, world without end."

"Amen," Mr. Lockey said firmly, preventing Mr. Harris from launching into further reverent exhortations. With relief, they dug in.

"Try the dressing, Mr. Harris," Alice's mother said. "It's a favorite in this house."

Mr. Harris took the serving bowl and helped himself to so generous a portion that it left little for anyone else. Rolling her eyes, Alice took the bowl and went to the kitchen to refill it. When she returned, she found her mother and Mr. Harris engaged in earnest conversation.

"Our Alice is maid to Lady Jemima, Mr. Harris. She earns near forty pound a year, ain't that so, Alice?"

"I'm sure Mr. Harris isn't interested in my wages."

"Why not?" Mr. Harris said. "Any man'd be curious."

"It's forty pound a year," Mrs. Lockey said, firmly. "Thereabouts. You know, I was in service myself—try the sprouts, Mr. Harris—it's fine preparation for the life of a farmer's wife. You learn to keep a house clean, you learn to talk proper and mind your manners with them that's higher up—gravy?—it serves a wife well, it does."

Mr. Harris sniffed. "Service be a lowly occupation. So many rough sorts."

"Not a lady's maid!" Mrs. Lockey insisted. "A lady's maid is ever so high a position, almost as grand as the housekeeper. And there's a bit of extra cash to be had from selling the lady's dresses. Alice's skilled with a needle. She made over that Sunday cloak you saw me wearing in church today. And she made over her own dress, too. Ain't it fine? You wouldn't know it weren't new. Such a lovely color!"

Alice looked down at her plate as if the roast were the most curious thing any girl had ever seen.

"Red?" Mr. Harris sniffed. "Not suited for a gal, I don't think."

"Oh, but beggars can't be choosers, can they, Mr. Harris?" Alice said. "A lowly servant has to manage with what her lady passes off to her."

He was not so stupid that he did not understand her tone, and it was now his turn to examine his meal.

"Come lend a hand with the pudding," Mrs. Lockey said to Alice.

"I'll do it, Ma!" Janet said, getting up.

"You sit!" Mrs. Lockey said sharply. "Alice. Now."

Once in the kitchen, Mrs. Lockey turned on her.

"What's wrong with you?"

"What's wrong with *me*? You'd better ask what's wrong with *him*. I can't abide him."

"You'd best learn to *abide,*" Mrs. Lockey said. "Because that man's farm brings him three hundred a year."

"I'd never marry him, not for a thousand a year!"

"You think you can do better'n Mr. Fred Harris, missy, you got another think coming. He's a solid man. Won't drink his earnings away. You'd do a lot worse."

"If I can't do better than Mr. Harris, I'll never marry. *Never.*"

"Oh, hush now, and bring out the custard."

The women came out to find Mr. Harris giving a long oration about his plans for a plot of land he had recently acquired.

"It'd bring in a fair amount planted in hops. Hops are better'n wheat, I always say. Better'n barley, too."

"Is that so?" Mr. Lockey said.

"You're in wheat and barley, ain't you?" Harris said. "You'd be better turning your field to hops."

Mr. Lockey gave his wife a pleading glance. It was not fair to expect a hardworking man to spend his Sunday listening to a boring man's parade of self-satisfactions and vague insults.

Alice pushed back her chair. "I must be on my way back up to the house before it gets too late. And I imagine your children need to get to bed, Mr. Harris."

"No!" cried Susan. "You said you'd stay over until the morning! You swore it!"

"I've got to do Lady Jemima's hair special for tonight."

"How'll you do it, our Alice?" Janet asked.

At this Alice launched into a long and detailed description of hairstyles, designed to make her seem as vacuous and silly a girl as ever crossed dour Fred Harris's path. She refused his grudging offer of a ride home in his wagon, and set off along the path back to the manor.

And so it was with unbearable disappointment that our heroine discovered that this unhappy day would now cost her one in Charlie's company. She moped for a bit; then a thought crept upon her. If Charlie would prey upon elements of his lord's character to engineer a visit to London, she could do the same. Our hero's and heroine's natures were similar, and she, too, vowed that once her goal was achieved, she would henceforth resist the lure of manipulation.

My reader will forgive another aside. In this covenant, Charlie was to be successful. But Alice, honest and straightforward Alice, would in her life go on to embrace wholeheartedly the power of coercion, though always in service of the greater good.

While dressing Lady Jemima the next afternoon, she asked after Mr. James Smythe-Roberts.

"Is he better, ma'am?"

"It seems so," Lady Jemima said. "Lady Harlowe wrote

to Mama that he was convalescing. And his wife has given birth to yet another son. The woman is a broodmare. By the time she is done, she will have more than the Queen. Poor Thomas."

"Is the family still in London?" Alice asked, knowing what the answer would be. Mrs. Smythe-Roberts had been determined to be treated with chloroform for the birth of her baby, a service that was only available in the capital. This had caused no small amount of talk in the servants' hall when the family had been in residence at Marlecombe Park, with the men wondering why a woman would make such a fuss ("It's not like getting a leg amputated, is it?") and the women nearly all resoundingly in favor ("You were sneezing a melon out your nose, you'd want to be knocked silly, too").

"I expect so," Lady Jemima said.

"Oh dear," Alice said.

"Why shouldn't they be in London?"

"No reason 't-all," Alice said. She went to the cupboard and pulled out two pair of boots. "Only I heard downstairs that Miss Mountjoy had gone up to London as well."

"What does it signify that the featherbrained Caroline Mountjoy is in London?"

"Nothing, I'm sure. Would ma'am like button boots or lace-up?"

"Buttons, in case I have to run after Merlin. I don't want to trip on my laces."

Lady Jemima was a member of the local hawking club and a famously accomplished falconer. She kept two birds, a peregrine falcon inappositely named Merlin, and a merlin falcon named Grace, after her sister, an appellation that she insisted was an honor but which Lady Grace knew full well to be an insult. Alice had once or twice seen her lady working her falcons, and had been impressed not only with the lady's skill but with her attitude. She took after her father, whom she admired terribly. Lord Alderwick's relationship with his raptors was far more romantic than that with his wife. Like him, Lady Jemima was imperturbable and easy when she had a bird of prey perched on her wrist, entirely unlike the Lady Jemima of indoors.

"Does Mr. Thomas Smythe-Roberts hawk?" Alice asked.

"He has no experience, but I let him wear Merlin once and he was excellent with him. He said he found it absolutely exhilarating."

"And does Miss Mountjoy?"

"Caroline Mountjoy? A falconer? Don't be ridiculous. She is not good for anything but rattling away at the pianoforte like a music-shop Sigismond Thalberg."

"I suppose 'tis why she is in London, then. Not liking the outdoors." With the boots buttoned, Alice moved aside so the lady could get up. "It's nice for Miss Mountjoy that she has Mr. Smythe-Roberts in London to entertain her."

Lady Jemima stamped her sour foot in its fresh-cleaned and scented boot. "I don't see why he had to go."

"To help his brother, I suppose," Alice said.

"How could he possibly be of any help at all? He is not a nursemaid! Lord and Lady Harlowe are there to take care of his brother. That is help enough!"

With that, Lady Jemima flounced out of the room, leaving Alice to hope that for once her lady's spirits would not be rejuvenated by an afternoon in the outdoors.

FOURTEEN

By noon the next morning, Lady Jemima and Alice were on the front step at Aunt Bennett's house in Warwick Place—an address Lady Jemima found less than desirable, but the only place Lady Alderwick would agree to let her daughter visit on her own. The front door opened onto a narrow entry, which led to a small drawing room stuffed with furniture upholstered in richly colored fabrics, Persian carpets, and embroidered draperies. Ornate inlaid occasional tables were scattered about the room, on each one a Grecian statuette or urn, or a bouquet of silk sunflowers. A lacquered Chinese cabinet took up an entire wall, and there was a low pillow-strewn divan positioned to allow a view onto the street. The opulence, though different in style, harked to Lady Alderwick's chocolate box of a sitting room, which amused Alice. She would have thought that Miss Bennett would have had more austere tastes.

At the sight of her aunt, Lady Jemima laughed. "Aunt Sarah! Are you on your way to a masquerade?" The lady was attired as if to conform with her décor, in a flowing Pre-Raphaelite gown of a vibrant shade of deepest emerald, embroidered with lemons and pomegranates, and tied with gold cord. It was nothing like the unadorned dresses Alice was used to seeing her wear. Alice imagined an entire cupboard of plain mouse-colored dresses marked "Marlecombe Park" gathering dust in an attic room, shaken out only for the lady's quarterly pilgrimage to her sister.

Alice had packed for Lady Jemima three large trunks stuffed with dresses and gowns, shoes, slippers and boots, and heaps of linen. There were half a dozen hatboxes and caskets of finery and jewels. As difficult as it had been to keep track of everything on the train and in the hansom from the station, it was that much harder to cram it all into the small bedchamber that Miss Bennett kept for visitors. Eventually, the hostess turned over her own room for her niece's use, a generosity Lady Jemima viewed as no more than her due.

"What does an old lady need with a room this size?" Lady Jemima said. The "old lady" in question had thirty-six years. "She must be so busy with her ridiculous meetings, art exhibitions, and comings and goings that she does not even make use of it. It is far better for it to be mine."

"I am indeed very busy with all sorts of ridiculous gatherings," a voice said dryly. Alice, busy taking Miss Bennett's clothes and objects from out of the cupboards and chests of drawers and replacing them with her lady's, turned to see the good lady standing in the doorway.

Lady Jemima looked abashed, but only for a moment. "If you would not *lurk* about, Aunt, you would not hear things said about you."

"I take note of your criticism, Jemima, and will endeavor to lurk less in my own home. I have come to tell you that you will be dining alone tonight. I have an engagement at the Somerville Club." The lady's voice was droll. In all, her manner in her own home was so much more relaxed than how she presented herself in Marlecombe Park, where her situation as a guest and her circumstances as a spinster conspired to make her not at her ease.

"Alone?" Lady Jemima said. "On my first night in town?"

"I expect it is I who will generally be dining alone while you are visiting here. One night of solitude won't harm you overmuch."

"Where are you going? Send a message that I will be joining you."

"You would find it entirely too dull."

"I should not!"

"I am dining at the home of Miss Bessie Parkes. After dinner, Mrs. Bodichon will be reading aloud from her novel and taking questions about her other literary works."

At the name of the author of the pamphlet she had so admired, Alice's ears pricked. She wished she could be in that room to hear that intelligent lady speak. Miss Bennett noticed Alice's attention, and for a moment wondered whether it might not be possible to bring the girl with her. Miss Sarah Bennett fancied herself an Aesthetic and a free-thinker. She had struggled through Mr. Heinrich Heine's *Deutschland. Ein Wintermärchen* in the original German, and though most of it was barely intelligible to her, she wholeheartedly condemned nationalism, militarism, and bourgeois obedience, and believed, at least theoretically, in the realization of the liberal ideal, so long, that is, that it would not rob her of the living she valued so highly, or of the neat little house of which she was so proud. However, for all her pretenses to modernity, Miss Bennett was a well-bred lady, the sister-in-law of an earl and the cousin (once removed) of a duke, and the idea of bringing a member of the lower classes to dine at the home of a friend of hers was so impossible that she was quite astonished that the thought had crossed her mind.

"A *reading*?" Lady Jemima said in horror, as though the invitation had been to a beheading. (Come to think of it, the bloodthirsty young lady would have mightily enjoyed that sort of event.) "I will write to all my friends and see if any of them are in town. There must be a table I can be squeezed round."

"I hope you'll not mind sleeping with me, Miss Lockey," the housekeeper said later that afternoon. "We're crammed in so tight there's nary a cupboard to put you in." What passed for a servants' hall in the house was a table set up in a corner of the kitchen, but it was cozy enough. It allowed cheerful Cook to be a part of every conversation, and gave ready access for all to the kettle and the biscuit tin.

"That suits me," Alice said.

"That eases my mind. We was all worried Lady Jemima'd be insulted to know her maid didn't have a room of her own."

"I don't think my lady has once in her life considered where I lay my head. It's possible she thinks I sleep hung by my ankles in a broom cupboard. I wonder, Mrs. Goodenough, might it be possible to post a letter?"

"The lad comes with the afternoon post round about four. If you'll give me your letter, I'll see he gets it."

Alice handed over a letter to Charlie. In it, she had written that she had succeeded in getting herself to London, and provided him Miss Bennett's address. She wrote that she did not know if she would be able to get away, or if her half-days would be suspended during their visit. Perhaps, if he was at liberty one evening, he might come to Warwick Place, and she would walk out for a bit while Lady Jemima was herself out for the evening.

Lady Jemima was also busy writing letters. The half-dozen notes she scribbled that afternoon were more than Alice had seen her write in her entire life, but by the last post she had only a single reply.

"Caroline Mountjoy," Lady Jemima groaned as Alice tugged her stays tight. The young lady's waist measured eighteen inches round, a feat accomplished only by Alice's significant effort. "Stupid, stupid, stupid Caroline Mountjoy. It will be torture." A torture, it seemed, that was less painful only than the prospect of dining alone.

Alice knotted Lady Jemima's stays and blotted the sweat from her own brow. "Perhaps Mr. Smythe-Roberts will be there," she said.

"I do not honestly know whether to hope he will or not. I hate to think of him dining regularly with that fat toad. But, oh, how I do miss him!"

"Does he yet know you are in London?"

"I wrote to his mother. I don't know if she is accepting callers, but I shall drop my card tomorrow. If nothing else, he will see it on the plate. If he does, he will pay a call, I am sure of it."

To Lady Jemima's chagrin, Mr. Thomas Smythe-Roberts was not at the dinner. This Alice discovered from Dick, Miss Bennett's man of all work, who accompanied Lady Jemima in the brougham hired to take her to and from the Mountjoy house. While waiting for the young lady, he took the cook of that establishment up on her offer of a cup of tea and a serving of bread with drippings, and proceeded to quiz the servants as to those who dined. Mr. Thomas Smythe-Roberts had sent his regrets, but Mr. and Mrs. Philip Ayres were in attendance, along with their spinster daughter, Olivia. There was an heir-in-waiting to an earl who was about to celebrate his centennial who might have been of interest to a young, unmarried lady had he not been near seventy years old. Also in the company were a bishop, a Mountjoy lady cousin, and to Lady Jemima's horror, Lord Wynstowe.

"The footman said the little lady was as pale as a trout's belly when she set her eyes on the lord," Dick recounted. "He nodded, curt as you please, and she turned in t'other direction."

"Is there history betwixt her and his lordship?" the housekeeper asked Alice.

Alice said, "I wouldn't call it history, but she doesn't care for him."

Dick said, "Care for him? She can't stand him, and him with fifty thousand pounds a year."

"Oh my!" the housekeeper said. "Such a well-to-do man! And so handsome, too, they say."

"I don't know 'bout handsome, but he's got sheep stations in New Zealand that bring him thousands, and word is he found a second seam o' coal on his place, and they say it'll make him as rich a man as any."

"And she can afford to turn her nose up at that, can she?" Cook said. "How much does she have?"

Dick said, "Twenty thousand pounds'll go to her husband. There's naught for her personal use besides her jewels, though folks expect his lordship'll set a bit aside for her."

"How ever do you know all this?" Alice asked.

"Old Dick knows all, missy," Cook said. It was true. Dick, in all other ways a man typical of the laboring class, liked to keep track of the comings and goings of the gentry. He was a devoted reader of *Punch,* though always a week or two behind, as he had to wait for Miss Bennett to be done with the journal. He knew his *Debrett's* backward and forward, and had committed to memory the names of all the titled aristocracy. He knew who was to marry whom, who wore what to whose ball, whose estate had been let and why. His employment in the house of a lady who eschewed all social gatherings other than the most obscure positively broke the man's heart, and he was only too delighted to have the opportunities Lady Jemima's visit provided.

Cook said, "Twenty thousand pound ain't *so* much. Who is she to turn her nose up at a viscount?"

"It's that Mr. Smythe-Roberts she's after," Dick said.

"Is that true, Miss Lockey? Is she carrying a torch for him?" the housekeeper said.

"She is," Alice said. "And I suppose he fancies her, too."

"Mr. Thomas's a rotten one," Dick said. "He keeps a lady in a house in the Ladbroke Estate. She's a singer, older than the young sir by a dozen years."

My reader may be surprised to read of the frankness of the conversation of those downstairs about the most intimate affairs of their masters. I assure you, this is no fiction. As the great French lady Anne-Marie Bigot de Cornuel, mistress of King Louis XIV, once said, "No man is a hero to his valet." We may add, nor any lady a heroine to her maid. Our servants know our innermost secrets, the details of our most clandestine assignations, the whys and wherefores of our most intimate acts, the corporeal humiliations we hide even from our spouses. Why are we so very sure of their utmost discretion? Do we maintain the same when it comes to them? Nay, we decry their faults and foibles at every turn, rant to our friends about the "servant problem," blame them when we misplace a bauble, trouble them without reference to their basic needs of sleep and sustenance, give them nary a moment to themselves. They are entirely dependent on our largesse for their bread and comfort. They may be dismissed at our whim without a character, or with one so lukewarm they are likely to find themselves without prospect of earning a living. If they gossip about us around the servants' table not out of malice but the way a child speaks of a parent, out of mingled fascination and fear, do you call it unjust?

"All right, now," the housekeeper said. "We don't need to bend Miss Lockey's ear anymore. We'd all best be abed. They'll be ringing soon enough."

The cook said to Alice, "The missus wakes not much past dawn, but yours'll sleep late, I reckon. Don't worry about breakfast. I'll keep you a plate warm by the hearth."

The boy handed Alice a hot flannel-wrapped brick of her own for the bed she was to share with the housekeeper, and the housemaid filled a pitcher with warm water for her to wash. They were all so kind, Alice thought. She hoped that Lady Jemima would stay with her aunt for a while, both so that she could see her Charlie, and so that she could remain in such warm and friendly company.

FIFTEEN

When Alice came down to the servants' hall for her dinner the next day, who did she find sitting at the table, dipping a biscuit into a cup of tea, but her own Charlie Wells.

"Mr. Wells," Alice said, her voice cracking with the effort of containing the tumult of her emotions.

"Dear Miss Lockey!" Charlie said, leaping to his feet.

Fortunately, there was no proper Mrs. Platt to scold, nor a Mr. Dale to give a disapproving glare down his nose at the young man's obvious delight. In this house, gentle, good-natured Mrs. Goodenough clucked and cooed like a pigeon. The housekeeper was a devotee of young love, despite her own sad experience, or perhaps because of it. As a girl, she had fallen in love with a Greek boy, a waiter in a coffeehouse. Cristos Katsourbos had returned the compliment, and proposed to her on the eve of his departure home to Heraklion to join the struggle for unification with Greece. He would send for her, he promised, as soon as liberation from the Ottoman

Empire was achieved. A week later, the owner of the coffeehouse himself returned to Crete, and so there was none to inform sad Miss Goodenough of the young revolutionary's death in the Cretan uprising, leaving her forever ignorant of her lover's fate. She knew only that he had gone away and not returned. The "Mrs." appended to her name as was the custom for a housekeeper never failed to give her a twinge of longing for the young man who might have made her a wife.

Charlie's eyes were the precise gray of Cristos's, Mrs. Goodenough thought fondly, a belief that was made no less enrapturing by the fact that her dead lover's eyes had been a nondescript brown.

Charlie took up Alice's hand, but then seemed not to know what to do with it. He inclined his head, and Alice thought for one horrified moment that he might kiss it like a medieval knight, but instead he satisfied himself with shaking it vigorously, as if they were two farmers sealing the deal on the sale of a calf.

"Sit down, both of you," Cook called from her station by the iron range. "There's no dinner upstairs, so I've done us a bit o' something special."

"I'd hoped I might take Miss Lockey out," Charlie said. He turned to Alice. "There is a chophouse not too far."

"Chops is what I'm serving you here, and they'll be better quality and cost you naught. Now, take your seats afore it gets cold."

Charlie looked as if he were again to demur, but Alice said, "We'd be happy to dine here with you, wouldn't we, Mr. Wells?"

"Pshaw!" Mrs. Goodenough said. "You'll not convince me that you're 'Mr. Wells' and 'Miss Lockey' to each other when you're on your own."

The housemaid served the meal, which was indeed a fine one. As soon as Charlie's plate was empty, Cook heaped it afresh, as if she knew of the tribulations Charlie suffered at the hands of Lord Wynstowe's cook, who had unfortunately traveled to London so that her lord could enjoy her absence no longer than necessary.

Only once Charlie had polished his plate twice, eaten more pudding than anyone other than Dick (who, though half his size, ate as much), and effused his gratitude to Cook and to Mrs. Goodenough, was he able, finally, to squire Alice out of the house.

"I am so happy to see you," he exclaimed, even as they were climbing the short flight of stairs from the servants' entrance to the street.

"I'm happy to see you, too."

He took up her hand again and squeezed it. Their joined hands sent a wave of desire through each, as though their bodies were pressed one against the other rather than connected merely by a small expanse of palm.

"How long do we have?" he asked.

"She won't return until midnight, I shouldn't think. Though, to be safe, I'd best be back by eleven."

"That gives us time enough."

"For what?"

"Have you ever been to a music hall?"

"A music hall? Is it . . . respectable?"

"I've not been myself, but I asked the haberdasher when I took Lord Wynstowe's gibus in for repair, and he promised there'd be no gaudy acts, nothing a girl would be ashamed to see. I've bought tickets for the stalls, because he did say the gallery might be rowdy."

Alice had never even been to a popular amusement, and

from the first moment they stepped into New Canterbury Hall, she was agog. She stared up at the sweeping staircases, crystal chandeliers, and gilded walls. Some in the crowd were indeed rowdy, but those most raucous rushed to the gallery. The stalls, where Charlie and Alice sat, were more sedate, though still festive. He settled her in her chair, and after receiving her assurances that she would be comfortable on her own for a few minutes, went off in search of refreshment. The plump lady seated next to her graced her with a smile marred only by a blackened lower tooth. Despite this misfortune, she was otherwise appealing—neat and tidy, with a fine peacock feather decorating her pretty ginger hair. She smelled of lavender and offered Alice an Allen & Hanburys Glycerine Pastille from a tin. Alice at first declined, but upon the lady's insistence took one and popped it into her mouth.

The lady then pulled from her reticule a scrap of white linen and a small bottle of lavender scent. She shook a drop of scent onto the handkerchief and handed it to Alice. "It can get pungent in here, especially as the hour grows late."

Alice accepted that as well, just as Charlie arrived with a chocolate biscuit perched atop a small tulip-shaped glass, and a pint of beer. "Sherry," he said, handing the glass to her.

"Did you bring nothing for yourself to eat?"

"Don't worry about me," he said.

She took a bite of the biscuit, washed it down with a sip of sherry, and announced, "Delicious!"

As the band began a lively musical overture, Charlie slipped an arm round her shoulders, and she settled back to enjoy the show. In ringing tones, the barker announced the audience's good fortune in being treated to the wonders of "Madame Lola the Serpent Lady," and a mysterious and exotic figure draped in shimmering silks took the stage, her hair adorned with gold coins that glinted beneath the lights. With a gasp, Alice realized that in her sinuous arms the performer cradled a large, coiled snake. "It's a python," Charlie whispered in Alice's ear as Madame Lola began to twirl with hypnotic fluidity. In her finale, the dancer brought the snake's head to her face, pursed her lips, and accepted the kiss of its long flickering tongue. The crowd burst into hysterical applause, tossing coins at Madame Lola's feet. She scooped up the offerings and glided off the stage, the curtains swaying shut behind her.

"Horrible!" Alice whispered to Charlie with delight.

The next act was a master illusionist who invited up a member of the gallery. He sat the lucky volunteer, a young lady with flowing blond hair wearing a diaphanous gown unsuited, Alice thought, to the evening's entertainment, in a chair, and swung a pendant before her eyes. He uttered a few sonorous words, and put her into a trance. With a flick of his fingers, he caused her to levitate above the crowd and float through the air over the gallery, her gossamer gown trailing behind her. The audience sat with their heads tipped up, staring in awe. When the magician gently lowered his volunteer back to the stage, Alice thought she noticed the pull of some kind of wire at the back of the woman's dress, but decided to put that out of her mind. Better to enjoy the fun than ruin it with skepticism.

The trampoline act left Alice gasping in amazement, the musical jester's songs were crass but undeniably entertaining, but the highlight of the show was the headliner, a tall man with a flamboyant mustache, wearing a silk top hat twice the height of any Alice had ever seen and a swirling velvet cloak. Champagne Charlie strode commandingly onto the stage, struck a pose, and launched into his signature song. Alice appeared to be the only person in the vast audience who did not know the words. In unrestrained unison the crowd sang along: "For Champagne Charlie is my name, / Good for any game at night, my boys!"

After this rollicking performance, Charlie told Alice that the hour was growing late, and they had to leave.

"But we haven't seen the Grande Finale!" she said.

"I promise we will come again, and stay through the encore."

They walked home, Alice's hand tucked up under Charlie's arm. As they passed out of each circle of amber light cast by the gas lamps, they leaned in to each other, taking advantage of the moments of darkness to press the length of their bodies together. When they stepped into the next glowing circle, they would shift gently apart. They were quiet, focusing on having their bodies move in synchronicity, until Alice finally sighed.

"I wish I knew when next I'd see you," she said.

"I wish I could see you every day."

She felt her cheeks, cold in the night air, grow warm with pleasure. They walked on, but soon she sensed a lag in Charlie's gait, a stiffness in his arm. Had she been too forward? Was he displeased?

"Alice . . ." His voice trailed away.

She waited.

"Alice," he said again, and again did not continue.

A church bell began its gloomy tolling. She counted one, two, three, and on until eleven, but still he did not speak. Chastened, she tried to slip her hand from beneath his arm, but he held it fast and cleared his throat.

"I am a poor man. I earn only fifty pounds a year."

"Fifty pound a year is not so little. Myself, I make only forty."

"Fifty pounds might be adequate to support a single man in service, but in my case it must stretch to sustain two more, my mother and my sister. Three people can barely manage on what I earn. To support four would be impossible. Oh, Alice . . ." He struggled ineffectively to contain his emotion. "I would ask you to marry me if only I could."

Sensible, practical Alice did not swoon, or even allow herself more than a moment's joy, because she knew this to be no proposal, only regret that one was impossible. Charlie was right. The life four would lead on fifty pounds a year would be penurious no matter their talent for economy. Moreover, even if Charlie were not encumbered with a mother and sister, the confines of his employment discouraged marriage. What form of wedlock was it in which a man slept elsewhere and saw his wife a single afternoon every other week, one full day a month, and that only when his lord was at home? What wife would content herself with such an arrangement, especially if there were children pining for their father? If only they worked in the same house they might see each other every day! Alice recalled Mademoiselle Lefebvre's offer to engineer Mr. Cahill's dismissal and Charlie's employment as Lord Alderwick's valet and thought bitterly that if she had that other young lady's casual relationship with morality she might have had a way to make herself content.

"If only Mr. Cahill were older," she said.

"Lord Alderwick's valet?"

"Were he ready to retire, we might find a way for you to take his position. But it will be a decade before he goes, at least."

Charlie halted, staring at her. She looked at him in puzzlement.

"What if Lord Wynstowe marries?" he said. "You could come to his house as maid to his wife! The house is not what you're used to, but if we are together, we can tolerate anything!"

"But any wife he'd have would bring her own maid," she said.

"What, then, if he were to marry your own lady?" He drew her to him, excitement replacing his prior woe. "This is the ideal solution to our predicament! We must make the two fall in love and marry, and then will we be able to as well!"

Alice laughed. "Lady Jemima love Lord Wynstowe? She'd sooner marry his carriage horse."

Charlie felt the prospect of happiness slip through his fingers. How could fate put such a girl in his way only to snatch her from him? He cursed his gentleman for being a tepid milksop. "Lord Wynstowe isn't entirely unappealing. There are things a young lady might value," Charlie said.

"Like what?"

They walked nearly an entire block as Charlie tried to come up with something. Finally, he said, "He is comely, is he not? And his estate is very good. Also, he is generous. Lady Wynstowe would never need to economize."

Alice considered this. "It is true that Lady Jemima is excessively fond of the things money buys."

"Fond enough to marry a man she despises?"

"We won't ever find out. She's expecting an offer from Mr. Thomas Smythe-Roberts, and then I'll be off with her to wherever he lives."

Gloomily, they resumed their walk. As they approached the house, Alice said, "If your lord were only like you, she could not help but love him."

"And if she were like you, even he could not resist her."

Then he swept Alice up in his arms and pressed his lips to hers.

Her first kiss! She had not once in her life been kissed by anyone other than her mother and sisters. Though not unaffectionate, her father was not physical with his children, and her brothers would sooner have kicked her in the shins than pressed their lips to her cheek. She had never returned the affections of any of the young men of the village who vied for her attentions, and certainly not allowed them such an intimacy. Charlie's lips were soft and warm; the faint stubble on his chin was rough against her skin. A kiss, Alice thought, was even more wonderful than she had allowed herself to imagine.

Unlike Alice, Charlie was not an innocent. He had kissed a few, and cuddled. (I warn the most delicate of my readers to skip ahead a page, lest the description that follows trouble their sensibilities.) Only once, however, had he fallen prey to the typical experiences of his sex. On the eve of his leaving the workhouse, his father had taken him to the room of one of the unfortunates who plied the oldest trade in a dark corner of the forbidding establishment. Though successful in achieving its ends, that experience had left our hero feeling as though he had sullied both himself and the sad-faced woman. All was made much worse by the fact that his father had entered the door as Charlie exited, leaving his son to run from the room to avoid the cacophony of grunts and moans all too similar to the ones he was used to hearing from his parents' pallet.

What Charlie felt kissing Alice was as unlike that experience as the giraffe of their excursion to the Zoological Gardens was to her elephant neighbor.

The trundling of wheels on cobblestones sent them leaping apart. Down the road, a brougham pulled up to Miss Bennett's house.

Alice took off at a run.

"We can't give up," Charlie called after. "We must at least try to encourage their love!"

Over her shoulder, she cried, "It can't hurt to try!"

She was down the stairs to the servants' entrance even as her lady alighted from the carriage.

SIXTEEN

There was no way to encourage Lady Jemima's receptivity to a suit by Lord Wynstowe as long as her attentions were focused upon Mr. Thomas Smythe-Roberts, so Alice determined that her first task would be to separate those lovers. While dressing her lady the next morning, she asked with feigned insouciance, "Has Mr. Thomas Smythe-Roberts yet paid a call?" She knew well that he had not, for Dick provided those downstairs with a full accounting not only of any guest who might have arrived, but of that individual's state of health, family history, approximate yearly income, favorite haberdasher, and any other detail of which he believed his audience should be aware.

"He has not," Lady Jemima said, with a sullen despair unfamiliar to Alice's ears. Her young lady was generally so brimming with self-love she rarely evinced anything resembling discouragement.

"Have you left your card for his mother?"

"I sent the man with it yesterday."

Alice shook her head in disapproval. “It’s not very nice for a young man to ignore a lady with whom he quite nearly had an understanding.”

Lady Jemima bit her lip. “It *is* rude, is it not?”

“I would say so. He’d be fortunate indeed were you to pay any attention to him at all.”

Lady Jemima’s sad expression hardened. “He certainly would.” There it was, the typical self-regard. All Alice had to do was water the narcissus blossom and the young lady’s loathing would surely flower.

“A lady with as many suitors as you need not tolerate such forgetfulness.”

“Indeed not.” But a worm of doubt had returned to Lady Jemima’s tone. “I think he might not have seen my card. Perhaps his mother kept it.”

No! Not this plaintive making of excuses! Alice gently pressed further, saying thoughtfully, “I wonder if there are some engagements he has accepted. Has he visited the home of Miss Caroline Mountjoy?”

At this mention of her nemesis, Lady Jemima revived. “She *says* he has come to dine, but I would not put it past her to lie.”

Time, Alice thought, to play the final card. Alice recalled that Mr. Thomas had described his relationship with his brother as other than cordial and concerned. She said, “Are the two brothers very fond of one another? Perhaps his dear brother’s illness makes Mr. Thomas so distraught he cannot contemplate social engagements.”

Lady Jemima’s shoulders slumped, but then she caught a glimpse of herself in the mirror. At once she smiled, revived by familiar vanity. “That is exactly what happened! His brother’s illness must have taken a sudden turn for the contagious after he dined with the Mountjoys. Yes! That's it. Oh, Alice! You do know exactly what to say to make me feel better." She flung an impulsive arm around Alice's neck. "Thank you!"

Desperate now, Alice fired another salvo. "I'm relieved. I didn't like to see you treated shabbily. And him only a younger son." She watched this arrow land. Lady Jemima thought of herself as deserving not only of attention and regard, but of the attention and regard of the most suitable people, which rarely included any gentleman not destined to inherit his family's fortune. "Don't fret, ma'am," Alice continued. "There are any number of young men who'd be grateful for your company, and many with fine estates and large incomes."

This appeared to snap Lady Jemima to attention and remind her of her worth and the young man's relative lack of standing. "Indeed there are. Fetch my habit. I shall go to Rotten Row. Everyone will be there."

Stymied again, Alice thought. For "everyone" did not include Lord Wynstowe, who was far too solicitous of his own comfort to ride out, even had he kept horses for his recreation.

"But you have no mount, ma'am!"

"Caroline Mountjoy promised me the use of her pony. Tell the man to go get it for me."

Having overplayed her hand, Alice did as told, and then returned to help her lady into her riding dress. As she was lacing Lady Jemima's boots, she had another thought. "Ma'am, would you care to share your engagements for the week with me, so that I might check the dress diary and prepare your gowns?"

Lady Jemima shifted through the detritus on the dressing table and handed Alice a stack of cards. "You brought me so few dresses, it will be some trick not to repeat." Alice had packed near two dozen dresses and a trunk full of trimmings to make each appear new and different.

"Pardon, ma'am."

Lady Jemima magnanimously forgave her. Once released, Alice hurried to the room she shared with Mrs. Goodenough and dashed off a quick note to Charlie, listing all of Lady Jemima's dinner engagements, as well as her plans to attend a musical at home at the Mountjoys' the following day.

That event, however, almost proved to be the undoing of all their plans. What we know about this near catastrophe we must assemble from moments observed by various members of the Mountjoy staff as relayed to Dick, as well as the account an exhilarated and shining-eyed Lady Jemima gave to Alice that evening.

Let us begin with dress, as is the custom in novels of this type. With her attention firmly affixed to the task of setting a snare for a husband, Lady Jemima was not eager to acquiesce to the modest expectations of the day. Nor, however, was she immune to fashion. On the contrary, she liked to be seen always as perfectly à la mode. This presented a conundrum, for a high-necked, long-sleeved day dress was de rigueur for an afternoon's entertainment. In a moment of inspiration, Alice resolved this dilemma by removing a panel from the bodice of a muslin dress and replacing it with one of transparent tulle. This allowed the young lady to display her décolletage while retaining the appearance of modesty. It also stood her in stark contrast to Miss Caroline Mountjoy, who was swathed in heavy velvet, her neckline so high that the ruffle of lace at the top caused an angry red rash to appear beneath her chin.

A great lover of music, the young hostess had engaged the violin virtuoso Joseph Joachim to entertain her guests, as well as a pair of charming if persistent sisters who performed a few too many Schubert lieder. The assembly's mien of rapt attention was further challenged by a tenor who, though he sang "Come Into the Garden, Maud" with great passion, could not hold a candle to Mr. John Sims Reeves, no matter how avidly he sought to imitate him. All pretense to enjoyment was finally utterly destroyed by Miss Mountjoy herself, who closed out the entertainment with a performance of such great prowess and little musicality that it inspired in the King Charles spaniel perched on the lap of the Duchess of Upper Wetwang a fit of cacophonous, near hysterical, barking. Little Patch's rhythmic yips were as an irresistible metronome to Miss Mountjoy, who increased the tempo of her playing to an incomprehensible frenzy.

In short, the afternoon musicale was a great success.

As the audience burst into an ovation more of relief than appreciation, Mr. Thomas Smythe-Roberts (for he was indeed in attendance) leaned over to whisper in Lady Jemima's ear. "I believe the pup's howled rendition of Thalberg's Fantasies was by far the superior."

Lady Jemima's unladylike snort of laughter caused the gentleman in the neighboring seat to turn on her a disapproving glare.

The ovations complete, the audience were finally served the refreshment for which they were pining. It was then that an event occurred which presented a most unfortunate contrast between Mr. Smythe-Roberts's dandified elegance and Lord Wynstowe's weakness of character, a distinction that set Alice and Charlie's cause so far back as to be, they feared, irredeemable.

It began innocently enough. A certain Miss Philippa Cromwell, descended from a lesser branch of that illustrious family, was sitting on an overstuffed sofa delicately sipping her tea when she was joined by the duchess and her canine companion. Poor Miss Cromwell's severe allergy to dogs was exceeded only by her fear of insulting one of such high rank, so she sat immovable, eyes streaming, a smile pasted to her lips. And then, horribly, she sneezed. As one of her hands was holding her teacup and the other its saucer, she was unable to bring her handkerchief to her nose, and thus the unfortunate young lady sent a spray of moisture through the air; much of it landing on the face of Lord Wynstowe, who was at that moment bending over a tray of seed cake, the better to select the most generous slice.

Lord Wynstowe had a horror of effluvia. Though lifelong, this revulsion was dramatically enhanced by an account he had recently read of a presentation in 1862 by Mr. Louis Pasteur to the French Academy of Sciences demonstrating that certain tiny entities are responsible for the fermentation and spoilage of food. Lord Wynstowe had read this account with great interest and mounting horror, and had become convinced that the world around him teemed with creatures intent upon crawling through his orifices in order to effervesce his innards. He believed, moreover, that these horrible organisms traveled through the air from one person to the next like miniature birds flying in terrible formation.

Dear Reader, you may laugh, but the monomania this created in Lord Wynstowe was genuine, if fantastical. And we must admit that even those of us with constitutions less inclined to agitation than the delicate Lord Wynstowe's might be disgusted were Miss Cromwell's torrent of droplets to land on our faces, noses, eyes, and mouths.

We might not, however, shriek. And, oh, did Lord Wynstowe shriek. He howled, then snatched up a cloth from beneath the cake knife, sending it clattering to the floor as he scrubbed at his face. The room fell silent, the footmen standing in amused attention at the catastrophe unfolding before them.

After a moment of red-faced horror, Miss Cromwell burst into tears and rushed from the room.

Still no one spoke, until Mr. Thomas Smythe-Roberts strode across the room in high dudgeon, grasped Lord Wynstowe's shoulder, and spun him round.

"Sir!" he said. "What do you mean by this ludicrous display?"

Lord Wynstowe, not willing to be insulted by a man he considered his social and intellectual inferior, launched into a lecture about the tiny, invisible creatures now crawling inside his skull. This went over as you might expect.

"Nonsense!" Mr. Smythe-Roberts said.

Lord Wynstowe persisted. Wee animals flying through the air, disease, etc., etc.

"Do you refuse to apologize, sir?" Mr. Smythe-Roberts interrupted.

"Apologize?" Lord Wynstowe looked genuinely confused.

"Apologize to the young lady for humiliating her."

"But why should I apologize?"

"You are a coward, sir! A foul coward who treats a lady ill."

Lord Wynstowe, taken terribly aback by this awful accusation issued before company, mumbled a few words and slunk from the room to find the object of his offense and press upon her his profuse apologies.

"He collapsed like a jelly left out in the sun," Lady Jemima told Alice, delighted. "Imagine believing that an invisible insect or lizard or some such can crawl from one mouth to another in a sneeze? It's too droll. He might look like the hero of a romantic novel, but Lord Wynstowe is the most strange, unpleasant, and cowardly man I've ever known."

SEVENTEEN

There was, Alice told Charlie, no possibility of kindling a romance between Lady Jemima and Lord Wynstowe. He had made himself absurd, and she had reveled in his humiliation. No two could be further apart.

They sat in a drafty corner of a chocolate shop, stealing an hour from the errands they were each running. Charlie pushed the delicate porcelain cup across the table toward her. Wanly, she lifted the cup and drank, leaving a froth of milky chocolate across her upper lip. Charlie took out a handkerchief and dabbed it away. This moment of casual intimacy did not go unobserved by the haughty French waiter, already predisposed to disapprove of young lovers so parsimonious that, though they took up two chairs, they shared a single cup. He made a great show of swabbing down the neighboring table with a filthy cloth and scowling at them, but Charlie was too concerned and Alice too low in spirits to take heed.

Alice said, "Soon enough, you'll be on your way back to Wynstowe, and Lady Jemima will marry Mr. Smythe-Roberts and take me off to live on whatever shore shiftless younger sons wash up on."

"Finish the chocolate," he said. "Before it's cold."

Alice sighed like a child and gulped down the rest of the cup. Charlie watched, entranced, as her tongue, pink as a cat's, darted over her lip.

"The way I see it," he said, "we have two problems, one nearly but not entirely insurmountable, and the other merely challenging."

"The insurmountable problem being that my lady despises your lord."

"*Nearly* insurmountable. Not entirely."

"Debatable," she said.

"Let's set that aside for now, and attack the other."

"The other meaning Mr. Thomas Smythe-Roberts, I assume," she said. "But that's no easier to solve. She's set her cap at him. She's in love."

"The Lady Jemima Alderwick you have described to me does not seem capable of love. Infatuation, maybe. Passion, perhaps. But love? Love that one feels when one's soul touches another's? Love that distracts from your work and your wants? Love that makes you prefer a stolen hour on a Tuesday afternoon in a chocolate shop to an entire year of Christmas Days? I doubt that."

Alice hid her embarrassment beneath a wry smile. "Are you going to start writing me poetry now, Charlie Wells?"

"I'm but a simple working man. I have no time for poetry."

"Shame. I do like poetry."

"Do you, now? Well, then, perhaps I'll try my hand. But until I do, we must turn our attentions to the problem of Mr. Thomas Smythe-Roberts. We know that he's a rake and a cad. And we know Old Dick says he keeps a mistress."

"Dick's never wrong."

"So we need to make the other lady's existence known to Lady Jemima, and then she's sure to reject him as not worthy of her."

Alice knew that her lady's vanity would not allow her to come second to another. She demanded to be the primary object not merely of attention but of envy. To know that someone else took space in her husband's heart would infuriate her. That this woman was of a class so far beneath hers would disgust her.

Charlie said, "I will find out from Dick who this mistress is and where she lives, and bring you some evidence of Smythe-Roberts's perfidy. You will present it to Lady Jemima. That will separate them, and afterward we'll figure some way to overcome our other problem."

"The nearly insurmountable problem."

"Nearly, but not entirely."

"I don't know whether to admire your optimism or despair of its foolishness."

"My optimism is not foolish. 'It is an ever-fixed mark, that looks on tempests and is never shaken.' "

At her puzzled frown he said, "Shakespeare's sonnet number one hundred sixteen. You see? You've turned me into a poet after all."

EIGHTEEN

Though Old Dick knew that the lady on whom Mr. Smythe-Roberts was lavishing his attentions was a singer, he did not know her name. Worse, much of the information he provided Charlie about her seemed doubtful. Charlie thought it unlikely that she was the natural daughter of Victor Emmanuel II of Sardinia, that she supplemented her income with jewel thievery, or that she had borne the children of both the Prince Consort and Prince Leopold, Duke of Albany. This last rumor was particularly improbable, as the stiff-necked and sententious father had died when the singer in question was but a child, and the son was far too delicate and tied too closely to the Queen's apron strings to father anyone's child.

Charlie, despite a childhood spent in part in the workhouse, had no connections to anyone in the city's demimonde who might have provided more accurate information, and thus determined that the best way to discover the identity of this lady of ill-repute was to follow her lover to her door.

As the likeliest time for Smythe-Roberts to wait upon his mistress would be after his evening's engagements, for much of the next week, as soon as his lord was to bed, Charlie went out and waited outside the dinners and clubs that Old Dick believed Smythe-Roberts most likely to frequent. Frustratingly, the young man attended not the apartments of his mistress, but rather a series of gaming halls and bawdy houses where, into the wee hours, he would gamble as he cavorted, or cavort as he gambled.

Charlie spent nights huddled against the cold, watching Mr. Smythe-Roberts on the town; the young gentleman generally ended his nights so thoroughly blootered that he could not walk unaided. His louche companions would load him into a hansom and send him home, ending Charlie's vigil in frustration.

One night, as Charlie waited outside Evans's Music and Supper Rooms, he realized that he was not alone in lurking in the shadows. Against a wall leaned a tall, portly man, wearing a checked suit of lurid green and yellow, so flashy and bright that it all but glowed in the periodic beams cast from the lanterns hanging on passing carriages. The man's eyes were so deep-set that in the gloom they appeared as black holes in his face. When the man noticed Charlie, he tipped his bowler and grunted. Charlie replied similarly. He was considering whether to call it a night and leave the man to his business when Mr. Smythe-Roberts exited the establishment.

The man near leapt across the road, astonishingly light on his feet considering his bulk, calling out, "Oy!"

Mr. Smythe-Roberts turned and then, seeing who it was who accosted him, took a step back.

"You've been avoiding me," the man growled.

"Indeed not, sir! It is only that I have not had occasion to come to your side of town."

"Your debt's due."

"Is it? I pay so little attention to the calendar." Mr. Smythe-Roberts was clearly trying to maintain a pose of smooth unconcern, but on the last syllable his voice cracked, causing the man to laugh.

"You'd better pay attention. You've been in arrears a fortnight now. I won't wait a minute more."

"You will have your money," Mr. Smythe-Roberts said. "I am a gentleman and pay my debts."

Again that bark of laughter. "If you paid your debts, you'd not have come to me."

"I have had a run of bad luck," Mr. Smythe-Roberts said. "But there is a horse running soon that I know for certain will win. If you advance me another hundred, you will have your money."

"Fool," the man said.

"One hundred pounds more, for a single month," Mr. Smythe-Roberts said, in a wheedling tone.

The man cracked knuckles, making a noise so oddly ominous that it caused even Charlie across the street to wince.

"Two weeks," the man said. "And your debt's now doubled."

"Impossible!"

"You'll pay me every penny or I'll have your fingers, one for each hundred you owe."

With that, the man stalked off into the night, leaving Mr. Smythe-Roberts alone in the dark. The young man staggered over to a nearby stoop and collapsed on a step. Charlie left him there, his head in his hands, so miserable a sight that he almost felt pity for him.

The sky was turning from its nighttime velvet black to a drab gray dawn when Charlie slipped through the servants' entrance into Lord Wynstowe's stately home. He closed the door quickly and quietly behind him in order to keep as little as possible of the cold air and noises of the awakening city from following him inside and disturbing the peace of the sleeping house. After slipping off his shoes to muffle his steps, he crept down the dark corridor past the servants' hall, the kitchen, the scullery, and the pantries. As he passed Mrs. Sweet's room, he heard the strike of a match and froze. A shaft of orange candlelight escaped the bottom of her door, and he ran, slipping on the polished floor and catching himself from falling only by pinwheeling his arms like a whirligig. He flung himself round the corner and out of sight just as the old crow stuck her head out of her door, calling querulously, "Who's there!"

The next morning, his fortune changed. Lord Wynstowe received in the post a letter inviting him to pay a visit to the Birmingham home of an esteemed eugenicist who shared his interest in physiognomy. The gentleman lived with two sisters in a very small house and had, Lord Wynstowe was told, no place to house a valet. In fact, the family employed neither a housekeeper nor a maid, and relied solely on the services of a village girl. Lord Wynstowe was dismayed by the directive to come alone, both because of his anxiety at traveling without the aid and comfort of his servant, and because of the unembarrassed, even cheerful tone with which Mr. Stiltstocking wrote of his circumstances. How, Lord Wynstowe wondered to Charlie, could such a venerable man fail to feel shame at his penury? Still, there was nothing for it. Lord Wynstowe craved membership in the Royal Society, and he was confident that, once he had the opportunity to share his theories with Mr. Stiltstocking, an invitation to join the scientific organization would be forthcoming. How could it not, given the conclusive proof he had accumulated about his family's physiognomic pre-eminence?

In order to guarantee his own freedom to indulge in nocturnal perambulations in pursuit of the object of his investigation, Charlie suggested to his gentleman that it might make sense for the other senior servants of the house to return to Wynstowe Manor. "For is it not a great expense, sir, to keep two houses open and running, the weather growing colder by the day?"

"Is it?" asked Lord Wynstowe, who thought little about money. As far as the viscount was concerned, funds appeared as if by magic in his pocket and accounts. He knew not how it happened, or how much of it there was, only that it was sufficient to purchase anything he desired, be it a complete set of the works of Plato bound in kid or a gold-plated caliper with which to measure his servants' skulls. Money was the purview of his estate steward and the manager of his coal works, and they were excessively talented in its accumulation and generous in its distribution.

"It surely is very dear, sir," Charlie said. "Coal for the fires alone costs the earth."

Lord Wynstowe looked puzzled. "But we produce our own coal. And anyway, why need we provide coal if it is only the servants who are in residence? My mother always said that they feel the cold less than normal people. Something to do with the effects of manual labor on the body's internal temperature."

This, Charlie thought, explained the bitterness of the attic rooms at Wynstowe Manor and here at the London house. Mrs. Sweet had learned her meanness at the previous lady's knee.

"It's not only the cold, sir," Charlie said. "Food in London is so dear, and in winter little can be sent from Wynstowe Manor."

"But I will not be here, so there will be no need to buy victuals."

To this, even quick-witted Charlie could find no reply. Did the man imagine that the cold to which he believed his servants immune froze their innards and made them impervious to hunger?

Lord Wynstowe said, "Oh well, I suppose, if you think it is best for you all to go home, then that is what you should do."

"Very well, sir. I'll tell the others. But, with your permission, I will stay here in town. I eat very little, and, as you say, I feel not the cold, and there is so much for me to do. I must supervise the apothecary's preparation of your winter remedies, and . . . and . . ." He struggled to come up with another task that could be claimed to require his presence. Fortunately, Lord Wynstowe had one at the ready.

"There is the matter of the edition of Alexander Morison's *The Physiognomy of Mental Diseases,*" Lord Wynstowe said. "The volume is critical to my research. You must attend upon Mr. Hatchard daily to impress upon him the urgency of the order."

"Yes, sir." When Charlie passed on to Mrs. Sweet the message that she and the others should leave for Wynstowe after Lord Wynstowe's departure, she scowled. "You'll be staying here, then?"

"I wish I weren't—the weather in Wynstowe Village is so fine this time of year, and my mother and sister are surely in need of my company—but there's nothing for it."

Mrs. Sweet gave a suspicious sniff, and Charlie scolded himself for having over-egged the pudding, but by the time he returned from seeing Lord Wynstowe off at the station, she and the others had shut up the house and were gone. To vex him, she had locked the door behind her, forcing Charlie to clamber through the kitchen window, soiling his trousers in the process.

Having missed his dinner in the rush to the station, once he was inside, Charlie went in search of something to eat, only to find that Mrs. Sweet had exacted a complete revenge. He found not a crust of bread or a jar of preserves, only a single wizened apple forgotten in the bottom of the bin. He wondered for a moment at the extent of the housekeeper's antipathy, then decided that it was nothing about him in particular that gave her affront, but rather his very existence—indeed, the existence of all humanity. She was as adept at misanthropy as her colleague Cook was incompetent in the kitchen.

Charlie ate the apple, borrowed an old and forgotten muffler from Lord Wynstowe's cupboard, and set out in pursuit of his object. It was early enough in the evening that he could rely on Mr. Smythe-Roberts not to have yet left home for his nightly entertainment. The family lived in one of a row of Gothic Revival terraced houses that strove for elegance with bits and pieces of stonework and cornices affixed at random to the front, and the odd gargoyle leering from the rooftops. Though new, the house failed in its quest for opulence, and Charlie wondered at the circumstance of the family. How long would they have either the will or the capacity to subsidize the younger son's excesses? If Old Dick was to be believed, Mr. Thomas Smythe-Roberts's expenses far exceeded his income, and he would not easily afford setting up his own household, even with a portion like what Lady Jemima would bring. That Smythe-Roberts's situation was precarious was all the better for his and Alice's prospects: if the man could not marry, he could not whisk away his bride and her maid.

Charlie slipped into a darkened doorway across from the house and shoved his hands into the pockets of his wool overcoat, a carefully mended cast-off of his former gentleman Mr. Stokes that he kept looking nearly new even though it was not much younger than he. He buried his chin in his muffler and stamped his feet to keep them from growing stiff with cold, wishing he did indeed possess a resistance to temperature. Sinking as deeply into the doorway as possible to keep his puffs of steaming breath from being visible, he was for once grateful for the murky haze that hung over the city like a noxious blanket. The thick and filthy fog might choke the breath out of a person, but it also made it easy to hide.

The door to the house opened, and Mr. Thomas Smythe-Roberts stepped out.

"Christ, it's frigid!" the man shouted over his shoulder to the companion who followed him.

The door banged closed after them, no doubt in wordless condemnation of his language.

The other young man said, "Let's to Eaton Square. There'll be a hansom there."

"Are you paying?" Mr. Smythe-Roberts said. "Because I'm skint. I should have had a sovereign or two, but the old lady caught mc going through James's pockets and made me return it all."

"I have nothing, either," the other man said sadly. "What are we to do? Go back inside?"

"And listen to my brother's wife hammer on the pianoforte and yowl like a stuck cat? I think not. We'll walk."

"It's miles!"

Mr. Smythe-Roberts pondered this for a moment, then said, "We'll go to Luciana's. She's good for a few shillings at least."

The other young man laughed. "*You're* taking money from *her* now?"

"I had Mappin & Webb send over a garnet choker last week that cost near ten pounds. She'll spare me a few bob or I'll pluck it right off her neck." He laughed. "It'll not be hers for long, anyway. I signed James's name, and soon enough the old booby will get the bill. He's too tightfisted to buy his wife so much as a cameo, so he'll know it was me."

The two men set off in the direction of the Ladbroke Estate, Charlie hard on their heels. Sound, unlike light, passed with startling acuity through the viscid air, and when they passed into a road devoid of passersby, Charlie's tread on the cobbles rang out like a bell. Mr. Smythe-Roberts spun around, causing Charlie to freeze.

"Did you hear that?" the young man said.

"Hear what?"

"Footsteps."

"You had too much port after dinner, old chap."

"For the past few days, I've had the damnedest sensation that I'm being followed."

The companion peered into the darkness. "Considering the sorts you owe money to, it's a wonder you haven't been chased down and strung up by a tribe of Spitalfields Jews."

As the two peered into the darkness, Charlie did his best to melt into the surrounding gloom.

Finally, the companion said, "I see no one."

The two turned into a narrow lane abutted by a public garden. Charlie stayed back, peering round the corner, until he saw them knock on the door of a small terraced house with a scrubbed front step that glowed white in the moonlight. He noted the location, and went back home.

The following morning, he returned to the house. A maid, no more than a girl, opened it to him. He had anticipated caution in admitting a stranger, or at least curiosity, and had prepared a story about a pocketbook that had come into his possession and which he desired to return to its rightful owner, but no interrogation was forthcoming. Without a word the maid let him into a pretty sitting room. He waited, gazing about him at the cherrywood secretary, the damask settee, the Venetian plaster. There was a fire burning cheerfully in what until he had arrived had been an empty room.

Soon enough, the mistress of the house came to greet him. She was dark-haired and olive-skinned, with liquid brown eyes and full lips stained an unnatural wine color. Her morning gown was of silk decorated with roses in various shades of red, and she had draped about her shoulders a black lace shawl of work so fine it was like a spider's web.

She looked, he thought, vaguely familiar.

Her voice was deep and mellifluous, as befits a singer, and she spoke with a thick and lovely Italian accent.

"May I help you, signor?" she said. "Do you have business with me?"

"Not precisely business, but I hope to speak to you of a matter of some urgency, to me at the least."

She lowered herself into a delicate armchair and motioned him to a spindly-legged settee, where he perched, feeling large and clumsy. He looked down at his shoes and noticed that they bore the dust of his journey. He knew that even the finest gentlemen could not help but attract city grime: after all, it was his responsibility to brush and polish it away from his gentleman's clothing and shoes. And yet he felt crass and uncouth, and imagined that this lady had sized up his class with the merest glance. He was not wrong.

"My name is Wells, and I hope to ask . . . I mean, to request . . ."

"To request?" she urged him on.

He was about to launch into his prepared tale of a pocketbook found in the gutter belonging to one Mr. Thomas Smythe-Roberts, in which there was a scrap of paper scribbled with her address, but he knew there would be no point. This lady looked so shrewd she would immediately see through his ruse. "I've come because I believe you can do me the greatest of favors," he said.

"How very *misterioso*. What favor?"

He peered at her face. She really did look uncannily familiar. "Have we met before, Miss . . . Miss . . . I'm sorry, I don't know your name."

"I am Signora Luciana di Galtieri. I come from Milano, where I performed with the Teatro alla Scala. Have you been to Italy?"

"No. I've never been outside of England."

"So it is unlikely that we are acquainted. Please continue, Signor Wells. What can I do for you?"

"It's a complicated story. I am valet to Lord Wynstowe, and my . . ." How to refer to Alice? "My dearest"? "My love"? "The one I think about every day"? "The key to any happiness I might ever attain, without whom I know my life will be nothing but drudgery and loneliness"? He said, "My special friend is abigail to Lady Jemima Alderwick. Her lady and my gentleman are so rarely in the same place at the same time, which means we see each other almost never. But if they were to marry . . ." His voice trailed off. When expressed beyond the confines of his and Alice's intimacy, the plan sounded impossible, even absurd.

But Signora di Galtieri clapped her hands delightedly. "You are a pair of *sensali di matrimoni,* arranging their marriage to further your own romance! How *delizioso.* But how can I help this charming scheme? I know neither you nor your *innamorata.*"

"You see, the ones we work for are not fond of one another. The truth is, they despise each other."

"Ah. This is a *grande problema.*"

"One we can overcome. I'm sure of it, if we only have time. But Lady Jemima has another suitor, and we fear, if we don't move quickly, she will soon be beyond Lord Wynstowe's reach."

"This Lady Jemima di Alderwick? She is supposed to be *molto bella.* But how exactly am I to help?"

"The suitor is Mr. Thomas Smythe-Roberts."

She gave a ringing trill of a laugh. "Thomas stands in the way of your plan! How *divertente.*"

"We have heard that you have a . . . a connection with Mr. Smythe-Roberts." Charlie cursed himself for his hesitations and stutters. He sounded a fool. He blundered on. "We hope you might discourage his attachment to Lady Jemima."

She laughed again. "This is also very charming. Mr. Thomas Smythe-Roberts is indeed my particular friend. But I cannot encourage or discourage his other *relazioni amorose.* Such is not the understanding between us."

"You are not to be married?"

Her laughter abated. "Are you really so naïve? You think a gentleman from a titled family like Thomas would marry an Italian singer, no matter how renowned? And even if he would, I would not marry him. He is a pleasant enough fellow, but he has nothing. Soon enough, he will exhaust his paltry resources. The only question is whether that will be before or after he grows tired of me and turns his attentions to another."

Her accent had faded, he noticed, and her words were suddenly devoid of their sprinkling of Italian. She seemed to realize this as well, and resumed, "I am sorry, signor, but there is nothing I can do to help you and your *innamorata*. You will have to find another way to be together. Perhaps you can look for employment in the same household."

"But it's so very rare that a couple will seek a new valet and a lady's maid at the same time. Or that we will even find other positions if we leave the ones we have."

He slumped on the settee, dejected. At that moment, a wail interrupted their conversation. The door opened, and a nursemaid entered, carrying a stout baby in her arms, its face the same pink as its gown.

"I'm so sorry, madam, but he won't be calmed. He's wanting feeding."

The singer held out her arms for the babe, who when deposited in them began snuffling at her bodice.

Charlie stared at the child, doing calculations in his mind. Could this be Mr. Smythe-Roberts's child? If so, what a stroke of luck! Lady Jemima might dismiss an assignation as youthful indiscretion, but surely the existence of a natural child would force an end to her affections. He tried to find words of delicacy to ask after the babe's parentage, but before he could do so, Signora di Galtieri stood up and swept out of the room.

Over her shoulder she called back, "I'm sorry your visit was in vain, Charlie."

He was out on the front step before he realized that he had not told her his Christian name, and in the main road before he remembered from where he knew her. Back then she was not Luciana di Galtieri but plain old Lucy Jones, a resident of the same workhouse as he, who was famous not for her voice, but for the finesse with which she could pick a pocket.

NINETEEN

The following day, too eager to wait until evening, Charlie went to Miss Bennett's house as soon as the sun rose in the sky. Even at that early hour, he found Alice awake, breakfasted, and sitting at the table in the warm kitchen, darning a pair of silk stockings. He took her hand. Cook cast a concerned eye on the couple. She hoped the girl had the wherewithal to withstand Charlie's allure, for though he seemed a decent young man, a man was still a man. Her own sister, a kitchen maid on a large estate, had entered into a misguided liaison with a stableboy and gotten herself in the family way. This fate befell all too many a girl, and she worried for Alice. While the two young people bent their heads together, whispering, Cook whipped up horseradish sauce and sliced cold roast beef, humming to herself, as if too occupied for eavesdropping, even as she cocked an ear.

After Charlie recounted the gist of his visit to Mr. Smythe-Roberts's mistress, Alice said, "I knew he was a scoundrel."

"We have no proof that the babe is his," Charlie said.

"Did she not say it was?"

"I did not ask."

"Oh, Charlie!" For the first time in their acquaintance Alice's voice contained a note of chastisement. Cook smiled, pleased to see evidence of the backbone that she hoped might protect Alice from a terrible fate.

Charlie looked suitably downcast. "I should have, I know. But might she not have taken offense?"

Alice allowed that the woman would likely indeed have been offended, and supposed that it spoke well of Charlie that he was averse to injuring the feelings of even such a woman as Signora Luciana di Galtieri, she who was once Lucy Jones. The problem was that, without knowing for sure who sired the child, they could not proceed with their plans.

"Give me her address," she said.

Cook gasped, and when Charlie and Alice looked at her, turned it into a cough.

"This horseradish is right pungent!" she said.

Alice got up, poured a glass of water from the pitcher, and handed it to Cook. She placed a hand between her shoulders and Cook had no choice but to continue her pretense and drain the glass.

"Thank you, dear. I'm all right now."

Alice returned to the table.

Once she was seated, Charlie, his voice lowered now to a whisper so that Cook could no longer hear, said, "You can't think to go to her. She is not an appropriate acquaintance for a person such as yourself!"

"Do you worry that I am so inclined to debauchery that a few moments in such a woman's presence will send me tumbling down to her level?"

"No!" he said.

"Charlie Wells, if we are to continue keeping company, you are going to have to accept that you can't decide for me what is appropriate or not. We must determine the parentage of that baby, and the mother is far more likely to confess it to me than to you."

That was perhaps the first time Charlie appreciated the full nature of the girl who so captivated him. Not only was she sweet, pretty, and witty, but also strong-minded. When her way was obstructed, she did not back down. He saw in her a similarity to his willful sister, Mary, whose lot in life was to contend with much sadness, and whose fortitude thus sometimes curdled into obstinacy. He was often impatient of this in Mary, but he determined that in Alice he would admire the quality.

"It is not an easy place to find," he said.

"Nowhere in this confusing city is easy to find," Alice rejoined. "The streets are higgledy-piggledy. They change names at random, bend this way and that. I know not how anyone dares step more than a minute from home, for fear of never finding their way back."

Charlie suggested that he escort her, which offer she initially refused.

"If she is to confide in me, I must be alone."

They agreed that he would take her only as far as the main road abutting the lady's lane, and wait for her there. Fortunately, Lady Jemima had plans on the morrow with Miss Mountjoy, and Alice was thus free to go.

After Charlie took his leave, Cook set down before Alice a cup of sweet, milky tea and a shortbread biscuit, then took the seat opposite. This surprised Alice, as she had rarely seen the good woman off her feet, running as she did all day from counter to sink to stove and back again.

"Miss Lockey, dear. I hope you'll not take it amiss, but I am old enough to be your mother, and I have seen much in my years."

"I can't imagine I would take anything you might say amiss, Mrs. Crispin, for you've been nothing but kind to me. I think you must be shocked by the things Mr. Wells and I were speaking of."

Cook did not deny it, only worried the strings of her apron and bit her lip. "It's so easy for a girl to find herself in difficulties."

"Difficulties?" Alice repeated.

"The kind a young man can bring."

Reader, those of our class take such pride in the virtue of our daughters that we send them into marriage wholly ignorant of their duties, the indelicate details of which often come as a dreadful surprise. How many of us have been visited by ashen-faced daughters the day after their nuptials, convinced they have married a barbarian, only to gasp in horror when informed that their own mothers have experienced the same indignities? But Alice was of a different class to ours. She grew up in a small house where the children slept close upon the parents, and so she knew precisely to which difficulties Mrs. Crispin alluded. For a moment, she took offense both on her own and on Charlie's behalf, but the sweet lady's expression was of concern, not disapproval, so Alice reassured her that she was not in danger of making so dreadful an error.

The following afternoon, as planned, Charlie escorted Alice onto the omnibus, where he insisted, over her objections, on paying her fare. They sat on a bench in the rear, far from the other passengers. He could tell by the high spots of color on her cheeks as they neared the Ladbroke Estate that her bluster concealed an agitation at the prospect of a confrontation unlike any she had ever had before, and squeezed her hand to lend her courage. When they disembarked in Ladbroke Grove, he pointed out the singer's house and, with a combination of admiration and concern, watched Alice set off resolutely down the lane. As she neared the house, she stumbled, and he nearly bolted to her side, but she kicked her skirts out of the way and stepped up to the door.

Even before she could knock, the door burst open and two burly men exited, to the accompaniment of a woman's shrieks. "Swine! May your poxed spickets rot!" The accent was pure Manchester Scuttler slang, and Alice assumed it was the maid's until a woman appeared, en déshabillé, ineffectually clutching round her a feathered peignoir. This, Alice realized at once, was the lady of the house.

One of the men nearly lifted Alice off her feet and set her aside, though with surprising delicacy. "Pardon, miss," he said.

The woman leaned against the doorpost and watched the two lumber down the lane. "Well," she said, finally. "Easy come, easy go." Only then did she notice Alice. *"Buongiorno,"* she said. And then laughed, shrugged, and in her natural voice said, "You'd best come in, deary."

TWENTY

Lucy Jones led Alice into her sitting room, calling over her shoulder to the maid to bring "tea and a tot, and look sharp."

"Let me guess," she said, once she had settled herself in her armchair. "You're Charlie Wells's girl."

Alice nodded, her eyes drawn to Lucy's wrapper, the golden silk stained in near perfect circles at the breast. Lucy yanked it closed.

"You'll be wanting to know about Thomas," Lucy said. "I'll say this. You have come at a good time. The blackguard's had me jewelry taken. And not only the blasted garnet necklace. They snatched near everything I got, and half of it naught to do with that wretched snake."

The maid came in with a tray on which there was both a teapot and a squat glass bottle. She put it on a small table within Lucy's reach and left. Lucy poured herself a stiff drink, knocked it back, and waved the bottle in Alice's direction with an inquiring expression.

"No, thank you," Alice said.

"Tea, then?"

"If you don't mind."

"If I minded, I'd not have offered."

Lucy splashed tea into a cup, dumped in far more sugar than Alice ever took, and handed it over.

"What are you wanting to know about the scoundrel? If he keeps me? He does. Or did. Bounder couldn't keep a turd in a piss bucket now."

"And your baby?"

"Little Tommy? Named for his father. Not that the rotter ever cared a hoot 'bout the boy, no matter that he pretends to when he wants something of me. He was back at me the day after Tommy came into the world."

Alice said, "I know I've no right to ask this of you, but it would help our cause if Lady Jemima knew about the boy."

"Might. Might not. These ladies, they're experts in looking t'other way."

"She'd forgive him an alliance, I think. But not a natural child."

"I don't know about that. To them, we're naught but garbage. They'd pay more attention to filth on the bottom of their boot." Lucy Jones's assessment of the consideration the gentry paid to those below their own station, though expressed with far less delicacy and far more outrage, was not too far off from Alice's own. Lucy continued, "Talking to your lady's more than my life's worth. Thomas has a vicious temper. I'll not cross him."

"Is he violent? Has he ever hurt you?"

"He's worse than most, better than some. Before Luciana di Galtieri made her debut, they felt free enough to knock old Lucy about. But few do now, at least not at first. Once they're comfortable, the game is up. Give him long enough, near every man'll raise his fist. You learn either to suffer it or to suffer alone."

Lucy read Alice's doubtful expression and shook her head wearily. "You'll see soon enough."

"My father never lifted his hand to my mother."

"So far's you know."

"I don't believe there aren't good men. Charlie's a good man."

Lucy sniffed, seemed about to speak, but was interrupted by a muffled cry.

"Bring him to me!" she called out. She looked down at her wrap.

"Damn it to hell! I put cloths in, but soon as I hear Tommy cry, I soak them right through. Look." The stains on the gown were indeed growing larger. "Pure French silk. Ruined."

The maid walked in with squalling Tommy in her arms. Lucy settled him on her breast. The babe burrowed, gulping and snuffling like a tiny pink piglet.

"I'd have a wet nurse in, only I'd not like to miss this," Lucy said, stroking the soft down on the baby's head. "When he nurses, it sends a jolt through your whole body." She shivered delightedly. "Better than what even the best man gives you."

Alice tried hard to present a mien of sophistication as she wondered if that was what her mother had experienced when she nursed Alice and her brothers and sisters. One thing was for certain, Mrs. Lockey would not have bared her breast before her own children, let alone before a stranger.

"And some men like it, too," Lucy continued, ignoring

Alice's discomfort. "Thomas is at me like a baby on his mother. Lapping it up."

At this, Alice felt a flush creep up her neck and suffuse her face bright pink. I imagine you are also flushed pink, dear Reader. But I will warrant you have experienced oddities like this and worse in your own bedroom, even if you wouldn't admit so.

Lucy laughed. "Poor thing. I've put you into a flutter."

"I'd use gall soap, with a bit of white vinegar," Alice said. "And put it in the sun to dry."

"Pardon?"

"On the stains."

"I'll tell my girl. But good luck finding sun in London. Not sure when's last we had a day that wasn't gray and thick as porridge."

"If you'll give the gown to me, I'll do my best. Silk's not easy. But I'll try."

"Would you?" Lucy said. "That's awful kind."

To Alice's astonishment, she stood up, shrugged off the gown, and stood there in her lace-trimmed drawers and an unlaced chemise from which one pink-tipped breast poked.

(Oh, my poor, long-suffering reader! I fear this account has lapsed into the obscene, and my apologies grow tiresome. Put it aside if you must, or, better yet, read it in the privacy of your own sitting room, where no one else will peek at its pages.)

Alice folded the gown into a neat parcel.

"I'll see if I can find a bit of paper and string for you," Lucy said. She held out the baby.

Alice took him, and she left.

"You're a sweet thing, aren't you?" she said. Tommy gave

her a gummy smile, and then belched. Alice snatched the tea cloth and blotted the burble of milk from the tot's lips before it could drip onto her own dress. She stroked the plump cheek. Tommy reached up and grabbed Alice's nose. She laughed and extricated herself from the baby's sticky clutch.

Lucy came back into the room, and smiled benevolently. "He likes you." She swapped a piece of brown paper and string for the baby. "You're a proper little cad, aren't you, Tommy, eyeing up the ladies?" she cooed. "I'll tell you what, dear. You go ahead and tell your lady about me and little Tommy, and I'll not deny it if asked."

"Would you write a letter? A few words?"

"Give you an inch and you'll ask for an ell, won't you?" She considered the request. "If Thomas sees a scribble of mine, he'll have my head. Worse, he'll tell all them society people, and then I won't be asked to the houses where I make my living."

"I don't think Lady Jemima will trust me without proof."

Lucy considered this for a moment, then said, "Come."

Alice followed her out into the hallway. The singer plucked an oiled silk umbrella from the stand, turned it over, and shook it; a handful of baubles fell onto the floor.

"I managed to save a few things from the greedy grubbers."

She picked a small locket from the pile, snapped it open, and showed it to Alice. On one side was a shockingly poorly executed miniature of a young man. Though the artist should not have been permitted within a mile of pen and ink, let alone oils, the features were not entirely unlike Mr. Thomas Smythe-Roberts's own. On the other were three locks of hair, one near black, one blond, and one a few fine strands of a baby's. On the bag was engraved *To L, with all my love, T.*

"He gave it to me when Tommy was born. It's tin, not

worth anything, but it was a sweet gift. Sweeter than I'd have expected, given its source. You can take it, but I'll want it back."

"I'll have it back to you with your gown. Thank you, Signora di Galtieri. This means the world."

"Oh, call me Lucy, why don't you. So long's we're alone. That's what Charlie knows me as, don't he?"

TWENTY-ONE

Alice knew that the bearer of bad news was more likely to suffer resentment for its revelation than to be thanked, and she knew her lady well enough to realize that if she were simply to tell her outright, the anger and shame would redound on Alice—if not immediately, then eventually. She considered slipping the information to that famous gossip-monger Dick, but had he been willing to share what he knew of the scoundrel with Lady Jemima, he would have done so already. Precious days passed as she considered and dispensed with various approaches. She had all but settled on an anonymous letter directed to Lady Jemima by a "concerned friend" when another avenue presented itself.

She was shaking out Lady Jemima's dresses, examining them for tears and stains, when Miss Bennett entered the room.

"Ma'am," Alice said, with a quick curtsy.

"I am sorry to disturb you in your labors," Miss Bennett said, "but I have need of a volume from my shelf." With a rustle of her vermilion skirts, Miss Bennett knelt in front of a lacquered bookcase and pulled out a book. "Have you read Mrs. Wollstonecraft?" she asked Alice. "This one is particularly compelling." She showed Alice the book. "*Maria: or, The Wrongs of Woman.* It is about a woman imprisoned in an insane asylum by her husband."

"My goodness," Alice said.

"Not one I would suggest for my niece, but I think you might appreciate it. It is very dramatic. I have promised the loan of it to my friend Mrs. Whishaw, but if she returns it before you leave London, you may borrow it. You must feel free to avail yourself of any book in the house. There is a red leather ledger in the drawing room. Write in it your name, the name of the volume, and the dates when it is borrowed and returned."

"Thank you so much, ma'am."

"You're very welcome." The lady suddenly wrinkled her nose. "My goodness, what is that awful stench?" She followed Alice's gaze to the pairs of Lady Jemima's dancing slippers, which the maid had assembled in order to endeavor to clean them. As the realization dawned, Miss Bennett burst out laughing. Alice bit her lips, trying to keep her face straight, but could not keep from allowing a giggle to escape.

Miss Bennett pressed a hand to her chest, contained her laughter, and said, "My goodness, your job is a difficult one. How have you enjoyed your stay here in London? Dick says you have an admirer who comes to call."

Alice should have known Dick would not have been able to restrain himself from gossiping about her.

"He's not an admirer, Miss Bennett. Only a friend I see sometimes. I am sorry if I've been indiscreet."

"I meant no criticism. And be assured, I'll not tell your

flighty lady. Even if she doesn't disapprove, she'll make your life a misery with her teasing. I'm very good at keeping confidences. I pride myself on it."

At this, a thought occurred to Alice. Might she have found a means of giving Lady Jemima the inculpatory information about her suitor? A word from her aunt would be far more credible to Lady Jemima than an anonymous letter. Could Miss Bennett be trusted not to reveal the source of her information? What choice did Alice have but to rely on Miss Bennett's attestation of her own discretion?

"May I confide in you, Miss Bennett? The issue is relevant not to me but rather to my lady. I would never want to discompose her, and fear that if I tell her myself I might cause her distress."

"Oh my, that does sound mysterious." Miss Bennett sat down on the bed. "I promise not to reveal anything you would not want me to."

Alice recounted to Miss Bennett the story of Mr. Smythe-Roberts's relations with the infamous singer.

"How did you come by this information?" Miss Bennett asked once she had finished expressing her disgust.

Alice knew she could not reveal her visit to Luciana. "Old Dick told me," she said, which was true enough. "And then my friend confirmed it."

"He confirmed the baby?"

"It is well known, and he had particular information confirming the truth of it."

"Gossip is an ugly thing. It is quite possible there is nothing to it at all."

Alice reached into the pocket of her apron and produced the locket. She handed it to Miss Bennett.

Miss Bennett snapped open the locket and peered at the

miniature. “Is this meant to be Mr. Smythe-Roberts?” she asked.

“It is, though I grant it is only the vaguest of likenesses.”

“It is only the vaguest of illustrations. People really should leave painting to the talented.”

“You can see that the child’s hair is blond, like its father’s,” Alice said. “And there is the inscription.”

Miss Bennett compressed her lips into a thin, disapproving line. “This is indeed compelling evidence, I grant you. Where did you come by it?”

“The lady herself gave it to . . . my friend. Oh, Miss Bennett. Lady Jemima expects an offer from him, and I fear she’ll accept it. But a man like that? It’s not what she deserves.”

“The minx could stand to be brought down a peg or two, but you are right. He is a bounder, and would cause more trouble certainly than he is worth.”

“He’s worth less than nothing! They say he’s plagued with debt. I fear that is why he is paying Lady Jemima his attentions.”

“Do you think so? There are young ladies with more of a portion than hers. But perhaps not so many who are as pretty as Jemima.” Miss Bennett got to her feet. “I will speak to her, and trust me, I won’t say how I’ve come upon the information. Thank you, Alice. It speaks well of you that you have your lady’s interests so close to your heart.”

At this Alice felt a twist of shame. The interests she had at heart were her own and Charlie’s. But, she told herself, to be married to a wastrel and a scoundrel would undoubtedly have made Lady Jemima desperately unhappy in the long run, so might not that mitigate the selfishness of Alice’s motivation?

Miss Bennett wasted no time in imparting to Lady Jemima

the ugliness of Mr. Smythe-Roberts's alliance. Alice prepared herself for the young lady's tears and fury, and for the possibility that they would repair immediately to Marlecombe Park so she could nurse her wounds in the bosom of her family. Alas, she overestimated her lady. It turned out that Luciana di Galtieri knew the gentry far better than did Alice.

That afternoon, Lady Jemima ran into her bedchamber. "Oh, Alice!" she wailed, throwing herself into a chair.

"There, there, ma'am," Alice said. They were off to a fine start, she thought, then scolded herself for feeling pleasure at the results of her scheming. She sprinkled some eau de cologne on a handkerchief and pressed it to Lady Jemima's forehead. "Don't be sad, ma'am," she said, soothingly.

Lady Jemima pushed her hand away. "I am not sad! I am furious! I am so angry, I could spit. My idiot aunt! Horrible woman. She is a gossip and scold."

This was not the turn Alice had hoped for.

Lady Jemima ranted on. "She is such a wrinkled old spinster. She understands nothing of the world. That she should insult Thomas so! Wretched woman!"

"What happened, ma'am?"

"She actually went so far as to produce a necklace that some bounder told her belonged to a wanton woman who claims she is his mistress! It is nonsense. Utter nonsense!"

"Miss Bennett is not one to tell lies, is she?"

The truth of this brought Lady Jemima up short, but still she would hear nothing bad of the man upon whom she had set her expectations. "She is too trusting, and believes whatever nonsense she is told. The painting is clearly of another man entirely. And 'To L, from T'? Ridiculous!"

With *all* his love, Alice corrected silently.

"There are millions of L's in the world and millions more

T's! Timothy. Theodore, Tristan, Terrence, Talbot . . ." She searched for more. "Theophilus!"

This nearly caused Alice to laugh, but, oh, catastrophe! Was Lady Jemima so very naïve?

"When I tell Thomas of this infamy being spread about the town, he will be most outraged."

Lady Jemima demanded to be dressed with even greater ostentation than usual, to prove to her aunt that the good lady's words had made no impression, and, Alice supposed, to impress upon Mr. Smythe-Roberts the resources of her family and self. She wore her finest gown, of pale green decorated with seed pearls and chips of diamonds, and had Alice hang about her neck a heavy gold chain with a gemstone-encrusted cross that was one of the Alderwick family jewels. If Lord Alderwick were to learn that Lady Jemima had brought the necklace to London, he would be furious, Alice knew. Lady Jemima demanded that her high-dressed hair also be festooned with valuable baubles. She looked opulent, if bordering on the tasteless. Still, Alice thought ruefully, it was the former that was most likely to send to Mr. Smythe-Roberts the desired message.

That evening, Alice sat alone at the servants' table, dejectedly nursing a cup of broth pressed upon her by Cook and watching the others rushing about in preparation for the small dinner Miss Bennett was hosting. Alice had not before seen Old Dick in anything other than a plain brown suit, but now he was stuffed into a shiny black formal jacket, his belly straining at the buttons. Mrs. Goodenough had ironed his black tie to a crisp. The maid of all work wore a brand-new white apron, and the boy, designated footman for the evening, wore beneath his coat an elegant striped waistcoat of which he was very proud, strutting importantly about the kitchen and thundering up the stairs with various items of porcelain and silver.

The servants were thrown even further into a tizzy when Miss Bennett herself appeared in the kitchen. She was garbed in a Grecian robe of burgundy velvet swathed with lace and cinched at the waist with a golden cord. By the freedom with which her various parts wobbled beneath the fabric, it was clear that she wore no corset, a fact that caused Old Dick's eyes to widen. Alice thought that if Mrs. Goodenough could have stomped on his foot to remind him of his manners, she would have. Instead, she rushed to her lady's side and showered her with a tumult of apologies, it was unclear for what.

Miss Bennett was herself in a state of agitation that matched that of her servants. "Mrs. Crispin!" she said. "I have received a note from Miss Davies. She will be accompanied this evening by Mrs. Faulkner!"

"Not to worry, ma'am," Cook said. "There's plenty for another lady."

"I'm sure there would be under normal circumstances," Miss Bennett said, "only Mrs. Faulkner is a member of the Vegetarian Society. She eats no animal products. Only vegetables and fruits."

"But the quail!" Cook replied aghast. "The butcher dressed it for me special."

"She won't eat the quail, or the lamb. How do you plan to serve the asparagus?"

"In a butter-and-lemon sauce."

"Leave off the butter. And find another vegetable to serve alongside. Otherwise, the poor woman will starve."

"Nothing from an animal at all, ma'am?" Cook asked.

"Nothing."

"Not the eggs and butter in the Bakewell pudding?"

"Absolutely not. Can you find something else to serve for afters?"

Cook kneaded her apron with mute anxiety. Finally, Mrs. Goodenough suggested gently, "Perhaps a bowl of preserves, Mrs. Crispin?"

The look of relief that passed over Cook's face was exceeded only by Miss Bennett's. Freed of her consternation, that lady turned to Alice. "My company tonight is quite eclectic. Miss Davies founded Girton College and was one of the ladies of Langham Place. She is now a prominent leader in the movement of ladies' educational reform. Mr. Alaric Watts, Jr. and his wife Mrs. Anna Watts will also be in attendance. She is a noted artist, he a writer, and they are both spiritualists. The conversation would be most edifying for you. I would not take it amiss if you were to listen in."

"My goodness!" Mrs. Goodenough exclaimed when her kind lady had gone away. "She does favor you!" Alice searched for a hint of envy, but found none in the housekeeper's smiling face. What an unusually warm house this was, Alice thought, without the competition too often evident even in such a generally tolerable place as Lord and Lady Alderwick's servants' hall.

Thus Alice found herself watching the goings-on from behind the swinging door between the pantry and the dining room, propped open a crack to allow her an unimpeded view. The conversation was at first dominated by Mr. Watts, who was taking great issue with the proliferation of mediums and spiritualists whose trickery and false promises, he said, reflected so poorly on those who, like him and his wife, practiced the art with sincerity.

"Wires!" he said. "Wobbling tables. Nonsense upon nonsense."

His diatribe, escalating in fervor, went on for long enough

that Alice was tempted to give up her seat by the servants' door, but soon enough he was interrupted by Old Dick and the maid, who slipped by Alice and into the dining room. Dick carried the sweets tray with the Bakewell tart over which Cook had labored, looking so delicious that it caused Alice's mouth to water. She wondered whether there would be some left for those downstairs to enjoy. The housemaid, her crisp new apron somewhat the worse for wear after an evening of serving, held a small dish of peaches in syrup. Alice watched her hesitate, looking from one lady to the next, until she finally set the dish in front of the one whom she deemed least forbidding, a girl of seventeen or so, with merry eyes, arched brows, and a mass of hair swirled atop her head. The girl looked puzzled, which flustered the maid, and she turned and left the room at a near run.

"Do you not eat cake, Emmeline?" Mr. Watts asked.

"I do," Emmeline said. "With pleasure."

Old Dick cleared his throat and said in a voice that Alice imagined sounded low to his deaf ears, but that rang through the room, "Them peaches are for the vegetable lady."

After a moment, Mrs. Faulkner, a wraithlike matron with a long, pale face, trembling fingers, and a general air of ennui, spoke up. "Vegetarian," she corrected Dick. Alice watched Emmeline suppress a smile and pass her the dish.

Dick, too, fled the room, leaving it to Miss Bennett to slice and serve the Bakewell tart, accompanied by a disquisition from Mrs. Faulkner on the horrors experienced by "innocent cows" who had their "bosoms" yanked and tortured in order to produce milk, butter, and cream. "Milk is more akin to pus than food!" she said, at which point Mrs. Watts set down her fork with a nauseated shudder. Do not, Mrs. Faulkner said, get her started on the eggs. But of course she did start.

"Naught but babes!"—torn from their tormented mama hens, day after day.

Miss Bennett, seeking to turn the conversation if not away from vegetarianism then at least to a version less likely to impair her guests' enjoyment of their meal, asked, "How did you find a cook adept at cooking without animal products? Or did you teach her yourself?"

"I did my best, but it was months before the wretch could boil a decent cabbage. Worse, in the end, my efforts were pointless, as I was forced to dismiss her."

"For smuggling pork fat into the potatoes?" Emmeline asked. Alice bit her lips to keep from laughing. She peered through the crack in the door, the better to see the faces of the assembly. The girl looked like churned cow pus wouldn't melt in her mouth.

Mrs. Faulkner pursed her lips. "She found herself in an unpleasant condition. And then, in the end, she died, so it was generally a disaster."

In a pleasant voice that belied the set of her jaw, Emmeline asked, "How did the poor woman die?"

"Of female trouble."

"In childbirth?" she pressed. Her manner made it clear that she knew the answer.

"In a manner of speaking."

Miss Bennett said, "Shall we turn our attention to more pleasant things?"

But the girl was having none of it. "Perhaps, if she had not found herself turned out of doors and forced into penury, the resolution of her situation might have been different."

"Young lady," Mrs. Faulkner said, "you know nothing of these things. My cook failed to protect her virtue. The outcome was inevitable."

"Aren't there many in similar circumstances whose positions allow them the opportunity for a different outcome?"

"Enough now, Emmeline," said a woman sitting across from the girl.

"I agree, Cousin Primrose," she said. "We have had enough of women suffering such terrible fates when the men who cause their ruin continue their lives unscathed. If we women had the vote, one of the many things we could do would be to protect the victims and call these vile perpetrators to account."

Miss Bennett said, "I think you will find general agreement round this table, dear."

Mr. Watts nodded vigorously.

"Hear, hear!" Mrs. Faulkner said. "I support suffrage for decent, upstanding women of the propertied classes."

"There is where we differ," Emmeline said. "My support is for *universal* suffrage. People of the working classes are as deserving as those who fancy themselves their betters, are they not? Perhaps even more so than many!"

And you, dear Reader? Where would you have stood on this issue? Would you have regretted your lack of opportunity to make your political opinions known outside the boundaries of your home? Or would the influence you wielded on your husband and sons have been sufficient for you?

Votes for women? Alice thought. It seemed as unlikely as votes for goats or horses.

"Miss Davies," Miss Bennett said, changing the subject, "I know we are all eager to hear about your work as cofounder of the Society for Promoting the Employment of Women."

"Thank you, Sarah," that lady said. "Our work focuses upon many issues, but one which I think will be of interest to this gathering is the plight of gentlewomen who must work to support themselves. What employment is there for such a lady be she temperamentally unsuited to the work of governess or companion? What can she do to maintain herself if she is denied an education or access to a profession?"

Alice wondered what it must be like to consider one's temperament or inclination in choosing employment. No one, not even she, had considered whether she was suited to her job. She was competent and able, and the job was a good one. Certainly better than others that might be available to her. She could have labored alongside her mother in the house and farmyard, but her wages were an important part of her family's household calculations. Out to work she was sent, following the reverend's exhortation to be grateful for the opportunity.

The conversation then turned to Mr. William Gladstone's Midlothian campaign, the size of the crowds, the extent and tenor of the newspaper coverage, whether it was really possible that the liberal former prime minister might be returned to office. The assembly was fervent in their admiration and cautiously optimistic, and by the end of the evening Alice felt herself a new devotee of the great man, eager to see him returned to the premiership.

So many novel ideas, unimaginable to her before she had seated herself on a small stool outside of a door opened a crack! When the guests had departed and those downstairs had shared the sliver of Bakewell tart that remained, Alice went to bed with her mind swimming. Not until her eyelids grew heavy did she realize that this was the first time since she had met him that her last thoughts had not been of Charlie. Though now she was thinking of him, she realized, not without some relief.

TWENTY-TWO

Over the next days, while Alice pondered the merits of women's suffrage, Charlie had his own concerns to occupy him. Lord Wynstowe returned from his visit to Mr. Stiltstocking brimming with inspiration. His fellow scientist had given him an exciting gift: a new set of small calipers modeled on those invented by none other than Leonardo da Vinci. Whereas the larger sets of calipers he already owned measured head size and shape, these new ones were, Lord Wynstowe explained, useful in ascertaining precise measurements of facial features, the area of his particular interest and, dare he say, expertise. He did not even wait to change from his traveling clothes, but insisted on measuring Charlie right away, notating to the smallest decimal the size of his servant's nose, eyes, mouth, and ears. Some of the wind was taken out of Lord Wynstowe's sails when it became clear that Charlie's features were remarkably regular. Regularity, Lord Wynstowe believed, was an attribute of nobility. It was the regularity of the features of the descendants of the first Lord Wynstowe that, he insisted, proved the family's superiority. To find this quality in a servant of ignoble birth was disconcerting.

Charlie, however, who had had occasion to observe at the closest of quarters all parts of his lord's anatomy, had noticed no unusual symmetry therein. On the contrary. Though Lord Wynstowe's features were indeed regular, and he was widely acknowledged to be well favored, only his valet knew that one of his ears not only stuck out farther than the other, but, if left unattended, would grow a thicket of stiff hairs entirely absent from its fellow. And there were other areas more intimate that differed by an amount so substantial that they might each have belonged to a different man. (You need not reach for your smelling salts, Reader, for I know you, like me, have noticed this common peculiarity.)

Lord Wynstowe took each measurement no fewer than three times, reaching satisfaction only when he discovered a decimal's difference in size between Charlie's nostrils.

"There is a marked difference in your nose," Lord Wynstowe said, his relief palpable. "Still, there is more uniformity than I would have expected, given your lowly station." He took another measurement, this time of the size of Charlie's canine teeth, jotted down the results, and then sighed heavily. "Your father was a watchmaker, you've said?"

"Yes, sir."

"And your mother's people? What was their background?"

"My mother hails from Cheshire. Her father was a dairyman, as was his father before him."

"An uneducated horologist and the daughter of a dairyman could not have produced a son with features like yours. There is only one explanation. Your father was not the man you thought. Your true father can only have been of noble birth."

Though he would have been happy to discover no biological connection to the father who had made so miserable the lives of his family, this affront to Charlie's mother's virtue angered him. He knew her to be the most respectable of women, one who had suffered much in her life as a result of her marriage to a man of intemperate habits and moral vacancy. Charlie suppressed his ire, though, reminding himself that his gentleman, even when not under the sway of professional excitement, had little sympathy inherent in his nature. He was not, however, malicious. It was more that emotion was for him a foreign language that he did not speak well. He was most likely unaware of having engendered any insult.

Lord Wynstowe took up his calipers. He again measured the length of Charlie's nose and the width of his nostrils, nodding in satisfaction. After making a few calculations, he asked Charlie to carry out the same measurements on him.

Lord Wynstowe was relieved by the comparison. Because he was descended from nobility on both sides, his was an ideal long, straight nose, he told Charlie. Charlie's, on the other hand, had on it a small lump, a consequence of his mother's lowly birth. Charlie did not point out that, to the extent that his nose was disfigured, it was likely a result not of his mother's class but rather of the punch he had taken on it from his sister Mary when he was but seven and she nine years old. Even at such a tender age, Charlie had refrained from returning the blow. He had seen on his mother's face the damage a man's fist could do. Instead, he had buried his head in his mother's lap and sobbed so hard that Mary had slunk over and pressed a penny she had been saving into his palm. He had exacted his revenge by using the coin to purchase a twist of Everton Toffees, half of which he ate with audible delight, the others he distributed to his younger siblings. Mary suffered the affront in an angry silence, but never again raised a hand to her brother.

The ratio of Charlie's fourth and second fingers as compared with his own provided Lord Wynstowe with more consternation, but he finally decided that, whereas a large enough differential was indicative of admirable masculine strength and grace, as great a one as Charlie's might indicate a tendency to brutality.

After verifying that Charlie had recorded all measurements in the calfskin-bound book Lord Wynstowe kept for this purpose, the viscount informed him that they were off to his club, where he intended to measure the faces of his fellow members. He desired specifically to examine those who had ascended to their peerages through royal patronage rather than by virtue of birth. Their faces, he said, would, like Charlie's, betray the baseness of their lineages. Charlie was disappointed that he would not have opportunity for an evening's visit to Alice, but relieved that his gentleman's industry foretold their continued residence in London.

Once at the club, Charlie, with the assistance of the porter, who received a generous gratuity for his efforts, set up an examination station with a chair, a small table on which to lay the various instruments and implements of Lord Wynstowe's explorations, as well as a pot of ink, a small stack of blotting paper, and a pen. The great man provided assistance by way of barking instructions and rubbing his hands together in delighted anticipation. He had often measured the painted features of his extended family as immortalized in the portrait gallery at Wynstowe Manor, refusing to consider that those visages might have been improved by a painter's desire to please his patron, but he had not before had the opportunity to measure actual living, upper-class faces.

He scanned the hall and then cried, "There is the Marquis of Drayton!" He rushed to the man's side, and though Charlie could not hear the conversation, Lord Wynstowe's pleading was obvious on his face. Unfortunately, so was the marquis's distaste on his own.

"I say, Wynstowe!" a rotund gentleman exclaimed after the marquis shook Lord Wynstowe off and entered the club. "I will sit for you!"

Lord Wynstowe assessed the man, short of stature, with a fleshy face and a lumpy potato nose. Before he could acquiesce, the gentleman clambered into the chair. Lord Wynstowe sighed heavily and took up his calipers.

"A new page," he said to Charlie. "The Duke of Feathersly."

Each measurement made Lord Wynstowe more morose than that previous, until, finally, he set down his calipers and released his subject. As he watched the duke go, he murmured, "Feathersly is awfully misproportioned."

"Do they not say, sir, that it is the exception that proves the rule?"

The viscount brightened. "They do! They do indeed."

Lord Wynstowe's travails continued for the rest of the evening. Even though he put his thumb on the scale by waving along both the more handsome newly ennobled peers and the less attractive scions of great families, there seemed to be neither rhyme nor reason to the shape and consistency of the features of those members of his club who deigned to seat themselves in his chair. There were so many snaggletoothed, lazy-eyed, and weak-digited men of noble birth that Lord Wynstowe was brought nearly to tears. Worse, the most regular features belonged to no less common a man than a shipping magnate recently appointed as a Knight Grand Cross of the Order of St. Michael and St. George by Her Majesty the Queen. This gentleman's visage was saved from perfect regularity only by a scar on his left cheek. Charlie wondered what importance could be drawn from this deformity as, like Charlie's nose, it was a feature not of birth but rather earned in a fight. Nonetheless, Lord Wynstowe was so relieved by its presence that even if Charlie were in the habit of doing so he could not have brought himself to puncture his lord's solace by questioning his conclusions.

The hour grew late, new arrivals grew fewer and further between, and Lord Wynstowe's face grew gray with fatigue. Charlie was about to encourage his lord to return home as surely he was exhausted from his journey when the club porter opened the door to admit none other than Lord Alderwick.

"Look there, man!" Lord Wynstowe said to Charlie. "It is Lord Alderwick. What good fortune! For is not his physiognomy most regular? And he is of such a long and noble lineage. I must measure him. Lord Alderwick! Sir! Please attend!"

Lord Alderwick looked not at all pleased to see him, a fact unsurprising given how poor an impression Lord Wynstowe had made when visiting Marlecombe Park. Charlie watched his master plead with the earl, wincing as the viscount clutched at the gentleman's sleeve, the better to draw him toward the chair. Lord Alderwick shook him off in the manner of a cow flicking at a fly with its tail, but, like the fly, Lord Wynstowe would not be dissuaded. Finally, Lord Alderwick allowed himself to be ushered over to the examination station.

"This won't take but a minute," Lord Wynstowe said, taking up his calipers. "A few measurements only. Wells! Open the notebook to a fresh sheet. Make haste, man!"

Charlie readied the notebook. Lord Wynstowe took up his calipers and measured the width and length of Lord

Alderwick's face from forehead to chin and ear to ear. "Compute the ratio," he instructed Charlie.

Fortunately, Charlie had been well schooled in arithmetic by his workhouse schoolmaster and made short work of the calculation. "One point six, sir."

"One point six!"

"One point six two, to be exact."

"My word! That's wonderful. *Wonderful.* Lord Alderwick, are you familiar with Euclid's golden ratio?"

"Whose what?"

"Euclid, the ancient Greek mathematician. It is a mathematical equation based on the Fibonacci series, where each entry is recursively defined by the entries preceding—"

"If that is all . . ." Lord Alderwick began to stand, but Lord Wynstowe pressed him back into the chair.

"It means that your facial proportions are perfection. Absolute perfection!"

Lord Alderwick settled back into his seat, indicating with a pompous nod of the head that this was no more than he had expected.

Lord Wynstowe measured from the top of the great man's nose to the center of his full lips, and from the lips to the bottom of his chin, reciting the measurements aloud to Charlie, and instructing him to compute their ratio.

"One point six one," Charlie said.

"Oh, this is remarkable, sir!" Lord Wynstowe said to Lord Alderwick with delight. "Your proportions are ideal." He paused, scruples demanding a slight qualification. "All but ideal! Very like my own, in fact."

Lord Wynstowe went through the remaining measurements. The distance from hairline to the upper eyelid was excessive, which caused some concern, until Lord Alderwick recalled that his hairline had receded since his youth and had once been, as he recalled, precisely the perfect measurement. The width of each eye was similar to the distance between the two. And his lower lip was the desirable amount fuller than the upper. The only concern was in the relative size of his nose and ears, but that measurement, Lord Wynstowe determined, was irrelevant. "In my research, I have learned that true aristocrats have long noses, such as yours and mine."

The calculations complete and the nobility of his aspect confirmed, a well-pleased Lord Alderwick walked through the doors into the club, Lord Wynstowe attentive at his side, leaving Charlie to stand uncertainly by the chair, wondering if he could risk the club porter's opprobrium by taking a seat. That man's stern shake of the head confirmed Charlie's fear that he was to remain standing until Lord Wynstowe removed from the club, which he did not do for near two and a half hours.

Charlie bided his time bent over the little table, writing a letter to Alice on a sheet of paper torn carefully from the back of the journal. He recounted his lord's and Lord Alderwick's increased amity, and wondered if this might not bode well for a connection between the families. Once they succeeded in deterring the relations between Mr. Smythe-Roberts and Lady Jemima, he wrote, their task might be easier than they imagined! His letter complete, Charlie was grudgingly sold a Penny Red at a tuppence markup by the porter, who then allowed him to place his letter among the club patrons' outgoing evening post.

TWENTY-THREE

The next morning, Charlie received a letter of his own, this one with troubling news. It was from Mary itself unusual, as his sister always left that obligation to their mother, who, though hardly a vigorous or educated correspondent, nonetheless managed a weekly scribble with a generally quite tedious recitation of the events of her and Mary's days alongside profusions of love and devotion. This beloved lady, Mary wrote now in a near-illegible scrawl, was ill. A few days previous, despite Mary's having left her with strict instructions to remain at rest until she returned from the shops, Mrs. Wells had determined to carry a load of laundered linen down to the yard to dry, and had slipped on the last few steps and fallen. Mary found her sprawled on the floor amidst the wet and now filthy washing. "Her ankle was swole up and she had a lump on her head," Mary wrote. "But it was the linen she was crying over."

Mary had almost to carry her up the stairs, then put her to bed and had the doctor in. He was unconcerned, and recommended only a comfrey poultice for the ankle and a cold compress for the head. Their ma had seemed all right, Mary wrote, considering, but in the night, she took a turn. She could keep nothing down, not even the beef tea the landlady brought. Then she began shaking, her eyes rolled back in her head, her heels drumming the mattress. The fits eventually stopped, mercifully, but she was now very weak, unable to rise from the bed, and not speaking other than to moan in pain and periodically call for Charlie. Mary had put off this letter for two days in hopes she would have better news to share, but now she feared Charlie must come home. Mary had looked into the timetable, and if he took the first train to Wynstowe from London in the morning and the last train back to London the next day, he would be gone for two days only; might Lord Wynstowe agree to spare him?

Letter in hand, Charlie rushed to Lord Wynstowe's bedroom, where he found the man rummaging through his clothes press.

"There you are!" Lord Wynstowe said, querulously. "I cannot say I expected to continue having to manage on my own once I came home." To his credit, however, the gentleman noticed Charlie's expression. "What is the matter?"

When Charlie recounted the contents of Mary's letter, Lord Wynstowe dropped his attitude of displeasure and said, "Pack my things. I will remove to my club, and you can take the evening train."

It was no small thing to allow a servant two days' liberty without notice, and Charlie's heart was warmed by his normally solipsistic gentleman doing so without a moment's pause.

Even as Charlie was across town packing both his lord's case and his own, Alice came down from dressing her lady to find his letter of the previous evening resting against her teacup. She felt a pang of remorse. She had scarce given thought to their project in the last days, so preoccupied had she been by the perplexing yet fascinating conversation on which she had eavesdropped. After that meeting, she had borrowed Mary Wollstonecraft's *A Vindication of the Rights of Woman* and John Stuart Mill's *The Subjection of Women* from Miss Bennett's small library and stayed up late into the night reading them. The arguments did not, at first blush, strike her as relevant to her own life. She found interesting Wollstonecraft's notion that a woman deserved an education as vigorous as a man's, but not even the boys in the village in which she had grown up had opportunity to pursue any education beyond what was offered at Miss Elliott's small school. She could think of no one who had gone on to a grammar school; such would have been beyond the means of all, and though she had heard tell of wealthy patrons who offered scholarships to the deserving poor, none in their village had been so fortuitous as to receive one. On the other hand, she felt keenly the truth of the lady's insistence that women were deserving of natural rights, for if justice demanded that a man's liberty should not be dependent on an accident of birth, why should a woman's? It amused her to see the great lady dismiss flighty ladies as "spaniels," prey to the vicissitudes of their sensibility. Women like herself, Alice thought, whose bread depended on their labor, had not the luxury of spanielhood. It was impossible to be frivolous while scrubbing stains out of another's dirty underclothes.

After reading Mr. Mill's pamphlet, she had snuffed her candle and, sleepless, considered how his words related to her own circumstances. Was Mr. Mill's version of equality, like

Wollstonecraft's, relevant only to those of Miss Bennett's class and circumstance, or was there something in it to which a woman like Alice might aspire? What might perfect equality look like in the life of a lady's maid? Was it a matter of earning the same as a man in a domestic position similar to her own—like Charlie, for example? Would that be sufficient satisfaction? What, Alice allowed herself to wonder, might become of a person like herself in a world of perfect equality and educational opportunity? Rather than go into service, might she have aspired to be the first in the village to continue her education? What then? Could she, in this fantastical society of boundless possibility, have become, for example, a clerk in a banking house? She imagined herself sitting hunched on a high stool in a dim room, her fingers black with ink, making meticulous notes in a ledger. That toil would be no less tedious than the worst of her current labors, though certainly less malodorous. Not a clerk, then. Might she have become a teacher, like her own Miss Elliott? That felt a more appealing prospect. She racked her brain for every profession she knew, imagining herself in a barrister's wig, a chemist's apron, a clergyman's collar. It was this last that brought her back firmly to earth. Absurd, she said to herself, pulling her nightcap down over her eyes and turning on her side to sleep.

Now, with Charlie's letter in hand, she reminded herself sternly to attend to activities that had effect on her own life, rather than fairy tales that, even if they were to become realities, would touch only the lives of ladies and gentlemen. She opened the letter, and smiled at Charlie's fond salutations. As she read, however, she worried at the excitement with which he related his gentleman's encounter with Lord Alderwick. She wished she shared his confidence that the bond between

Lady Jemima and Mr. Smythe-Roberts could be severed. It had, if anything, grown stronger in the face of Miss Bennett's opprobrium. The young gentleman had vigorously denied the accusation, dismissing the miniature in the locket and the lock of hair as belonging to some other T. He was sure he had heard of a Theophilus or two of dubious character. In the wake of the accusation Mr. Smythe-Roberts's attentions had, if anything, increased. He visited each morning and accompanied Lady Jemima on various outings in the afternoons. He was indeed ever-present.

Lady Jemima firmly refused Miss Bennett's offer to assume the duties of chaperone, so it had fallen to Alice to trail after the couple. Lady Jemima and her gentleman spent an afternoon in the National Gallery, which would have interested Alice but for the speed at which the two galloped through the rooms. They paid marginally more attention to the displays of the International Exhibition of Modern Marvels at the Alexandra Palace, which Mr. Smythe-Roberts referred to as the "Ally Pally," lingering especially at the photography exhibit. Alice's spirits brightened at a moment of discord, when Lady Jemima demanded coquettishly that Mr. Smythe-Roberts pay for her image to be captured, and he declined. It was clear to Alice and, she hoped, to Lady Jemima that his refusal had naught to do with his claim that the invention was "silly," but rather, that the man lacked even the handful of pence to commission the photograph. Still, within a few minutes, Lady Jemima had ceased to pout and was back on Mr. Smythe-Roberts's arm.

Despite such incidents, it was on these excursions that Alice was finally able to see for herself what attracted Lady Jemima to this man who should have been beneath her notice. His good looks were indeed part of his magnetism, as were the admiring glances they received as a couple, both so fair and haughty, gliding through crowds like a pair of swans among a flock of ducks. His manner with her was elegance personified, but what was truly enchanting was how engrossed he seemed, looking into her eyes when she spoke as if he had never met anyone so fascinating, laughing at her witticisms, bending toward her confidentially, and whispering into her ear, his words for her alone. He performed attentiveness with a virtuoso's brilliance, and Lady Jemima drank it up. To be the focus of such single-minded attention, Alice thought, was a flattery so delicious that even her lady, long used to the regard of men, was powerless before it.

No, Alice thought, rereading Charlie's letter as she drank her morning tea, it would not be so easy to separate the two. Just then, she heard the jangle of the doorbell and a muffled man's voice coming from above. She strained to identify the speaker. The voice was too deep to belong to Mr. Smythe-Roberts, she thought. Her curiosity was satisfied when the maid arrived downstairs, breathless with news of Lord Alderwick's attendance upon his daughter and sister-in-law. He had come to London, it seemed, especially to scold Lady Jemima for drawing so profligately upon her allowance. As the maid told the story, the young lady had seemed not at all pleased to see her father, though she had quickly assumed an expression of supposed delight. He had not deigned to notice the charade, but immediately launched into his criticisms.

"The steward tells me that he has received no end of milliners' and other bills, and that you have three times exceeded your allowance," he said. "Your expenditures are outlandish."

"If they be outlandish, as you say, Papa, that is only because London is so very dear. Everything costs three times what it does at home, and one must look three times as fine! You wouldn't want me to be outshone by the likes of Caroline Mountjoy, would you?"

"I have near as much confidence in your beauty as you do yourself, and so do not credit that concern."

"You are the dearest papa who ever lived," she simpered. "But beauty means less here in town than do fine dresses and jewels."

"Were I a girl who had raided her mother's jewel box, I would leave that subject alone."

The maid told the servants gathered in the kitchen, "She didn't even go red in the face! Just flicked 'er 'ead like it were nowt at all, and her accused of thievery!"

Alice was surprised to find herself defending her lady. "I'm sure her intention is to return to her mother all of the jewels she borrowed."

The maid reported that Lord Alderwick had informed Lady Jemima, "You must go attend to your mother. She is hardly a model of economy, but you will find fewer claims on your purse in the village." Then he asked, "Where is your aunt this morning?"

"She rises at dawn and sets out on what she calls her constitutional. You will not believe it when you see her, Papa. She looks a fright, swathed in silks, like an opera singer in her boudoir."

With this, she succeeded in her attempt to earn a grudging albeit sour smile from her father, who was always willing to sneer at his wife's sister.

Miss Bennett's servants, however, were outraged to hear of the disparagement of the dear lady of whom they were so fond. Cook expressed her affront by clanging a pot on the stove, and Mrs. Goodenough by shaking her head and frowning, an expression so unfamiliar to her features that it could last no more than a moment before being replaced by her habitual placid and pleasant one.

The maid's breathless tale was interrupted by a ringing at the front door. She threw up her hands. "All this to-ing and fro-ing's like to drive me mad!" She rushed up the stairs.

"At a walk!" Mrs. Goodenough called after her. "I can't blame the girl," she said to Alice. "This is more excitement than we've had in this house in a month of Sundays."

At the door was Mr. Thomas Smythe-Roberts, come to pay a call. His surprise at finding himself in the company not only of his lady but of her forbidding father, Alice could only surmise. She strained, without success, to make sense of the mumbling from above.

Mrs. Goodenough said, "If you don't mind, dear, could you take this . . ." She glanced around the room, pounced on a silver sugar server, and held it out to Alice. ". . . and put it in the pantry alongside the rest of the silver?"

The housekeeper could barely contain her smile as Alice took the bowl and crept silently up the servants' stairs, arriving at her perch in time to hear the young lady say, "London is far more diverting than home, Papa, but I do sometimes wish for a greater variety of acquaintance. Perhaps you might take me out with you so that I can meet more people."

There was a small silence after this comment, and Alice imagined Mr. Smythe-Roberts looking busily down at his hands, or out the window, anything to avoid the eye of the lady to whom he was paying suit. Perhaps he was wondering whether this last was a gentle gibe, a subtle message that Lady Jemima had not accepted his denial of an attachment to Signora di Galtieri. She knew that the arrogant young man would dismiss this thought quickly, determined to believe the comment to be no more than thoughtless. He was, Alice considered, the sort of person who would not tolerate any concern at odds with his own comfort.

"Alice," Mrs. Goodenough whispered, appearing by her side. "Come quickly. Your young man's come to call."

Almost grudgingly, Alice followed the housekeeper back to the kitchen, where she found Charlie being fussed over by Cook.

"You'll have a bowl of porridge, won't you, Mr. Wells? With stewed prunes and a bit of barley sugar."

"I'm afraid I haven't the time, Mrs. Crispin."

Charlie did not look like himself. His expression was fretful. "What's happened?" Alice said.

Charlie told her quickly about his mother. He thought he would be gone no more than two days, he said, but it was possible that Lord Wynstowe might decide in the interim to return to Wynstowe Manor.

"I didn't want you to wonder why I wasn't calling."

Alice wished they were alone so she could press her lips to his forehead, the way her own mother did when she was inconsolable about something. She satisfied herself with taking his hand and squeezing it.

"You'll write and tell me how she is?" she said. He nodded, but any further conversation was interrupted by the chime of the bell.

"It's Lady Jemima," Mrs. Goodenough said. "She must have gone up to her room."

"I have to go," Alice said. But she could not bear to let loose his hand.

Mrs. Goodenough said, "She'll not be pleased to wait. Don't worry about Mr. Wells. He'll get home to find his mother right as rain, to be sure."

Impulsively, Alice leaned over and gave Charlie a quick

kiss on the cheek. Then she rushed upstairs to wait on her lady.

Lady Jemima was pacing back and forth, wringing her hands.

"Alice!" she said upon hearing the door open. "Where have you been? I need you urgently."

"I'm so sorry, ma'am. I came as soon as I heard the bell."

"My father is here! And Thomas has come! He will use this opportunity to ask for my hand, I am sure of it. I pretended to be in urgent need of a moment's privacy to give him time to make his petition."

"Very exciting, ma'am," Alice said, her heart sinking.

"You must go downstairs and listen at the door. I want a full report on their conversation."

"But what if they were to see me? Surely your father will not take kindly to my snooping?"

"Then make sure you are not seen. Go! Before they finish!" She jutted her chin in the direction of a filled chamber pot. "And take that with you." She shuddered. "How can Aunt Sarah live like this, without a proper place to do her business?"

Alice wondered if it even occurred to Lady Jemima that this particular discomfort caused Alice far more trouble than it did the lady herself.

"It really is unfair that I am expected to live like a Black man in the wilds of the West Indies."

Alice doubted that those who toiled in the sugarcane fields made regular use of porcelain chamber pots, or even of a privy like the small brick one in Miss Bennett's garden, with the image of a lone rose carved into the cheerfully painted wooden door; the whole place was kept in a state of such good order and cleanliness that, but for the odors emanating from the pit, it might be confused with a gentle lady's boudoir. Alice knew better than to suggest that Lady Jemima make use of it, however more pleasant that might be than squatting over a pot.

Alice rushed to dump out the contents of the pot and scrub it clean, then returned to the pantry, from which she could eavesdrop on the two gentlemen. She arrived in time to hear an unusually voluble Lord Alderwick say, "Tell me, good sir. Is the making of a fortune beyond your younger son's portion a part of your plan? Or do you prefer to live modestly?"

"Oh, you know. I make my own way."

"Do you?" Lord Alderwick sneered. "How so?"

"I win a bit at cards."

"Cards?"

"And the races."

"I have always found that those who rely on luck to fill their purses inevitably find themselves the worse for it. Odds do not tend to favor a man for long. If you cannot live within your means, you would be better off securing an income. You might take my brother's example. He made his fortune, such as it was, in Ceylon. He owned a tea plantation."

"Did he, sir? How very adventurous of him."

"Philip did not have an adventurous bone in his body. He was scared of his own shadow. How he managed in a land full of tigers and marauding natives I don't know. Though he seemed to be doing well enough. That is, until he died."

"Was he killed by a tiger, then, sir?"

"A *tiger*? Good God, man. Don't be an idiot. He died of the Asiatic cholera. Our mother was quite prostrate with grief. She had not wanted him to go, but then, Philip was determined to better his fortune, and how else is a younger son to earn his living but to take such risks? If you don't have the brass for adventure in the Indies or Africa, I suppose you might take orders. Does your brother possess a living he might bestow on you?"

Mr. Smythe-Roberts laughed. "I? Take orders?"

Though the conversation seemed to Alice one that a gentleman might have with one who had asked for his daughter's hand, what followed disabused her of that impression.

"Have you considered marrying? You would do well to find yourself the daughter of an American industrialist. I understand that there are hordes of them scurrying about the drawing rooms of the city. Perhaps you will find one willing to settle for the younger brother of a minor member of the landed gentry."

"I will take this advice to heart, sir," Mr. Smythe-Roberts said.

Lord Alderwick must have discerned the pride and irritation in Mr. Smythe-Roberts's voice, for he said stiffly, "I will take my leave. Tell Jemima she can expect me on the morrow."

Alice heard the scrape of a chair on the floor. She shrank back into the gloom of the pantry, listening as Lord Alderwick trod heavily down the front passage and out the door. After another moment, there was the peal of the bell, and the maid rushed up the stairs and into the drawing room.

"Should I call for Lady Jemima, sir?" she asked.

"Get me my coat," Mr. Smythe-Roberts said. "And be quick about it."

The maid left, and within a moment, the young man was gone.

"But did he ask my father or did he not?" Lady Jemima said after Alice had recounted the conversation.

"I cannot know for sure, ma'am, but it did not seem so. He

did not give the impression of a man disappointed, nor your father that of one declining a petition."

"I think you must be correct. My father would not have jested about Ceylon and American ladies had he received and declined an offer on my behalf. Thomas must have lost his nerve. This is most vexing."

TWENTY-FOUR

Charlie knew his dear mother was dying as soon as he walked into the small bedchamber she shared with his sister. Beneath her frayed sleeping cap, with its cheerful decoration of faded cherries embroidered by his long-dead youngest sister, Mrs. Wells's face was as gray as the ashes in the cold grate; her cheeks were sunken, her lips cracked and dry.

"Why is there no fire?" Charlie asked Mary.

"Because the boy who brings the coals has not come, and I've been afraid to leave her side to fetch any myself."

"I'll go."

"Sit, Charlie. She needs you here, not running about the district. I'll be back in a few minutes." She handed him a bowl of water and a clean muslin cloth. "She isn't able to drink, but you can try to wet her lips."

Charlie sat down on the edge of his mother's bed, dampened a corner of the cloth, and held it to her mouth. The water dribbled unnoticed onto her chemise. He dabbed it away and took his mother's hand. It was as familiar to him as his own.

Her fingers were long and might even have been elegant, like Alice's fine hand, but they were marred by the lumps and scabs of half-healed chilblains. He traced his own finger along a scar that crossed his mother's palm. Though he had been a small boy, he recalled clearly the incident that caused it. His father had received a hefty payment for the repair of a lady's French ormolu clock and had counted out the coins and notes on the table, crowing with pleasure. The entire family had stared at the heap, imagining the delights that could be purchased with it. The children were hungry, so their fantasies were of food: Macaroons or a seed cake from the baker. Meat pies, one for all, even the little ones. Charlie supposed his mother's imaginings were of a payment of the arrears on the rent of their small lodgings. But Mr. Wells had swept the money into his hand and left, returning hours later with empty pockets and a belly full of whiskey. Charlie watched, astonished, as his mother picked up the bowl of soup that she had put aside for her husband, potatoes floating in a liquid more water than broth, and flung it at him. Though her aim was poor and she succeeded only in smashing the bowl to the floor, his father's response had been to roar, snatch up a knife from the table, and lunge. She had lifted her hand against the blade, and it had sliced open her palm. The streaming blood had frightened or shamed Mr. Wells, and he had staggered from the room, banging the door shut behind him. As soon as he was gone, Mary and Charlie had leapt from their pallets. Mary had bandaged the wound with a scrap torn from her chemise while Charlie dried their mother's tears on his shirttails.

Now he lifted her scarred palm to his lips and gently kissed it.

"I'm here, Ma," he said. "It's your Charlie come to see you."

He thought he saw a flicker behind her eyelids. He leaned closer. Her breath grew ever more labored. Suddenly there was a loud gurgling in her throat, a sticky rattle. And she was gone.

He heard a crash behind him. Mary stood in the doorway, the scuttle turned over on the floor, hunks and chips of coal scattered across the bare planks. With a wail, she rushed over, fell to her knees, and laid her head on their mother's chest, weeping.

The church was all but empty, with only the landlady, her son, and a handful of servants from Wynstowe Manor in attendance. Charlie and Mary sat in the second row, the first being by custom reserved for the great family of Wynstowe, even when none were in attendance. The service itself was finer than Charlie had anticipated. The vicar knew Mrs. Wells, and so his homily was warm, even fond. He praised her for her modesty and kindness, and said that she approached death as she lived, with Christian faith, fortitude, and quiet dignity. He even recalled the names of Charlie's long-dead younger brother and sister, which made Charlie's eyes fill. Mary had exhausted her tears on the day Mrs. Wells died, and the only evidence of her distress was two spots of color that caused the pocks on her cheeks to glow an angry red. She remained silent even as the pallbearers—two men from the village and a footman from the Manor—helped Charlie lower the rosewood coffin, for which he had paid too much, into the fresh-dug grave. Stone-faced, she ignored Charlie's entreaties to come away when the service over the grave was done. Only when the gravediggers had done their grim work and the hole was filled would she agree to return to their lodgings.

Before church, Mary had prepared a tray of bread and butter and sent Charlie to the public house for a pitcher of small beer. Now she brewed a pot of tea, the landlady appeared with a Madeira cake, and they readied themselves to receive visitors. The vicar arrived, as did a handful of others who came to comfort the grieving and partake of the refreshments. Mary sat stiffly, her hands folded in her lap. To Charlie was left the obligation of conversing with their company. He accepted condolences, agreed that the weather was unusually chill even for the time of year, that Lord Wynstowe's wreath was indeed evidence of the utmost generosity, that they were fortunate that the weather had cooperated, etc. etc.

When the few visitors were finally gone, Charlie, feeling as though the walls were closing in on him, asked his sister, "Shall we take a walk?"

"You go. I have things to do here."

"What things?"

But she provided no answer.

Charlie took a meandering path through the small copse of trees between the village and Wynstowe Manor, wishing, as he dodged puddles, that he had changed into everyday shoes. The funeral had depleted his savings, and if he ruined these, he would have nothing with which to purchase a pair for new best.

As he tromped through the gray afternoon, moving briskly against the cold, he imagined Alice walking beside him, her arm in his, quiet and comforting company. Take heart, he told himself. Their plan would work, it *must,* and then Alice would be his wife, and he need never again suffer such painful solitude. Whatever tragedies life brought, they would face them together.

His eye was caught by a small patch of snowdrops, and he gathered a posy to take to Mary. It would comfort her, he hoped, to see that even in the midst of winter some blooms were brave enough to defy the gloom.

By the time he returned to the house, the sun was low in the sky. As he climbed the rickety stairs to the family lodging, he heard voices. Who, he wondered, had come so late to pay their respects? He opened the door to find none other than Alice, dressed in traveling clothes, perched on one of the two chairs pulled up before the fire now blazing in the grate.

She had left for Wynstowe immediately upon receiving the mourners' card that Charlie had posted the morning after his mother's death. Mary had purchased a dozen of these cards from the stationers, paying an extra shilling for one with a motif of drooping lilies in addition to the usual black border. She and Charlie had filled them in with the details of their mother's funeral and internment and sent cards to the vicar, the landlady, the butler and housekeeper at Wynstowe Manor, a few of the village shopkeepers whose establishments Mrs. Wells frequented, and two ladies she knew from church. That left them still with three cards. Charlie had addressed one to Alice, causing Mary to arch an eyebrow.

"Is she your sweetheart?" she had asked.

He nodded.

"Are you betrothed?"

"I hope to be."

"And she? What does she hope?"

"She hopes the same."

"So you've asked her?"

"We have talked about the possibility."

"You're thinking I'll move in with you and your lady? Keep your house for you? A spinster sister no better than a servant?"

"Why would you say such a thing? I am a servant and not ashamed. So is Alice. She's abigail to Lady Jemima Alderwick."

"You can't marry if you are both servants."

"We have a plan," Charlie said. He took up the envelope

before it was ready, causing the ink to smudge. "Damn it!" He tore up the envelope, the card still in it.

Mary handed him another card and another envelope. He addressed this one, blotted the ink, and then took up the rest of the cards.

"Is there someone to send the last of them to?" he asked.

Mary shook her head.

"Do you want to save it?"

"I need no souvenir to remind me that our mother is dead."

Mary was a most devoted daughter and had never shown any resentment of the effort required to care for their mother, but she was, without a doubt, the least sentimental person he had ever known.

"I will keep it, then," he said.

Now, seeing Alice unexpectedly sitting with his sister, he could not restrain himself. He crossed the room in two long strides and swept her up in his arms, kissing her on the mouth.

They lingered in their embrace until Mary's dry cough interrupted their reverie. Though they moved apart, Charlie could not bear to lose his love entirely; his hands hovered atop her shoulders.

"You came," he said.

"I planned to be here in time for the service," Alice said. "I left before dawn, but the train was delayed something awful."

"No matter. I am only glad to see you. Mary, is not Alice kind to come?"

"She is," Mary said.

Mary had surprised Alice by knowing immediately who she was. "You are Charlie's own Alice," she had said when she opened the door. "Come all the way from London. You'll be perishing for a cup of tea."

Alice had followed Mary into the plain sitting room, with

its old but serviceable furniture, the rough Hessian upholstery covered with a profusion of tatted lace doilies. Mary knelt at the hearth and swung the kettle on its crane over the coals. Then she busied herself with a teapot and cups.

"We've no milk left," Mary said, "and only a bit of sugar. The vicar et nearly the whole loaf. I've never met a man with such a sweet tooth."

Alice said, "I like it black." She did not, really, but she did so wish Charlie's sister to be favorably disposed to her.

"At least it's good tea," Mary said. "Charlie bought Darjeeling for a treat."

"Lovely," Alice said.

"I don't know 'bout 'lovely,' but it's better than the usual."

The two drank their tea—lovely it was, as Mary knew well how to brew a cup—in silence unbroken until Charlie burst through the door.

Now Alice said, "I fear I need to turn right around. I promised Lady Jemima I'd be back to dress her in the morning, and the last train is in less than an hour."

"I will come with you," Charlie said. He turned to Mary. "Will you be all right, sister?" Only then did he notice that Mary, too, was clad in traveling clothes, by her side a carpet bag, its broken handle tied up with string.

"I'm coming with you," Mary said.

"To London? But that's impossible. There's naught for you there."

She took from her bodice a scrap of newsprint and handed it to Charlie. It read:

Reliable and industrious women required for employment. Duties include operating machinery, sewing, and general factory tasks. No prior experience necessary; training provided.

Must be in good health and of sound character. Apply in person at J. Smith & Co. Textiles, 12 High Street, London, or send inquiries to the above address.

"Don't you worry, sister. You need not go out to work. Your circumstances will remain unchanged. You'll stay here in your home, in the village where you have friends to keep you company."

"I have no friends, and I want to earn my own keep."

"So you do, and so you always have. With Ma gone, you can take in more sewing, that'll give you more to spend. Haven't I always taken care of you? I always have and I always will. Alice knows that, don't you, Alice? Mary's my responsibility."

"Don't you see that I don't want to be your responsibility!" Mary said, her voice harsh.

On his face was an expression of hurt and confusion, open and innocent like a child's. "I've not made you feel bad about it, have I? You are my responsibility, and I'm glad of it."

"To be honest, brother, I care not whether you are glad or not glad. I have long desired to leave this place and see London. Now, finally, I'm free to go."

"Is it only that? London is a filthy place. The air itself is unsuitable for a girl to breathe. Unpack your bag. Next time I am given leave, I will take you to London. We will visit the Zoological Gardens. Alice and I went there and found it most agreeable."

"I don't care about zoological gardens and I don't want to visit. I want to make my life in the city. Anyway, the air can't be as putrid as you say if Alice breathes it. If you won't let me travel with you, I'll wait until tomorrow and take the morning train. You'll be hard-pressed to find me then, and by the time you do, I'll have me a factory job, and that's that."

Charlie was annoyed by his sister, but refused to give evidence of his emotion, as he knew it would cause her only to set her face more firmly against him. Instead, he tried for a tone that was calm and informative. "The mills are terrible, nasty places. They work their girls near to their deaths."

"Not all. Some are better than others."

"That may be so, but you'll not be able to discern good from bad until it's too late."

"You underestimate me. You always have."

Frustrated, Charlie rubbed his hand through his hair, making it stand on end. Alice fought an urge to smooth it back into place.

"You're proud, Mary," he said. "When you get an idea in your head, you won't budge."

"What's wrong with wanting to earn my own way?" She lifted her chin and crossed her arms, as if to prove his point.

"Nothing at all. It's admirable. Do you not think so, Alice? That Mary wants to earn her way speaks well of her."

"I'm sure it does," Alice said.

To Mary he said, "I'll speak to Mrs. Sweet. I'll ask if she'll take you on at the Manor."

"I wouldn't work for that woman if she paid me a king's ransom. And I told you. I won't be a servant. Not yours, not your Lord Wynstowe's. I'm going to London, and that's that."

Charlie cast a beseeching look Alice's way, but she could think of nothing to say. Mary was determined.

"Mary, please!" He was by now distraught. "How will you find suitable lodging, even if you find a job?"

"There are boardinghouses where women and girls live," Mary said.

"What do you know of boardinghouses? How long have you been planning this escape of yours?"

"Escape?" Mary said angrily. "Is that what you call it?"

"What do you call it, then?"

"My *life*! Which I have spent till now caring for our ma."

"But you love Ma!"

"And I was happy enough to be with her, but now she's gone, and I must make my way in the world."

"I keep telling you! You don't need to make your own way; you have *me*!"

Alice, her voice soft and soothing, said, "Perhaps you can ask Lord Wynstowe if Mary can stay with you for a few weeks, until she finds employment and lodgings?"

"So you are in agreement with this harebrained scheme?" Charlie said.

Agree or not, Alice could see that Charlie was destined to make no headway with his sister. Also, she could not help but admire the woman's pluck. In her turn, Mary looked astonished to receive Alice's support, and Alice felt a moment's satisfaction at having so obviously exceeded her expectations.

"As Mary is determined," Alice said, "it's far better that she travel with us. The way is long, and she's never been on a train before." She turned to Mary. "Have you?"

"No, but I have dreamed of it."

Alice said, "It's settled, then. There is little room where I stay, but if Lord Wynstowe won't have you, I can perhaps ask if a pallet can be made up on the floor of the kitchen for tonight. And then, tomorrow, you can look for lodging and employment."

"I won't allow it," Charlie said, his voice raised.

Alice looked at him, surprised. She had not before seen him attempt such a dictatorial protestation. It fit him ill, and she decided to ignore it. "Come, you two. If we miss the train, I will be in the most severe difficulties."

This kind of recalcitrance Charlie was used to from his sister. From his love, however, it was a surprise. Against the two of them, how could he do battle?

"But don't you see?" he said, all bluster gone now from his voice. "We're all that's left, Mary. Ma and the others are gone, and if anything happens to you . . ." His voice trailed off. He felt a burning in his eyes. Were these tears? he thought, horrified. He had not cried since he was a child and would not now, no matter that his mother was dead and his sister determined to worry him beyond all that was reasonable. Sensing his distress, Mary grabbed him roughly round the shoulders.

"Nothing'll happen to me, brother. And if anything does, I'll come running to you—how's that?"

After a last moment's resistance, he returned her awkward embrace.

"Anyway," Mary said gruffly, pulling loose. "You've got more than only me. There's Alice now, isn't there, Alice? Charlie's got you, too?"

His tetchy and unmannered sister had given voice to the very thought that had comforted Charlie over these last long days. Alice nodded, a small tuck of her chin that washed him in warmth and comfort. He held her gaze for a long, sweet moment until, finally, she said, "One might think you two were conspiring to see me miss my train!"

"So that's it, then?" the landlady said moments later, as she held open the door for them to leave.

"Yes" was Mary's simple reply. She handed over the key. "You may take what you like and give what bits and bobs remain to the almshouse."

Charlie turned to the landlady. "If you would save what is left until Mary's return, we'd be most grateful."

"I won't be back," Mary said, and walked out the door.

"She's not herself," Charlie said, pressing a shilling into the landlady's palm.

"Methinks you've not been home overmuch, for you've forgotten your own sister," the landlady said.

TWENTY-FIVE

Charlie and Mary arrived at Lord Wynstowe's house well past midnight. He led his sister to the top of the house and put her in a housemaid's room. Though she insisted she did not need it, eventually Charlie found linens for her bed in a cupboard heaped with the worn sheets and rough blankets that were all Mrs. Sweet allowed the servants under her supervision. He counted himself fortunate that the unpleasant old woman was not in residence. She would have evicted his sister in a trice, caring not if Mary was thus reduced to sleeping in the street.

In anticipation of Lord Wynstowe's return, Charlie had engaged temporary servants from Miss Telfer's Registry Office, and in the morning the substitute cook set before them mugs of tea and bowls of porridge served with a dollop of preserves and a splash of cream, far tastier a meal than anything Wynstowe Manor's cook had ever managed. They were famished, not having eaten much at their mother's makeshift wake, and so bent over their bowls, trying and failing not to gobble. There was a similarity to their posture and gestures, if not to their appearance, which made clear their relationship.

Cook refilled their bowls—the very first time, Charlie thought, that a ladle in this kitchen had served out a second portion.

His meal done, he told his sister that he was off to inform Lord Wynstowe of his return. "You're not to go traipsing from factory to factory willy-nilly. Alice and I will consult and find you a decent place."

Charlie found the gentleman at his club, ready to return home. To Charlie's astonishment, rather than hire a hackney for the journey, Lord Wynstowe insisted on walking home through Regent's Park, a distance of no less than two miles, farther than his feet had carried him in as long as Charlie had been in his employ. Charlie wondered at this change, and worried that he might not have time to request from the chemist a cream to treat the blisters that were inevitably to sprout on his gentleman's delicate heels. As they walked through the park, Charlie considered whether Lord Wynstowe might not be in his cups, so merry were his spirits. What, he wondered, was the source of the lord's good cheer?

"Guess whom I have been in company with, Wells! No, you will never guess. Lord Alderwick! Of Marlecombe Park! None other!"

On the first evening of Lord Wynstowe's residence in the club, the gentlemen had found themselves dining alone at proximate tables. While waiting for his soup, Lord Wynstowe had effused to Lord Alderwick again about the delight of measuring his elegant features. Such symmetry indicated the most superior intellect and breeding, finer than anything he had seen. Lord Wynstowe now confided in Charlie that he had exaggerated about this, but only a bit. Though Lord Alderwick's measurements were on a par with his own and those he extrapolated from the portraits of his ancestors at Wynstowe Manor, they were of course not *more* exceptional. Still, the white lie had been worth it, and Lord Alderwick had been appropriately flattered and had invited Lord Wynstowe to join their tables together. The two had spent the meal in delightful conversation, the topic of Lord Alderwick's physiognomy and the excellence of both his progeny and his ancestors inexhaustible. After their meal, they had repaired to the clubroom, where they joined two others at euchre. Lord Wynstowe was pleased to discover that Lord Alderwick frowned on gambling as much as he did himself, so the table played only for pence.

"At the end of that night and each subsequent, the victor would put his winnings toward a bottle for the table," Lord Wynstowe said. "You might be surprised to hear that one evening it was I who was given that honor!"

"Congratulations, sir."

"I have invited Lord Alderwick to abide with us while he is in town," Lord Wynstowe continued. "Far more comfortable than at the club." He paused, struck by a terrible thought. "Mrs. Sweet and Cook have not returned, have they?"

"No, sir, but worry not. I have arranged for a complement of temporary servants."

Lord Wynstowe looked exceptionally relieved. "Excellent. The cook is decent, I hope. Lord Alderwick is a bit of a gourmand, and I wouldn't like to expose him to my own cook. Her repertoire is so limited."

And its taste so foul, Charlie thought to himself, wondering why the gentleman persisted in employing the two wretched women. He said only, "If this morning's servants' breakfast is any indication, the temporary cook prepares an excellent table."

The viscount looked for a moment nonplussed, and Charlie wondered if he was for the first time considering the very notion of a servants' meal, if he perhaps imagined that those in his employ foraged for scraps or lived on air, but such was Lord Wynstowe's mood that he nodded amiably and commented on the fine weather, a shard of sunlight having broken through the leaden clouds to illuminate their path ahead.

Thus encouraged, Charlie allowed himself to petition his gentleman that Mary be permitted to stay until she found lodgings of her own. "To earn her keep, she can help the maids," Charlie said. "She is a strong girl and used to heavy work."

"Yes, yes," Lord Wynstowe replied, far too full of plans for the entertainment of his guest to pay any real attention to his man.

Alice was similarly occupied with the circumstance of Mary Wells, hoping that she would have a moment to speak to Miss Bennett privately about the girl. Fortunately, that morning Lady Jemima announced that she would be again gone through luncheon. Miss Mountjoy's father had purchased a brand-new Thrupp & Maberly carriage for his daughter's exclusive use, and though Lady Jemima was "spitting green with envy," she was glad to join her despised friend in exhibiting the fine vehicle to the beau monde. Once Lady Jemima was off to Rotten Row, Alice straightened her dress, repinned her hair, and tapped on the door of the drawing room.

"Come," Miss Bennett called.

Alice entered to find the good lady clad in a diaphanous morning gown of gold and silver, on her head a turban decorated with an ostrich plume that floated over her face, oscillating with each puff of breath.

"How may I help you, dear?" Miss Bennett said, spitting out a bit of feather. "I saw that you took me up on my invitation to borrow books. How did you find the John Stuart Mill?"

"Oh, Miss Bennett, is it not remarkable! The idea that a mere woman might be left to choose her direction as freely as a man? It is at once incomprehensible and necessary!"

Miss Bennett laughed. " 'Necessary'! My word. You have indeed become an acolyte."

Chastened, Alice rued that she had allowed herself to deviate from the attitude of reserve that was required of a maid, even by such an indulgent lady, and hoped she had not harmed her chances of earning another favor. But Miss Bennett continued with seeming sincerity, "I admire your sedulousness. No teacher could wish for a more diligent pupil."

"Thank you, miss. I am sorry to bother you, only I hope I might ask for your advice."

"The last time you made this request, I could provide little in the way of assistance. I fear my conversation with my niece served only to strengthen her in the belief that her suitor has no faults."

"It is not about Lady Jemima that I seek your counsel. I have an acquaintance, a Miss Wells, newly come to London from the country. She is seeking employment."

"As much as I might wish to assist, you know I have no space for another servant. We are as tightly packed as a tin of sardines as it is."

"Oh no, miss. My friend hopes to find a place in a factory."

Miss Bennett set down her pen and urgently said, "Factory

work is most taxing to the body and deleterious to the mind. You must discourage her from this path."

"She is quite set on it. I recall Miss Davies, your guest, speaking about the Society for the Employment of Women—"

"The Society for *Promoting* the Employment of Women. SPEW they call it, a horrible acronym." She shuddered.

"Do you think the society might assist my friend in choosing employment? Only there are so many factories looking for girls, and some must surely be better than others."

"Are you sure you cannot dissuade her, dear? It might be the death of her!"

"I wish I could, miss, but she's stubborn. Not even her own brother could make headway with her."

Miss Bennett opened her address book, took a scrap of foolscap, and wrote down an address. "Have your friend contact Miss Davies. She is of democratic character and won't consider a letter from a factory girl to be a presumption."

"Thank you, Miss Bennett."

"Now, don't you think of leaving my niece and joining your friend. I know you, Alice, and you wouldn't like factory work one bit."

"I would never, miss."

"My niece may lack tact and sensibility, but she is at heart a decent girl and, I think, an adequate mistress."

"Oh yes, miss. I am most fortunate in my employment."

"You are indeed. And, of course, you must continue to feel at liberty to borrow books from my library." Miss Bennett turned back to the letter over which she had been laboring when Alice walked in. Alice, dismissed, ran to the kitchen, where she begged a page of paper from Mrs. Goodenough and wrote to Miss Emily Davies on behalf of dear Charlie's sister.

TWENTY-SIX

Upon returning to her aunt's house, Lady Jemima stormed up the stairs to her bedchamber in yet another fit of temper. Alice fetched her a glass of barley water, which she drank down with a gulp and a shudder.

"It is too awful!" she said, wiping her mouth on her sleeve. The ladies, she recounted, had come upon Mr. Smythe-Roberts on Rotten Row, as they had hoped. He had been afoot, which she found surprising, but he explained that his horse had thrown a shoe and gone lame.

"He is devoted to the beast," Lady Jemima told Alice. "Won't ride another."

He is skint and can't *afford* another, Alice rejoined, though only in her mind.

He had leapt aboard the landau and spent, Lady Jemima cried, upwards of an hour exclaiming over its virtues. Such a fine carriage! Such an elegant pair!

Lady Jemima said, "*We* were not the pair he so admired. It

was the horses! Then he waxed eloquent about the carriage's leather fittings, the paint. He praised the *springs*!"

That the young man she viewed as her suitor and hers alone was devoting so much energy to flattering Miss Mountjoy, or at least her possession, was bad enough, but when Lady Jemima asked if Mr. Smythe-Roberts had yet called upon her father, he claimed that, though he certainly desired to again pay his respects to Lord Alderwick, he had been loath to frequent the home of Lord Wynstowe.

"It is not as though I don't understand his feelings," Lady Jemima said. "Lord Wynstowe may look like a prince, but he is a toad. Still, Thomas should value his connection with me more than his distaste for him."

"It is disgraceful that he does not, ma'am."

Lady Jemima scowled. "I would hardly call it *disgraceful*. Perturbing, yes. Exasperating indeed. But Mr. Smythe-Roberts could never be a disgrace to anyone. You overstep, Alice. You must watch your manners. I have reminded you of this before."

"My apologies, my lady. Only I hate to see one whom I esteem so very highly treated in a manner that verges on disrespect."

Lady Jemima's attitude turned again. "Perhaps he *is* disrespectful. Perhaps he is even a little cowardly when it comes to Papa. Papa is very fierce. Oh, what shall I do?"

Lady Jemima could not legally marry without her father's permission, but, more than that, Alice believed that her lady valued the great man's opinion more than anyone's other than her own. She had more than once told Alice that she was certainly her father's favorite child, even including her small brother. It provoked her much to think that the earl might be immune to her lover's good qualities.

Alice considered how she could put this antipathy to good use. Mr. Smythe-Roberts was not the kind of young man who improved on further acquaintance. Much the opposite. Perhaps if Lord Alderwick were to be more frequently in his company, and thus more exposed to the young gentleman, the father would find the suitor's character even more wanting than he did now, and forbid the match. There was a risk, she supposed, that Mr. Smythe-Roberts could wile his way into Lord Alderwick's good graces, but might not there be a circumstance in which he would reveal his true nature, a nature which Lord Alderwick was sure to dislike? The scene Charlie described of Mr. Smythe-Roberts being threatened by the turf accountant came suddenly to mind. Lord Alderwick did not gamble and had a poor opinion of those who did. Should he have opportunity to see this evil quality in action, he was sure to reject the man as suitor for his daughter.

Alice said, "Perhaps, if the two spent time together, his fear would abate? Lord Alderwick is not so very forbidding."

"Papa is only a bear if you don't know him." A niggling doubt at the dubious veracity of this statement troubled Lady Jemima for a moment, before being firmly dismissed. "But where would they meet? My father disdains Rotten Row, and Mr. Smythe-Roberts is not a member of Boodle's, more's the pity. Their paths are not likely to cross anywhere other than at Lord Wynstowe's home, and Thomas has already said he won't go there!"

Alice laid her trap: "Is your father not fond of the steeplechase?"

"He is."

"Might they not meet at the races, then?"

Lady Jemima's face broke out into an unladylike grin. "Oh, that is a most excellent idea! They might meet at Alexandra

Park!" She rushed over to the small table on which Alice had placed her combs, brushes, and other intimacies and rummaged around until she found the filigreed silver case stocked with her visiting cards. She scribbled a note on one and handed it to Alice.

"Take this to Mr. Smythe-Roberts. Make sure you give it to him directly—not to his mother, and most assuredly not to that vile brother of his, or his broodmare of a wife."

Alice waited until she left the room to read the card: *Sir. Would not an outing to Alexandra Park be a fine idea? Let us make a day of it. I know my father would very much enjoy it. If you seek to make a good impression on him, you might invite him to join us. Does that not sound fine? Yours, J.*

Alice took herself to the Smythe-Roberts home, but when she arrived she dithered at the tradesemen's entrace. How exactly did Lady Jemima imagine that she, a servant, would be granted access to the family residence in order to accomplish the task of delivering the card to Mr. Smythe-Roberts's hand? She had no choice but to beg the butler's indulgence of her errand.

"If you might take it to Mr. Smythe-Roberts himself, I'd be so very grateful. My lady will take it amiss if I leave without ascertaining that her card reached its intended recipient."

The butler, though unimpressed by Lady Jemima's urgency, agreed. Perhaps, Alice thought, he took into consideration the possibility that this lady might end up a member of the family, with authority over him. At any rate, he accomplished her request and returned with a piece of letter paper folded over itself but not sealed.

"For Lady Jemima," he said.

Once Alice was away from the house she unfolded the paper: *An excellent idea from a beautiful lady, and most for-*

tuitous as there's a horse running Saturday next that I already planned to see. I will invite your father to join me. With a mountain of love and a heap of kisses, Your Tommy.

Dear God, Alice thought. Things had progressed even further than she had imagined. That he called himself "Tommy" was terrible. But love? And *kisses*? If she and Charlie were to have even a hope of success, they needed to act now.

TWENTY-SEVEN

The next morning's post contained a note that distracted Alice from her primary purpose. Miss Davies agreed to see Mary that very afternoon at the offices of the Society for Promoting the Employment of Women. Fortunately, it was Alice's half-day, so, after completing her duties, she donned the best of the warm clothes she had inherited from her lady, a Harris tweed bodice whose moth-eaten holes she had carefully and near invisibly darned, a wool skirt over a bustle, and a high-collared cloak, and set out for Lord Wynstowe's house. She found Mary in the servants' hall, mending a pair of the viscount's britches. While a willing footman went in search of Charlie, she told Mary of the letter she had written to Miss Davies and of the reply she had received by return post.

"I wouldn't feel right asking a lady like her for help," Mary said. "Better I go directly to the factory that placed the advertisement."

"Miss Bennett said that Miss Davies is an approachable

person. And you will have me with you. Together, we'll muster courage enough, don't you think?"

Mary looked as if she wanted to argue her case further, but finally nodded in acquiescence. "You're very kind, Miss Lockey."

"Do call me Alice. After all, your brother uses my Christian name."

Said brother arrived at that moment, his forehead damp with perspiration from his race down the stairs, so eager was he to see her.

Alice said, "I have news."

Charlie held his hand up, silencing her. "Is Alderwick's man here?" he whispered to Mary.

"Off to the haberdashers," Mary said. "In search of a new set of handkerchiefs."

Relieved, Charlie turned to Alice. "Your news is good or ill?"

"It is an opportunity. Mr. Smythe-Roberts will be inviting Lord Alderwick to the steeplechase at Alexandra Park on Saturday. Lord Wynstowe must not only attend, but issue the invitation first, so that he is host to the affair rather than Mr. Smythe-Roberts. It would be much to his benefit to be seen in that role, I'm sure of it."

Charlie's eager expression faded. "Lord Wynstowe does not frequent the races. He is afraid of horses. And dogs. And mice. And badgers, though to my knowledge he's never seen one."

Cook, passing through the servants' hall, chortled. Charlie felt for a moment abashed at his disloyalty in mocking his lord, especially as the gentleman was so kind as to allow Mary to stay.

"Is there no way to convince him?" Alice said. "Otherwise, I fear Mr. Smythe-Roberts will press his advantage."

"I will do my best to come up with something."

Alice turned to Mary. "I am happy to see you settling in."

"I'll not settle in here. I'll get my own lodging as soon as I have work." Mary bit off her thread with her strong, yellow teeth.

This woman, Alice thought, rough-voiced and ill-tempered, could not be more different to Charlie. Alice reminded herself that Mary had only recently lost her mother. It was no wonder she was out of spirits. Perhaps at other times she had, beneath that crabbed exterior, as warm a personality as his own. And, whether Mary was sour or not, Alice was determined to be her friend.

"Your stitches are very fine," Alice said.

"I should hope so," Mary said. "I've been sewing since my fingers were too small for the thimble."

So much for flattery. "We must be off," Alice said. "The walk is long." Mary picked up from the back of her chair a thin shawl not at all suitable for the damp cold of a London winter. Alice supposed that Charlie had spent his savings on the funeral and had nothing left for his sister's wardrobe. She unclasped her own heavy woolen cloak. "Wear this," she said. "I am quite warm and don't need it."

"I'm fine as I am," Mary said.

"I insist."

Mary wavered, and finally allowed Alice to place the cloak around her shoulders.

Though she was not likely to receive any warm outerwear from Lady Jemima before the end of the season, perhaps, Alice thought, she might barter with Mrs. Goodenough for one of Miss Bennett's cast-offs. She could not help but smile at the thought of Mary clad in that lady's swaths of crimson velvet or gilded cashmere.

The walk across the city was as bitterly cold as she had

feared it would be, though fortunately the rain held off. The SPEW offices were not much warmer than the outdoors, and the young lady seated behind the reception desk was wrapped in her own brightly colored Indian shawl and gloves, with a thick muffler wound round her throat. Alice immediately recognized her as the girl who had spoken up so forcefully at Miss Bennett's soirée.

"If you are in training to embark on an Arctic exploration, you are most welcome to SPEW," the young lady said. "Otherwise, might I suggest you run for your lives? The chimney is blocked, the sweep unresponsive, and I am mere moments away from dying of the cold."

"I'm afraid we have no choice but to risk ending up in the grave alongside you," Alice said. "We have an appointment with Miss Davies."

The girl smiled broadly, clearly pleased Alice had joined in her fun.

"I am sorry, but Miss Davies is not here." The young lady looked down at the watch pinned to her bodice. "She has, shall we say, a flexible relationship with the hour. I hope she will not be long delayed. With whom do I have the pleasure of speaking?"

"I am Alice Lockey, and this is Mary Wells."

"I am Emmeline Goulden. What can I do for you?"

"Miss Davies invited us to come to seek consultation about suitable places for employment. Mary is looking for work in a factory, and we have heard that some have better working conditions than others. We know not how to choose."

Emmeline said, "What type of employment do you seek? I don't recommend the soap and candle factories, as they are full of awful smells and the ingredients are caustic to the skin. There are match factories, but"—she shuddered—"there's a girl who came in a few days ago, poor thing, her chin is fair rotted away from the phosphorus."

"Neither a soap factory nor a match factory," Alice said firmly. "Mary is a very fine seamstress. Perhaps she can make use of that skill?"

"The hours are long and the pay is poor in the garment factories. Better a textile mill, I think. The hours are no worse, and the pay is better."

"Is there one such place that treats its employees with more consideration than the others?"

"I am afraid I don't know much about the different places, but there are a few girls who come regularly to our meetings who work in the mills. They will know better than anyone which to avoid. If you come to a meeting, I will introduce you to them."

"But I can't wait for a meeting. I must find a place right away," Mary said. "I have no time to waste."

"Well, then, you are in luck," Emmeline said. "We are meeting this very evening. Eight o'clock, after the workday ends."

Mary looked at Alice, perturbed. "Is that too late for you? Do you have to get back?"

Mrs. Goodenough had already agreed to step into her place to dress Lady Jemima, and the young lady would be out for the evening and not likely to return until eleven or even midnight. "I can stay," she said.

A clap of thunder rang out, and the three looked out the window as the sky opened and sheets of torrential rain fell to the earth. Alice did not fancy making their way home and back again in this storm. "Might we sit here until the meeting, Miss Goulden?" she asked. "Only it's bucketing down and we have just the one umbrella between us."

"Absolutely not. It is far too cold. We will write a note to Miss Davies, telling her we have gone in search of a fire, and you will come with me. I am staying at the home of my cousin around the corner," the girl said.

Alice hesitated. She did not want to receive an invitation not her due, and, given her fine attire, it was possible that the young lady had mistaken her for one of her own class. How could she correct her without embarrassing them both? She must make clear her position.

"Miss," Alice asked, "did you not attend a soirée at the home of Miss Sarah Bennett not long ago?"

"I did indeed. A very dull affair. Why do you ask?"

"I work in the house. Or, rather, I stay there now with my kind lady, Lady Jemima Alderwick of Marlecombe Park. I am her abigail."

"Are you?" Emmeline looked delighted. "She is meant to be quite a beauty. You must tell me everything about her. Is she kind? Does handsome do as handsome is?" She took Alice's arm in her own. "You and I will share my umbrella. Mary, you stay nice and dry beneath Alice's." And she led the two out of the offices and into the blustery day.

By the time they reached the modest house of Emmeline's cousin, far from being "nice and dry," the three girls were wet through. As they surged through the door into the small entryway, Emmeline announced to the maid, "Hullo, Bridget! Are we not a trio of drowned rats?" She shook her skirts, spattering water.

The maid rushed away and returned with an armload of linen towels. The girls sopped up the worst of the wet, and Emmeline led them into a small parlor. She instructed them to prop their boots up on the grate and spread their skirts. She said, "Please bring nourishment at once, Bridget! I cannot decide which we will perish from first, the cold or starvation!" Years later, in moments of black humor, Alice would remind her friend of this comment given so cheerfully.

"You'll be wanting tea, then?" Bridget said.

"Yes, please. And bread and butter." To her new friends Emmeline said, "By the thermometer, Manchester is far more bitter than London, but there is something about the cold in the capital that sinks into my bones."

"You are from Manchester?" Alice said.

"I am. And you? Where is Marlecombe Park?"

"In ——shire."

"That's in the south?"

"Yes."

"I've not been south. Is it very pretty?"

"In spring and summer it is. And in autumn, too. Winter is gray and cold, like everywhere."

"My brother lived in Manchester," Mary said. "He was employed in the house of Mr. Arthur Stokes. Do you know him?"

"The name rings a faint bell."

"He owns a factory. Textiles."

Emmeline said, "My father is also in manufacturing. Though he is not overfond of other men of his situation, and so we do not dine with them often. You see, we are reformers, and so few men of business are. But tell me, why have you not considered asking your brother's former gentleman for employment? Manchester is a far more welcoming city than London. At least, I have found it so."

"Charlie regularly comes to London with Lord Wynstowe, but never to Manchester. I'd be all alone there."

"That sounds delicious. I have no fewer than nine brothers and sisters and am never alone. I am home only during the school holidays, and still I must visit my cousin here in London to clear the ringing in my ears. They are all so very unpleasantly loud!"

Alice noticed that Mary was shifting her feet ever closer to the grate. Alice's own stout boots had kept her feet dry, but Mary was not so lucky. Her boots were old and, though clearly well tended, had leaked.

Emmeline must have noticed the same, because she leaned down and unlaced her own. "My boots will never dry if I keep my feet in them," she said. She propped her completely dry boots against the grate and wiggled her toes in her stockings. "You must do the same. Come, Mary. Take off your boots so they will dry faster."

Gratefully, Mary removed them and leaned her feet in their soggy stockings up against the grate.

"You, too, Alice," Emmeline said.

As Alice was complying, the maid came in with tea, buttered toast, and a cake bursting with sultanas. Emmeline clapped her hands in delight.

"Oh, Bridget, you dear thing, you have brought us all my favorites. We will stuff ourselves silly! But wait!" She took up the knife, sliced a large piece of the cake, put it on one of the small plates, and held it out to Bridget. "You must take a piece now or there will be nothing left. You know what a glutton I am."

"I couldn't, miss."

"You most certainly could. I insist."

Bridget took the plate, shaking her head but smiling fondly at the girl. This young lady's manner, Alice thought, was unlike any she had before experienced. She was talkative and frank, like Lady Jemima, but with a jolliness that made her a most appealing companion.

"Now, tell me, you two," Emmeline said. "Do you like to read novels? What are your favorites? Have you read *Uncle Tom's Cabin* by Mrs. Stowe? She is from America. It is not a new book, but it is my absolute favorite. I love it so well that when I was a girl my mother would tell me the tale for my bedtime story near every night."

"I'm afraid I have not read it," Alice said.

"You must! My family are abolitionists, one and all. Or we were, when there was still slavery. And one of the characters is my namesake, which makes it all the more wonderful, though of course she suffers dearly. Mrs. Stowe's Emmeline is a poor slave girl of but fifteen, bought for the villain master's enjoyment. But she is very brave and hides herself away in an attic and thus avoids his abuses. I never wept so, reading a book! I soaked at least a dozen handkerchiefs. Though, of course, it is awfully sentimental—how all those horrible slaveowners become devoted Christians and freed their slaves, when we know that the vast majority of them were happy to go to war and kill near one million people in order to avoid doing so. Oh, you must, you must, you must read it!" She leapt to her feet and rushed over to the bookshelves, scanning the volumes. "There it is!" She took up a chair and, before Alice could warn her to take care, had clambered upon it, taken out the book, and jumped down, holding up her skirts to reveal beneath them a bright-red flannel petticoat. "Here," Emmeline said.

"But won't your cousin object to our taking it away with us?" Alice said.

"She is kind and generous, and I will vouch for your honesty and reliability!"

"But you don't know me at all!" Alice said.

"I am a very fine judge of character," Emmeline said. "Oh

dear. You must think me terribly conceited. I am not, I assure you." She frowned. "Though I wonder, is it conceited to consider oneself *not* conceited?"

At this Alice could not help bursting into laughter. "Thank you so much for the loan of the book," she said. "I will read it right away and return it to you."

Mary said, "My brother told me how Mr. Stokes visited the plantations in the Americas where his cotton came from and said the former slaves' situation was bad as can be—even now, after abolition."

"Your brother and his gentleman sound very wise indeed. My brothers are impossible. Well. Not Walter. He is the most sensible of the bunch. But the rest of them. Maddening! And to think, as girls, we are constantly told that it is our place in the world to make ourselves attractive to them. Ridiculous. Why not *they* make themselves attractive to *us*? Tell me more about your brother. Is he kind or cruel?"

"My Charlie is very kind, though he bosses me about awfully."

Alice said, "It is only that Charlie worries about you, Mary."

Mary said, "Alice won't hear nothing bad of Charlie, because he is her sweetheart."

"Well, then, it is you who must tell me what he is like, Alice. A woman knows her sweetheart near as well as his sister does. Why haven't you eaten more cake? You must be famished. I know I am." She put slices on both girls' plates. "Tell me everything about your young man, Alice."

"He's kind, as Mary says," Alice said. "He's intelligent and thoughtful."

"Does he care about the important things? Is he a suffragist?"

Mary laughed. "Can a man be a suffragist?"

"Of course he can! John Stuart Mill, for one."

"Mr. Mill! He is wonderful indeed!" Alice said. "I've only just read *The Subjection of Women*."

"It is a most inspiring book. I have been a confirmed suffragist since I was ten years old. All my family are. Are you a supporter of votes for women?"

Alice said, "I am afraid I don't know enough to have an opinion."

"You need not know any more than that you are as good as any man!" the girl cried. "You know that, surely."

"I know it," Mary said. "I know that there's not a man better than me, and many worse."

Alice looked at her friend with surprise and not a little admiration.

"Good for you, Mary!" Emmeline said. "You must help me to convert your friend to our cause. We shall make a believer of her yet. And then, Alice, you will bring your Charlie around so that you can be partners in the struggle, like Mr. Mill and his wife. Is your brother the sort of man to join us, Mary?"

Mary said, "I can't say."

"If he is as good a man as you say he is, then he will. I am sure of it."

Was she herself so confident? Alice wondered. She loved Charlie and knew him to be good and kind. On that first night of their acquaintance, he had not condemned her defense of the rights of the working man, had actually agreed with her, but even if he believed her own judgment deserving of respect, would he extend that consideration to womankind as a whole? How many men, after all, were like Mr. John Stuart Mill?

TWENTY-EIGHT

While Alice and his sister were discussing topics theoretical, Charlie was consumed with finding means of convincing Lord Wynstowe that an excursion to Alexandra Park to watch the steeplechase would be neither disagreeable nor onerous. As a matter of policy, their walk from the club through the park notwithstanding, Lord Wynstowe avoided the outdoors at all costs, treating a drop of rain on his shoulder as a matter requiring immediate medical attention. Moreover, he abhorred the raucousness of crowds. The prospect of the crush of race day and prolonged exposure to the hoi polloi was more than Lord Wynstowe could normally tolerate. Eventually, however, an idea occurred to Charlie, one that might convince his lord to brave these unbearable elements.

"Sir," Charlie asked while unrolling Lord Wynstowe's stockings for the night, "I know my understanding is unsophisticated; I am after all but a poorly educated servant. But

I have been thinking long about your work, and wondering whether it might not be applicable beyond the race of man."

Lord Wynstowe groaned and wiggled his toes. "Fetch the basin. I want to soak my feet."

Charlie filled a copper basin with hot water, stirred in a generous amount of Epsom salts, and gently settled the gentleman's feet into the soothing bath. Then he continued: "If a man's breeding and superiority can be extrapolated from his features, might it not be the same for horses? Might a horse that is truly excellent be of more symmetrical and pleasing appearance than less superior beasts, just as the attractive countenance of a superior gentleman such as yourself is evidence of the finest intellectual and physical vigor?"

The physically vigorous gentleman wriggled his toes in the hot water and groaned with pleasure. "I must have the doctor in; my feet pain me so at the end of the day. What were you saying?"

"Horses, sir, and their aspect."

"Ah yes. Those awful beasts." He shuddered. Then, after a moment, "It is common knowledge that attention to breeding improves the quality of a horse, and we know from my research that symmetry of feature indicates quality. It stands to reason, then, that the most symmetrically featured animal is likeliest to be the swiftest and of the best temperament. But why this interest in horses?"

"I was considering how very much Lord Alderwick loves the races, and how he must be eager to attend the steeplechase in Alexandra Park, which got me thinking about horses and how some are so much finer than others."

Lord Wynstowe began to look intrigued. "It might be an interesting experiment to measure a truly excellent horse and compare it to a nag."

"What an idea, sir! Perhaps Lord Alderwick might know of such a horse available for examination."

"It would have to be one who can be assured not to bite or kick."

"Of course, sir. If only you might attend the races at Alexandra Park together. He would surely introduce you to the owners of the very best beasts."

"The steeplechase? The idea . . ." He shuddered.

"A dreadful prospect, sir, I'm sure." Charlie feigned a thoughtful mien. "Ah well. I'm sure there are other gentlemen of science who will pursue this line of inquiry and satisfy the curiosity of the public." He removed the viscount's feet from the basin and wiped them dry on a soft towel. "Shall I use the methylated spirit or the camphor cream?"

"Camphor. The spirit makes my heels itch." Lord Wynstowe looked increasingly thoughtful. "Is the weather at Alexandra Park very ill this time of year?"

"They say it's often balmy on race day."

"Is it very crowded?"

"I understand the boxes are most comfortable." Charlie began massaging the camphor cream into the bottoms of Lord Wynstowe's fleshy feet, soft as a babe's, with no arch to speak of. The feet of a man who took as little exercise as possible.

"A box might not be *too* unpleasant," Lord Wynstowe said.

"Indeed, sir. We could arrange to augment the refreshments with hampers. The new cook is so fine, I'm sure she could prepare an excellent picnic."

Charlie watched Lord Wynstowe's expression grow ever more thoughtful.

"Shall I tell Cook?" Charlie said. "Saturday next, sir? No time like the present."

Lord Wynstowe leaned back, closed his eyes, and released himself into the sensation of Charlie's firm thumbs working the muscles, such as they were, of his feet.

"Sir?"

"Yes, Saturday next," Lord Wynstowe mumbled. Then his head slumped. He was asleep.

TWENTY-NINE

These next chapters in our story bring about its climax, so I suggest to my reader that she find time away from friends and family to enjoy the solitude that close attention requires. It began when Alice returned to the home of Lucy Jones bearing the locket and the peignoir, which she had not only cleaned but returned to its original condition by replacing the tired feathers, repairing the dragging hem, and shortening the sleeves, having discerned by their grubby condition that they were too long. Lucy was so well pleased by Alice's work that she insisted she stay awhile and partake of a glass of sherry before returning to Lady Jemima.

"My lady believes me only to have gone to the milliner's and will resent my lingering," Alice said.

"Do have a drink!" Lucy insisted, and splashed a generous amount into a glass. "You must tell me how your marriage plot's coming along. Tommy's not dared to show his face since you were here, so I know something's gone on."

"I fear we have not made much progress," Alice said. "Mr.

Smythe-Roberts denied your connection and convinced Lady Jemima that it was gossip and not to pay it any mind."

"I'd not have expected otherwise. He is really and truly a bounder, ain't he?"

"Charlie and I have one last iron in the fire. We arranged for Mr. Smythe-Roberts to join Lord Alderwick at the steeple-chase. We've heard he can't resist a bet, and Lord Alderwick doesn't approve of gambling. He won't so easily consent to his daughter marrying one of whom he thinks ill."

"That's a top idea," Lucy said. "Tommy'll not be able to dodge the bookies. The scoundrel owes money all over town. He even owes me twenty quid, if you can believe that!"

Alice set down her glass and rose. "I must be off," she said, "before Lady Jemima misses me."

"At her beck and call, you are," Lucy said. "Don't know how you can bear it."

Alice shrugged. What choice did she have?

THIRTY

The day of the National Hunt races at Alexandra Park was as fine as one could hope for in the season. The weather could, if one was not unwilling to exaggerate, be deemed temperate, though "a notch warmer than freezing" was perhaps a more accurate description. Charlie had dressed Lord Wynstowe in a double layer of woolen undergarments and fur-lined gloves and boots. They had debated together the merits of the various of Lord Wynstowe's coats and determined that, though the sable was both the finest and the warmest, the sealskin would repel any rain that might dare to fall. In the end, they took both. Thus attired, the gentleman was comfortable, if a bit red-faced and sweaty, and was in fine spirits.

To celebrate the festive excursion, Lord Wynstowe presented Lord Alderwick with a fine pair of Carl Seitz binoculars, a match for his own. The earl was delighted with the gift, exclaiming, "I can see the beast's fetlock, even the buckles on his saddle! Marvelous!"

"They are from Negretti & Zambra scientific-and-optical supply," Lord Wynstowe said. "The very best available in London."

Eyes fixed to his binoculars, Lord Alderwick waxed on about individual horses, their owners and trainers, their lineages and records. Lord Wynstowe seemed genuinely fascinated by the proceedings as elucidated by his companion, and the two were happily occupied while Charlie supervised the laying out of the contents of the hampers and took care that the wines and spirits were served with alacrity and appropriate flourish.

That they were diverted was fortunate, because it was near ninety minutes that the gentlemen waited for Lady Jemima and Mr. Smythe-Roberts to appear. Those two, accompanied by Miss Bennett as chaperone, had arrived at the racetrack at the same moment as a barouche in which rode a gentleman and a foreign lady. As Old Dick, riding in the brougham, later reported to Alice and Charlie, though the two gentlemen were quite clearly acquainted, Mr. Smythe-Roberts seemed unwilling to acknowledge his friend. The second young man gave him no choice, however, greeting him by name and bringing over his companion to introduce her to their party.

"What are you about, Phillips?" Mr. Smythe-Roberts had muttered.

"I believe you are acquainted with Signora Luciana di Galtieri," Mr. Phillips said. In his eye was a twinkle. When hearing the story, Charlie wondered if the gentleman might not be the very one whom he had seen accompany Mr. Smythe-Roberts to Lucy Jones's house. "And you must be the famously beautiful Lady Jemima." Mr. Phillips took her proffered hand and grazed it with a kiss.

Lady Jemima, however, had eyes only for the elegantly if

flamboyantly dressed singer. Lucy smiled and in her best Italian said, "*Piacere di conoscerla.*" She then turned to Mr. Smythe-Roberts and said, in thickly accented English, "What a surprise to see you, Thomas. When you said you would be in the *campagna* for the rest of the month, I assumed you meant farther away than Muswell Hill."

Mr. Smythe-Roberts blushed beet-red and took Lady Jemima's elbow. "We must go. We are already late."

After a lingering glance at the lady whose identity, it can be surmised, she immediately realized, Lady Jemima allowed herself to be led away, with Miss Bennett following behind.

"Good morning, Papa," Lady Jemima said as she swept into the box and kissed her father on his cheek. "Forgive our tardiness. I was very naughty and kept Mr. Smythe-Roberts and Aunt Sarah waiting for well over an hour, and then we were waylaid by his friends."

"A famous singer," Miss Bennett said. "A shame you have not introduced her to us before, Mr. Smythe-Roberts. She seems a remarkable woman."

Mr. Smythe-Roberts's jaw twitched with the effort of not scowling, but Lord Alderwick, adept at ignoring what interested him not, nodded only vaguely in his direction, and resumed instructing Lord Wynstowe about the merits of various steeds. Meanwhile, Lady Jemima looked about her at the ornate wood paneling, the wallpaper with images of horses leaping fences and their jockeys clad in various bright shades, the high-backed upholstered chairs, their gold velvet matching that of the tasseled curtains, the merry fire burning in the grate.

"What a comfortable box you have arranged for us, Lord Wynstowe! Do you not think so, Thomas? Shall we invite your friends to join us? It would be too ungenerous not to share our comfort with them." Her voice had a sharp edge to it. Charlie was well pleased at the evidence of dispute or disagreement between the two.

Mr. Smythe-Roberts made much of peering through the windows at the race. "They would not like it. It is so difficult to see the horses from this distance."

This Lord Alderwick did hear, and he scowled at the young man.

"Perhaps if you had opera glasses you wouldn't find our vantage point so displeasing," Miss Bennett said, removing a pair from her reticule. The lady took great interest in the proceedings, glancing from her racing form to the track and back through her glasses again. When one of the horses stumbled, she gasped.

"Up you go, Vixen!" she called out, then groaned when the horse failed to recover and came in dead last. "What a disappointment," she said. "Jemima, come help me choose a horse for the next race. Shall it be Miss Mowbray or Regalia?"

"What, good lady, is your theory of selection?" Mr. Smythe-Roberts asked. "Are you championing exclusively fillies?"

"And if I am?" Miss Bennett said.

"If loyalty to your own sex trumps horseflesh, you are bound to lose," he said, with a disparaging laugh. "Is your aunt not amusing, Jemima?"

But Lady Jemima was not paying attention to him. Her eyes were instead on her father and his companion. She looked as though she was assessing what this unlikely friendship could signify. Charlie wondered if she might not even be considering if there was not something about the viscount that she herself had missed. Might she be thinking that she had been perhaps too hasty in her dismissal of the possibility of his having good qualities, and too eager to condemn his faults? Or was that too much to hope?

"I say, Jemima, do you also cleave to your own sex when it comes to horseflesh?" Mr. Smythe-Roberts pressed.

At this, Lord Alderwick turned, scowling. "*Lady* Jemima," he said, stressing the honorific, "has no opinions on the matter."

"Oh, but I do, Papa!" She pointed to a delicate horse prancing beneath its rider. "I like that one very much."

"That is Majestic Lass, out of Gallant Spirit," said Miss Bennett, consulting her race card. "A filly." She smiled blandly at Mr. Smythe-Roberts. "Shall we place a small wager, Mr. Smythe-Roberts? Majestic Lass versus whichever you consider to be the finer animal?"

"Can I, Papa?"

"A very small wager," Lord Alderwick said.

Lady Jemima clapped delightedly. "Which horse do you choose, Mr. Smythe-Roberts?"

"Ironclad Valor is the horse to beat," the young gentleman said.

Miss Bennett said, "Jemima and I wager half a crown that our Majestic Lass shall beat your Ironclad Valor."

Lady Jemima said, "I shall buy a new hat with my winnings."

"I must go place my bet," Mr. Smythe-Roberts muttered.

"You are placing a real bet?" Lady Jemima asked. "With an actual bookmaker?"

"I am indeed. I will be back in a few moments."

"We will go with you," Miss Bennett said. "We will much enjoy watching the race from the rail."

Mr. Smythe-Roberts said, "It is far more comfortable to watch from here."

"Surely you don't begrudge us that finer vantage point. Come, Jemima." The ladies gathered their parasols.

"Do come on, Thomas," Lady Jemima said. "We will miss the flag start."

The three left the box and made their way to the bookmakers' pitch at trackside.

They had not been gone long when Charlie noticed that the crowd at the rail was restive. Looking closer, he saw that the members of their party were in the thick of the disturbance. "Sir," he said urgently, pointing to the bookmakers' pitch. "Look."

Lord Wynstowe trained his binoculars in the direction of Charlie's pointing finger and gasped. "Lord Alderwick!" he said. "There is trouble!"

Down at trackside, a burly man in a loud checked suit had Mr. Smythe-Roberts by the collar and was shaking him like a fisher shaking a rabbit preparatory to ripping out its throat. It was, Charlie realized, the very man he had seen accost Mr. Smythe-Roberts on that dark night. The young man was batting ineffectually at the brute's grip and appeared from this distance to be choking. Miss Bennett and Lady Jemima were huddled off to the side, expressions of horror on their faces.

Without a word, Lord Alderwick rushed out of the box. He set off down the grandstand, shouting, "Out of the way!" and pushing people aside. Charlie followed in his wake. As he ran, he was astonished to discover that Lord Wynstowe was at his heels, coming ever closer to the massive animals of which Charlie knew him to be frightened, and from whom he had hitherto maintained the distance allowed by binoculars.

They arrived trackside as Lady Jemima was flinging herself at the battling pair, beating Mr. Smythe-Roberts's abuser's back with Miss Bennett's racing form, which she had rolled up into a baton. Before Charlie could even step into the fray,

Lord Alderwick had grabbed the violent man's balled-up fist and wrenched it aside.

"Stand down!" Lord Alderwick shouted. But the lout shook him off and landed a punch square on Mr. Smythe-Roberts's aquiline nose. There was an audible crunch. The crowd gasped, and the young man bleated in pain. Now Charlie joined in, doing his best to restrain the assailant, but the man landed another punch, this one sending Mr. Smythe-Roberts tumbling backward directly into the path of Lady Jemima. Lord Wynstowe launched himself between the young lady and the falling man, arms outspread. Mr. Smythe-Roberts thus landed full on Lord Wynstowe, who planted his feet and bore the weight, protecting the young gentlewoman from harm.

Charlie and Lord Alderwick between them wrestled the bellowing man to the ground. Charlie sat on his chest and Lord Alderwick pinned his arms until two police officers arrived. The uniformed men wielded truncheons, which they used liberally and without discretion, so that Charlie had to dodge the blows. He rolled away, and the officers, between them, finally subdued the man.

"What in the name of God is the meaning of this attack?" Lord Alderwick said.

"That nob owes me a monkey and a grand!" the man snarled.

One of the policemen whistled. The other translated: "Fifteen hundred pounds."

Lord Alderwick looked aghast, then turned to Mr. Smythe-Roberts. "Is this true?"

The young gentleman, blood streaming down his face, had not even the grace to look ashamed.

Lord Wynstowe said to the bookmaker, "You have attacked a gentleman and will now face prosecution by the Crown.

Unless we can reach an agreement." He looked at the policemen, who shrugged. Lord Wynstowe continued, "I will repay Mr. Smythe-Roberts's debt to the tune of one thousand pounds, and you will call it even and trouble him no further. Do you accept these terms, sir?"

Charlie stared, mouth agape. Had he been asked half an hour before what Lord Wynstowe was likely to do under these circumstances, he would have confidently replied that the man would cower far from the skirmish. He would never have imagined that his gentleman would actively engage the aggressor.

The burly man growled, but finally agreed to Lord Wynstowe's terms.

"Shake hands, then," Lord Wynstowe said.

The policemen loosed one of the man's hands, and he extended it to Mr. Smythe-Roberts, who waved it away.

"Show some spine and shake the man's hand," Lord Alderwick said.

Grudgingly, Mr. Smythe-Roberts followed orders.

Lord Wynstowe took his mother-of-pearl card case from his pocket, withdrew a visiting card, and handed it to the bookie. "Come to my house tomorrow at noon and you shall have your money."

"Off with you, then," one of the policemen said, releasing the man and giving him a kick. He scrambled away.

"Are you hurt, Lord Wynstowe?" Lady Jemima asked urgently. "Your trousers! They are torn!"

They indeed gaped at the knee. And, worse, blood seeped through the tear. Charlie waited for Lord Wynstowe to collapse, for he had a horror of blood, but the gentleman merely said, "I am quite well, Lady Jemima." And then, further to Charlie's astonishment, he continued, "My word, what pluck you showed! Had we not arrived, I believe you would have subdued the man yourself!"

She gave a modest but charming laugh, which curdled when Signora Luciana di Galtieri rushed upon them, Mr. Phillips in her wake. "Thomas!" the singer exclaimed, clutching him to her, and then, in an echo of Lady Jemima, though her words were directed in a far less deserving direction, "Are you hurt?"

He shook her off.

"Had you not best be off home, Mr. Smythe-Roberts?" Lady Jemima said in chilly tones, no longer indulging in the familiarity of his Christian name. "You look an absolute fright. I am sure your lovely friend will happily nurse you."

Mr. Smythe-Roberts made as if to argue, but Lady Jemima's withering glare made clear there was no point to him remaining in her company. He turned and, followed by his friend and his mistress, slunk away.

Lord Wynstowe said, "I for one am very much in need of refreshment. A hot cup of tea will do us all good."

"Personally, I require something a bit stronger," Miss Bennett said.

"Rest assured, we have plenty of that, too," Lord Wynstowe said.

THIRTY-ONE

Alice took advantage of Lady Jemima's day at the races to take Miss Emmeline Goulden up on her invitation to luncheon with the young lady's parents at her cousin's home. The invitation had been issued to Mary as well, but she had begged Alice to allow her to refuse. She would not, Mary said, be comfortable at such a genteel gathering. She was bound to say something wrong, spill soup on herself or, worse, on someone else.

Though the maintenance of soup in its bowl was generally within Alice's capacities, she herself was not at all confident that she would not misstep, and she wondered if it would not be better to make her own excuses. She pushed aside her anxieties, however. She was intrigued by Emmeline. She felt the difference between their ages, but even so the girl knew so much more than Alice did, if not about how to survive the world as it was, then certainly about what the world could and should be.

On the day of the engagement, she dressed with even more

meticulousness than usual, in a repurposed day-dress of Lady Jemima's in a subtle plaid of ochre and forest green. She debated complementing the dress with a brown pleated bonnet trimmed with a bit of velvet fur, a cast-off of Lady Grace's that had never been worn, the elder sister having informed the younger on its first outing that she looked like a potato with an upside-down teacup on its head. "Potatoes don't have heads," Lady Grace had said, but never wore the bonnet again. Alice was not remotely potato-like, and the bonnet was unlike a teacup except from a certain angle, and so she wore it, though not without a certain trepidation.

In attendance in addition to the hostess, Miss Primrose Lyle, whom Alice recognized from eavesdropping on Miss Bennett's evening, were Emmeline's parents, Mr. Robert and Mrs. Sophia Goulden, and her younger sister, Mary Jane, a much quieter person than the vivacious Emmeline. Also in attendance was a Mr. Richard Pankhurst, a founding member, Emmeline said when introducing him, of the Manchester branch of the National Society for Women's Suffrage.

The parents were more like Emmeline in their animation than like her subdued sister, and they treated Alice with as much good-natured inquisitiveness as they would have an adventurer returning from the Amazon. They wanted to know all about her, where she was from, how she came to be a lady's maid, what was the nature of her work, and how did she feel about it.

"Is your mistress kind?" Miss Lyle asked.

"'Mistress' is a word I so dislike," said Mrs. Goulden. "It implies a kind of ownership."

Alice had not considered this before, but was that not indeed the very word slaves in the New World had been compelled to use for those who presumed to own them? She determined never to use it again, and she would tell Charlie not to call Lord Wynstowe his master anymore.

"My dear lady is generous," Alice said, "though sometimes fickle and often demanding. But yet I am here today, and there are many in my position who wouldn't be given liberty to attend a luncheon." That she had not in fact asked leave from Lady Jemima, but rather made away with the excuse of errands to run on her lady's behalf, Alice did not mention.

Mr. Pankhurst asked, "And are you satisfied in this position? Do you imagine anything more for yourself?"

Alice found herself bristling. "My place is a good one," she said.

Mr. Goulden said sternly, "Service is honest and honorable work and nothing to be ashamed of. I myself have done work far more humble!"

"Mr. Goulden began his career as an errand boy," his wife said.

"And my mother was a fustian cutter," he said.

Alice smiled at them gratefully, and regretted that she had not known of this before. Perhaps Mary might have come, had she been told that her host's mother had a job like her own.

"Is your work satisfying?" Miss Lyle asked. "Do you find your day-to-day tasks absorbing?"

Alice considered. "I am indeed satisfied when I accomplish something I set out to do, if too often that thing is itself not of particular interest—trimming a bonnet or repairing a bit of lace, for example. But I would say that most often I am less absorbed in the tasks at hand than I am in my own thoughts."

"That is true of me, too," Mary Jane said.

Emmeline laughed. "You can certainly spend hours staring out the window at nothing, Mary Jane! Though I have often wondered, when you do so, if you are thinking of anything at all."

Mary Jane looked more resigned to this ribbing than affronted by it, but her mother chided Emmeline. "Only a child believes that her own mind is busy with thoughts while others' are an incomprehensible blank. Adults understand that each of us possesses a mind equally complex and engrossing."

"Not *all* of us, surely," Emmeline said. "Would you say that Lord Elcho's mind is complex and engrossing, for example?"

"Lord Elcho," Mrs. Goulden told Alice, "is the member for Haddingtonshire."

"And a famous empty-headed buffoon," Mr. Goulden said.

"I rest my case," Emmeline said.

"If the world were just," Mr. Goulden said, smiling fondly, "it would be our Emmeline who was called to the bar, not her brother."

Mr. Pankhurst took this not as the joke it was intended and said, with utmost seriousness, "First we will get women the vote, and then we will demand that all professions be open to them."

"Hear, hear!" said Emmeline. "Let it be in my lifetime, for I should very much like to be a barrister." Alas, this was in retrospect to be a poignant comment, for though the future Mrs. Pankhurst would live to see a limited suffrage granted women, fully equal voting rights would come an agonizing and ironical two weeks after that lady's death.

As the luncheon progressed through various courses and topics of conversation, Alice, even as she listened, could not help but be troubled by the feelings Mr. Pankhurst had unwittingly stirred in her. Had she not in fact always chafed against the confines of her circumstances? What had her life been but grasping at a series of escalating ambitions? First she had left the farm for the manor; then she had striven for a more exalted servant's position. How many under-maids became lady's maids? She had not met another. Then, when she met Charlie, together they had imagined bettering themselves. She would become a housekeeper, he a butler. One day they might open a shop or another kind of establishment. What, she wondered, would happen once they achieved that mutual goal? Would she be content, or would she continue to strive, and if so, for what?

Alice had always suffered from a suspicion that she was different to those around her, not merely in her goals or capacities or even in her ambitions, but in some other, deeper way. She knew few servants who craved the stimulation of books and tracts as she did, who found inspiration in the works of George Eliot and Mary Wollstonecraft. Not even Charlie, who had initially gained her attention when he noticed the book she was reading and recommended one of his own.

She was interrupted in her musings by a scraping of chairs as the ladies rose to their feet. She hurriedly stood and followed them into the sitting room, leaving the two gentlemen to their port and cigars.

Emmeline took Alice's arm and pulled her onto the settee next to her. "What think you of Mr. Pankhurst?" she asked.

What did Alice think? That he was stuffy and sanctimonious. That he had unsettled her and seemed not to mind it. "He is a very interesting man," she said.

"He is. He truly is," Emmeline said. And then after a moment, "He is not so *very* old, is he?"

"I suppose he has forty or fifty years," Alice said.

"Surely not!" the young lady cried. "He is so vigorous a man!" She blushed, then sighed dramatically. "I wish I did not have to return to school."

"Do you not enjoy it? Is it not exciting to live in France?"

"I do, very much, but there is much *work* to do here. You must come to visit me when I return home, and stay for a long visit in Manchester. There are so many of us in my house, one more won't even be noticed. And you and I can together work side by side with Mr. Pankhurst and the other members of the society."

Alice felt keenly the difference between her friend and herself. No matter Emmeline's father's lineage, only a lady of a certain class could imagine that someone like Alice could pay a long visit anywhere, without upending her life and ruining her opportunities for employment. Still, Alice thought, as she accepted a cup of pale tea from Mrs. Goulden, how nice it would have been to avail herself of the opportunities offered by this invitation. Working side by side with Mr. Pankhurst was hardly an appealing prospect, but working on the cause so dear to the hearts of all in this room, a cause that she was beginning to be suspicious might one day be dear to her own, would be marvelous. If she were only a different person from a different background, a person with the liberty and resources to devote herself to important work rather than labor consequential only because of the life its salary allowed.

So novel and engrossing was the luncheon that Alice almost forgot before she left to return the copy of *Uncle Tom's Cabin* that Emmeline had lent her. Miss Lyle, whose library Emmeline had freely pillaged, accepted the restoration of the book to its place on the shelf only on condition that Alice take another, and the company had great fun assembling a pile for Alice's edification that included pamphlets by Miss Lydia Becker, Mr. Pankhurst's partner at the Manchester Society for Women's Suffrage, as well Mrs. Josephine Butler's volume *Woman's Work and Woman's Culture.*

"As a working woman yourself, I believe you will find much to identify with in Mrs. Butler's words," Mr. Pankhurst said.

"Is that very lady not speaking next Thursday at Exeter Hall?" Mrs. Goulden said.

"She is indeed," Mr. Pankhurst replied. "Alongside Henry and Millicent Fawcett. It promises to be a fascinating evening. I only wish I did not have to return to Manchester before then."

"Alice and I will go," Emmeline announced.

Alice was about to tell her friend that the chances of her effecting another escape so soon were slim at best, when the grandmother clock on the mantel struck four. Alice blanched. It was long past time for her to return. Even if she ran the whole way home, she feared she would arrive after Lady Jemima, and, no matter Mrs. Goodenough's assurances that she would step in if necessary, Alice knew her lady (never again her mistress) well enough to know she would be perturbed by her maid's playing the truant.

"Allow me to flag a hansom for you," Mr. Goulden said, and was up on his feet and out the door before Alice could protest. She could not imagine how dear such a ride would be, though she knew her purse could not withstand the assault. Without fuss or comment, however, Mr. Goulden anticipated her circumstances and paid the fare. Such a kind man, Alice thought, and vowed to herself to repay him as soon as she was able.

THIRTY-TWO

That night, Lady Jemima returned home aflutter with the news of her own day's activities and did not at first notice Alice's distraction. It was only when Alice took from the cupboard a day-dress in lieu of one for the evening that Lady Jemima said, "Alice! What on earth has possessed you?"

"Forgive my preoccupation, ma'am. I am very relieved you are unharmed. Thank goodness for Lord Wynstowe! He comported himself with courage, did he not?"

"He did indeed. In stark contrast to Mr. Smythe-Roberts, who shamed himself." Lady Jemima paused, a small smile passing over her lips. "I must say, Lord Wynstowe's behavior today matched his countenance in a way I have not before seen."

"He is indeed fine-looking, is he not?" Alice said.

"Most distinguished," Lady Jemima mused. "One might even call him elegant."

"Gallant?" Alice murmured.

"Assuredly."

There was at that moment a rapping at the door, and Miss Bennett popped her head in. To dine with her brother-in-law and Lord Wynstowe, she had resumed her Marlecombe Park mufti, all traces of her preferred aesthetic style gone. Her gown, creased from the cupboard, was of sober and muted tones, her hair drawn back in a severe bun.

"Are you ready, dear? The carriage is waiting."

"As you can see, Aunt, I am not ready. Surely the coachman's job is to attend me, or do you suggest mine is to attend him?"

Miss Bennett ignored her niece's rudeness and looked about the room. "Alice, have you not yet begun to pack? Lady Jemima requires her things be moved this very night!"

"Oh yes, Alice," Lady Jemima said. "I forgot to mention that I will be removing to Lord Wynstowe's house. Papa says it is well for me to join him, as I will be much more comfortable there. You do live so very far away from everything, Aunt. And in such an incommodious establishment. I don't know how you can stand it."

"It is a miracle I can bear up at all," Miss Bennett said.

The two ladies swept out of the room, leaving Alice reeling with astonishment. She was to stay in the same house as Charlie! Moreover, if the admiration she heard in Lady Jemima's voice continued to blossom, and if the young lady grew in Lord Wynstowe's estimation as he had in hers, if all aligned and progressed, then she and Charlie might finally be together permanently! She pushed away all thoughts of the events of her afternoon and spent her next hours in a frenzy of packing, with Mrs. Goodenough and the young maid conscripted to the effort. Clothing was folded between sheets of packing paper, powders and creams were wrapped in muslin, shoes and boots put into their cases. Lady Jemima had purchased so much London finery that Alice was forced to borrow not only all of Miss Bennett's trunks but Mrs. Goodenough's own case, which the lady lent with some trepidation, only moderately mollified by Alice's assurances that she would return it.

"It has served me so long," the good lady said, "and I cannot easily afford another."

Alice thought how unfair it was that one young lady possessed so much that she could not only fill a room full of cases, but would be hard-pressed to notice if one or two boxes or bags were missing, and another, no less deserving, could own so little that a single empty case was a prized possession. She recalled Mr. Pankhurst's words about the power of women's suffrage, and thought that if that gentleman were right, the vote would grant a person like Mrs. Goodenough a dignity neither more nor less valuable than Lady Jemima's, and would better the circumstances of all working men and women. But Alice's tasks were too numerous to allow time for political musings, and after repeated assurances that she would guard the good woman's possessions as if they were her own, she was away.

When Alice, along with Lady Jemima's mountain of cases, boxes, and bags, finally arrived at the home of Lord Wynstowe, she ignored Dick's proffered hand and clambered down from the carriage, and rushed to the servants' door even as Charlie flung it open. She skidded to a halt, but he had no such compunctions; he swept her up in his arms and spun her round, laughing with excitement.

"It's happened!" he said. "You're here!"

She laughed and wriggled out of his embrace, glancing back at Dick, who was taking keen-eyed note of it all. Within hours, all of England would know that the valet of Nigel

Deverell, seventh Viscount Wynstowe, and the maid of Lady Jemima, daughter of Earl Alderwick, were in love.

As they entered the kitchen, Charlie said, "Did she give you an account of the incident? How Lord Wynstowe leapt to her rescue?"

"She did," Alice said.

"I was flat-out flabbergasted. Lord Wynstowe! Swift-thinking and courageous! That is a wonder I never thought I'd see."

"It is indeed remarkable," Alice said.

"And now we are together in the same house, you and I, just as we always hoped to be. I can feel it, dear Alice. Our victory is close at hand! Lord Wynstowe assigned the very best bedchamber to Lady Jemima. His mother's own!"

"He must esteem her very much."

"Exactly so!"

At this moment, Mary bustled in. "I did what I could to air the room, but it's been closed for donkey's years. I put sachets in the drawers and set a pot of vinegar and lavender to boil on the fire. I hope it'll suit your lady."

"It will suit her very well, I'm sure," Alice said.

"Come, Alice. I will help you with the unpacking," Charlie said.

"You'll do no such thing," Mary said. "Lady Jemima'll not want a big galumphing boy rifling through her bits and pieces."

"What do you imagine I do all day, sister, but rifle through Lord Wynstowe's bits and pieces?"

"A lady's things ain't the same as a gentleman's, are they, Alice?" She led Alice away and up to the room, which was as lovely as Charlie had promised, if a bit redolent of vinegar and lavender.

"When do you begin at the mill?" Alice asked.

"Monday next."

"Are you anxious? It would be natural to be."

"The girls Miss Emmeline introduced me to say that this is the best of all the mills to work in. The foreman who hired me is stern, but he's said to be fair. He doesn't play favorites or hold your wages back or make you work too many extra hours without pay."

"What about your accommodation?"

"My place at the rooming house opens on Saturday. There are three other girls in the room, but one works at a bakery, so she is gone by midnight and does not return before morning. Since she's the one I'm to share with, I'll have a bed to myself almost the whole night."

"What does Charlie say about it all?"

"My brother still tries to convince me to go back to Wynstowe and seek a position in the house, but I won't. That life isn't for me, and I'm only too glad to see the back of the village. I prefer it here in London. And in a factory my time will be my own after the workday is done. I might even attend the University Extension Scheme! There's nothing like that in the country."

Something like envy stirred in Alice. Her position was inarguably superior to that of Mary, but to own the leisure of one's evenings, and to spend that time learning new things or in conversation with others sympathetic to the same causes? Soon enough, Lady Jemima would return to the quiet of Marlecombe Park, and, if Alice and Charlie were fortunate, after that to Wynstowe Manor. Either way, Alice would be once again so many miles from the fascinations of the city that the hours she had spent in the company of suffragists like Emmeline Goulden and Mr. Pankhurst would be a memory as distant as if it were a different life. But she would have her Charlie. And that was so joyful and exciting a prospect that it must surely outweigh all others.

When Lady Jemima retired to her chamber that night, she was in an unusual mood, more pensive than Alice had ever seen her. She allowed herself to be undressed all but silently, her only words a compliment for the chamber allocated to her.

"It belonged to Lord Wynstowe's mother," Alice said. "His man says it is a mark of his highest esteem that he has given it to you."

"It is most pleasing," Lady Jemima murmured, staring dreamily at her reflection in the glass as Alice brushed her hair, oiled it, pinned the curls at the front, and plaited the rest for the night.

"That must be her portrait." Lady Jemima pointed at a large painting of a thin-lipped woman clutching a sinuous, furred stoat. "She is very beautiful. I see her son in her features, don't you?" Lady Jemima continued.

The execution of the portrait was so poor that the lady looked less like her son than she did the animal she held inexplicably in her arms. Take issue as one might with his manner, Alice thought, it could not be said that Lord Wynstowe looked like a stoat.

"Papa says he is very earnest and intelligent. He is sober, but is sobriety not a desirable quality in a husband? One can always look to one's friends for diversion, but to one's husband one looks for care and security. Do you not think so?"

"You are a far better judge of husbands than I, ma'am."

"To think I once imagined that Mr. Smythe-Roberts would be a good husband!" the young lady said, drawing up the bedclothes. Then, exhausted from the excitement of her day, she closed her eyes and fell asleep.

After dropping the dirty linen in the scullery, Alice repaired to the servants' quarters. Having taken long with Lady Jemima's toilette, she was the last upstairs, and the long corridor was silent, everyone else abed. Or almost everyone. Down at the end of the hallway in the men's section, a beam of yellow light shone from a cracked open door. She looked up and down at the others to make sure they were all closed tight. Then she unlaced and stepped out of her boots. Holding them in her hand, she crept soundlessly down the corridor in her stocking feet. She stopped at the open door, suddenly afraid. Would her visit be welcome? Was this who she was? She screwed up her courage, took a breath, and pushed the door open.

THIRTY-THREE

Charlie sat on the edge of his bed, hands clasped, head bent. There was a whorl of hair at the crown of his head that she had never before noticed. Did he even know it was there? Might she be one of the only people to have noticed it, for who other than a man's mother, lover, or barber had the opportunity to scrutinize the top of a man's head? She smiled at this thought, but then too soon remembered that there was one other who regularly looked down at this dear head. Lord Wynstowe had perused this cowlick on hundreds, perhaps even thousands of occasions as her dear Charlie bent before him, buckling his shoes, unrolling his stockings, picking up his discarded clothing, and emptying his chamber pot.

You must stop it, she told herself. She would not allow Lord Wynstowe or Lady Jemima to intrude on this moment. Right now, in this small room, she and Charlie were not as they were in their waking hours—servants—but a man and a woman, lovers and beloveds.

She stepped into the dim, wavering light cast by the single candle guttering in its dented brass holder, and he looked up.

"You came," he said. "I didn't know if you would."

He seemed suddenly to remember his manners and began to rise, but she crossed quickly to the bed and pressed his shoulders down. She stood between his knees. As her skirts were voluminous and heavy, they allowed no warmth from his body to reach hers. There was simply too much cloth between them. She unfastened her dress at the throat, the horn buttons slippery beneath her fingertips. She, who buttoned and unbuttoned her lady three or four times a day, found herself awkward, near bumbling. Charlie put his hands on hers, stilling her fingers.

"Do you not want me?" she asked.

His hands loosed hers in wordless answer. She resumed her work, fingers suddenly flying. In a moment she was undone. She shrugged her dress off, and it puddled at her feet. Still, there was so much between them! She thought longingly of the loose robes and caftans Miss Bennett favored in her city incarnation, and made as short a work possible of her bodice, petticoats, and corset. Finally, she stood before him only in chemise and bloomers. He traced the row of embroidered bluebells along the neckline of her chemise, and she trembled, gooseflesh rising on her skin, whether from his touch or from the bite of the winter's cold she did not know. She was near naked, vulnerable; he was wrapped in layers of cotton and wool, firm and strong. Gently but firmly, she pushed him back onto the bed.

Afterward, they huddled beneath the threadbare blanket, bodies pressed together. The blood drying on Alice's thighs was sticky, and she wondered how badly stained the linen would be. She had no idea if she had left behind a smear or a flood. What excuse would Charlie make for his ruined linen? She would take the sheet with her, she decided. Bloodstains on her own bedding would go unremarked.

She felt his limp, damp penis move against her belly as if of its own volition. Curious, she took it in her hand, causing him to startle. It was soft, the skin silky and wrinkled. She wondered how something so small and innocent could have pierced her with such power. She squeezed it. Charlie shifted against her.

"Does that hurt?" she asked.

"Not exactly."

To her surprise it began to grow in her palm.

"Again?" he asked.

"Again," she said.

The sun was not yet risen, but the black of the night had started to turn to the steel gray of dawn. Through the window Alice could see the lamplighter extinguishing the gas lamps one by one.

"I'd best go," she said. "Before the house wakes."

"Someday soon, we won't need to creep about," he said. "We will go to sleep and wake in one another's arms."

She sat up, accidentally elbowing him in the stomach. "Oof!" he said, and laughed quietly. "I will insist that they give us a bigger bed once we're married."

"Are you so confident that it will go thus between Lady Jemima and Lord Wynstowe? They will marry and so we will be able to?"

"He is wealthy, she is pretty, and they no longer loathe one another."

"And that's enough?"

"For them." He kissed her shoulder. "How lucky we are that we have so much more."

"What if they don't marry, Charlie? What then?"

"Then you will leave your job and move to Wynstowe Village. I managed on my salary to support my mother and sister. Mary is working now, so all I have will go to you and our children. We will live frugally and save what we can, and someday we will have enough to open a shop in the village." He kissed her shoulder. "I can't live without you, Alice. Even before tonight I knew I couldn't. But now? Now I won't. I love you."

"I love you, too." She kissed his brow and then his lips, soft beneath hers. Then she stood up and quickly began to dress.

He propped himself up on an elbow and watched her. What had he done to deserve this good fortune? he wondered. He thought of his childhood. His father's violence, his mother's despair. The years of hunger, and the misery of the workhouse. The loneliness of his years of service. Alice was compensation for these tribulations of his youth. He had suffered, and now he had been granted his reward. His own remarkable girl.

"Give me the bed linens," she said. "I will exchange them with my own so no one will be suspicious."

He got up and stripped the bed. Naked before her, his body was long and white; his shoulders were broad. There was a mole on his shoulder that Alice longed to kiss. She took the bundle from him and started out, but paused with her hand on the doorknob. "I've much enjoyed London," she said.

"I, too, for it has given us opportunity to be together," he said, misunderstanding her point, or, perhaps better to say, not understanding the scope of reasons for her burgeoning attachment to the city.

"Would you ever want to live here?" she asked.

"I long to return to the country. Once you are there, you will see. The air is fresh, the breeze redolent with flowers, much like your home. And the people of the village, if not the house, are friendly. Nothing like this city full of strangers and foul fumes."

"Once they are married, I expect Lord Wynstowe and Lady Jemima will spend at least part of the season here."

"Soon enough, she will be with child, and the comforts of home will appeal more than the tribulations of town."

"I think you underestimate the pull society has on my lady."

"Lord Wynstowe very little likes it here, and she will come to understand that she must give way to his preferences."

"Why must she give way? Why not he give way to hers?"

Charlie laughed. "Even Lord Wynstowe is not so weak-willed as to indulge a wife at the expense of his own comfort."

Need a man be weak-willed to consider his wife? Alice wondered. She turned to leave, and again turned back. "You and I might find work together in a house in London. Or in a shop. Whiteleys in Westbourne Grove is expanding, Old Dick says."

"Alice, what are you about? We would never earn enough as shop assistants to support ourselves, nor would they even let you work there as a wife. I promise you, whether they marry or not, we will soon be together every night as we have been tonight."

She was an innocent, he reminded himself, and in the

light of the sun might rue her nighttime behavior and fear she might be condemned among the servants of the house or the people of the village. Worse, she might fear that he would act as so many men might and leave her now that the deed was done.

"We are as husband and wife," he said. "In heart and soon in law. I promise you. You will love Wynstowe, whether you come there as abigail to Lady Jemima or merely as Mrs. Wells of the village. The country is beautiful, the villagers are kind, and together we will survive Mrs. Sweet. You are much stronger than she, and will have the protection of Lady Jemima and of myself."

She nodded but still hesitated in the doorway.

"Would it be possible for you to ask Lord Wynstowe to give you liberty this Thursday evening?"

"I will do anything you ask." An idea occurred and he smiled. "Let's go to the music hall! We will take Mary with us. She's never seen anything like that in all her days."

"Not the music hall. There is somewhere else I would like to go. Thursday at six. You'll ask him?"

Without waiting for his answer, she rushed out the door in the very nick of time, for moments later he heard loud knocking as the butler passed along the hall, waking the servants to their day.

THIRTY-FOUR

Unfortunately, on the morning of the lecture, Emmeline sent a letter saying she was forced to return to Manchester because her mama was suffering a touch of catarrh, and "hordes of wretched Goulden children" were "running rampant over the lands." Her father had written, insisting on her return, and "as soon as I can procure a horsewhip" she would be on her way home. "You must go to the lecture anyway," she wrote. "Lucky girl! I am envious. Someday I will lead my own life and never subordinate my wishes to anyone, not even those I love."

The attraction Alice's young friend felt for the much older Mr. Pankhurst suddenly made sense. A man as firm in his commitment to the rights of women as Mr. Pankhurst would likely make a point of deferring to his wife, and so she would not be compelled to temper her own desires in favor of his, as even Alice's Charlie had said a wife must.

When Alice and Charlie walked into the meeting hall, they found, as if to affirm the trepidation he had expressed at the prospect of an evening in company with a roomful of suffragists, a bustle of formidable ladies in comfortable shoes and rational dress. She noticed Charlie's eyes widening, and the truth was even she, who spent her days undressing and dressing a lady, was taken aback by the sight of so many bosoms unrestricted by corsets. Why is it so rarely those whose forms are likely to be appreciated who most readily adopt the artistic dress? Depend upon it, the bust that wobbles is never the one that gives least offense.

The Mrs. Jellybys of the audience were festooned like marshals of Napoleon's Grande Armée, with multicolored sashes, ribbons, buttons, and badges boasting slogans such as "Touch Not the Cup!," "Small Hands Deserve Books, Not Chains!," "End Animal Cruelty!," "BWTA!," "IOA!," "RSPCA!," and other proof of the depth of their commitment, not merely to the rights of women but to those of animals and children, to temperance, to Social Purity, and to all the various acronymic societies, committees, leagues, associations, federations, and guilds to which a woman of ideals and passion (and leisure time) might devote her considerable talents. Have you found as I have, dear Reader, that so often public affirmations of allegiance are inversely correlated with productive activity? But let me not impose these observations on Alice, who was too young and too newly exposed to this world to have developed a cynicism like my own.

Meanwhile, Charlie, a flush creeping up his neck to his cheeks, tried valiantly to keep his gaze affixed on his own hands and not on the unfettered bosoms in the room. Alas, the poor man could not avoid his discomfort for very long, for the couple was set upon by Miss Lyle, herself clad in a pair of bloomers which revealed a good four inches of ankle. Alice had heard of these split skirts, but she had never seen one in the flesh, so to speak. At first blush, the costume seemed to her absurd, but within a moment it occurred to her how much liberty such attire would provide. Imagine walking through the streets of London without worrying about one's skirt's trailing in the mire of mud, dust, excrement both animal and human, and all the filthy rest that streams through the streets of even the most gracious neighborhoods! How much easier would it be to maintain one's lady's clothing if her hems were not soiled with such grime. This last brought another smile to Alice's lips, as she imagined Lady Jemima swanning through Mayfair clad in bloomers.

"You came!" the eccentrically clad lady said to Alice. She turned to Charlie, "I am Miss Primrose Lyle." She reached out her hand and shook his so firmly that Alice swore his gloved hand crumpled in her grip. So busy not wincing was he that he failed to respond.

"May I introduce Charlie Wells," Alice said.

"Well done, Mr. Wells!" Miss Lyle said, pumping his arm up and down. "I like to see a man take a stand in favor of suffrage for all!" Charlie had not the need either to accept her acclaim or to demur, for she was distracted at that moment by an elderly woman who scurried into the room like a mouse on the run from a tomcat. "Evelyn!" Miss Lyle bellowed. Unceremoniously, she dropped Charlie's hand and rushed to scoop up her friend and hustle her to a pair of seats in the frontmost row, from which she summarily evicted a couple who had unsuspectingly taken the place she considered her own.

"Can an amputee be an adequate valet?" Charlie asked Alice. "Because I fear I have lost all use of my right hand."

Just as Alice laughed aloud, a woman stepped up to the dais and the room hushed, which caused no few heads to turn in their direction. Charlie gazed at her in mock disapproval, shook his head, and shrugged as if to ask, what was a man to do with so rude a companion?

As speaker after speaker took the stage, Charlie found himself growing ever more confused and uncomfortable. It was not that the young man disagreed with the opinions expressed by the orators, only that he wondered both at their vehemence and at the exuberant approval of the crowd. To him, they all seemed excessive, even embarrassing in their effusiveness. Such exhortations to equality and liberty had been justified when a horror like slavery was their object, but could they really apply to the circumstances of women? With the speaker who decried the plight of factory girls, he nodded in agreement, and also with a gentleman who bemoaned the evils of drink, for he knew the devastation his father's drunkenness had wrought, but he failed to see how votes for women would alleviate so many ills. Should not they be demanding protection of women in their fragility and purity, not thrusting upon them the responsibilities of suffrage? Women should not be pushed defenseless into the world but rather nurtured and shielded from harm. To that cause he would gladly devote himself. But to the vote? What good would it serve?

He would explain all this to Alice, he thought. She would certainly agree. But Alice, when he turned to her to whisper his disapproval, was staring rapt, on her face an expression akin to awe.

Eventually, the keynote speakers were introduced. Mr. Henry Fawcett, Member of Parliament for Hackney, and his wife, Mrs. Millicent Fawcett, social reformers and staunch advocates for women's rights, took the stage, Mrs. Fawcett leading her husband, his hand resting lightly on her arm.

"Is he blind?" Charlie murmured in amazement.

"It seems so," Alice said.

"How remarkable!"

A woman in the row behind them tapped on Charlie's shoulder with her fan. "Shh!" she hissed imperiously.

Mr. and Mrs. Fawcett bowed their heads in gratitude for the wave of applause. Then, before either could utter a single word, there was a loud crash. The doors to the assembly room smashed open, and a gang of ruffians surged inside. They were not, as one might assume from what next ensued, rogues of the lower classes. On the contrary. These were fine gentlemen in elegant attire, their well-tended mustaches and trimmed beards adorning faces contorted in fury. It is not impossible that you, dear Reader, might be acquainted with some of them, as shocking as that might seem.

The brutes set about the crowd with truncheons and walking sticks, battering without regard for the sex of their victims, blows landing on the heads of women and girls as often as on their male escorts. They shouted words of abuse I will offend neither your sensibilities nor my own by noting here. They grunted and howled like the animals they were, and even bellowed in laughter at their victims' shrieks of terror and pain.

Charlie hauled Alice from her seat. With one arm about her, and the other fending off blows, he steered her through the mêlée. The other men in the audience were likewise trying to cover the bodies of their female companions to protect them from the violence, but they were too few and the devils too many.

Charlie pointed toward a small door to the right of the stage. "This way!" he shouted. On the stage, Mr. Fawcett, able only to hear the cacophony, looked confused and frightened, his wife even more so as she gazed round in terror. Half a dozen women and men from the audience rushed to the front of the room, linking arms before the stage and facing the roiling crowd, a human shield to protect the couple. When Alice saw what they were about, she turned to join them, determined to lend her body to the fray, but Charlie, intent on reaching the door, did not release her.

"We must help them!" she cried.

Violently, she broke loose and ran to where the line of defenders stood. She linked arms with an elderly gentleman as the savages reached the stage. A man shoved his red face into hers, and she felt his spittle on her cheeks. The brute grabbed her breast and twisted it violently, screaming, "Slut! Whore!" (I know I said I would refrain from recounting these ugly words, but if poor Alice was forced to hear them shouted in her ears, then you and I must have the fortitude to read them on the page.)

Charlie launched himself at her assailant and brought him down to the ground. He punched the man's face again and again, crushing it beneath his fists. Alice was astonished at the violence of Charlie's response, but felt no urge to stop him. On the contrary, a bloodthirsty rage rose in her, and she would have landed a kick on the parts of the man's body that would have felt it most had not she been knocked aside by a copper, who struck at Charlie with his nightstick, missing his face but landing a blow on his back and shoulder that sent him flying. Fortunately, the copper's attention was then attracted by the shriek of a lady who clutched at the torn bodice of her dress.

Alice helped Charlie to his feet and they ran toward the door. He stopped suddenly. In their path, an elderly woman sat on the ground, her legs splayed before her, her hat askew. Charlie bent and unceremoniously picked her up. Staggering under her substantial weight, he continued toward the door.

Alice flung it open, and they emerged into a narrow, dark alley. Others surged out behind them, and they were carried along with the fleeing crowd to the main road.

A gentleman rushed up to them calling, "Mother!" The woman in Charlie's arms moaned, and Charlie set her down gently, holding her steady.

"Thank you, sir!" the gentleman said.

The shriek of a dozen whistles announced the appearance of the police, and the young gentleman hustled his mother away.

"The tube!" Charlie shouted. Holding hands, he and Alice ran down the street to the gaslit entrance to the Underground.

They raced down the stairs and up to the ticket office. Charlie requested the cheapest tickets and fumbled for his purse. Only then did Alice realize that his left arm hung all but useless by his side. In the frenzy she had not even noticed that he had carried the poor old woman in one arm. Behind them, she heard the pounding of feet on the stairs. She took out her own purse and paid for their fares, snatching up the tickets as a pair of coppers came up behind them. Alice smiled at them, and took Charlie's right arm.

"Come, dear," she said brightly. "Mother's kept us so late, the children will think we've been spirited away!" The two walked briskly to the platform. Only the whiteness of Charlie's lips revealed the extent of the pain he was in. Otherwise, they might have been any young couple returning home from a visit to a relative.

Though it felt like hours that they waited on the platform, studiously ignoring the Metropolitan Police officers racing up and down, it was in truth mere moments before a train arrived and they could disappear into a third-class carriage.

The clattering of the train echoing through the tunnel

made conversation impossible, and so they did not speak until they were once again aboveground.

"Do you think Mr. and Mrs. Fawcett were hurt?" Alice asked once they were in the relative quiet of the road.

Charlie did not answer. He must, she thought, be in too much pain to speak.

"It must have been dreadful for Mr. Fawcett," she said, conscious that she was being uncharacteristically loquacious, filling Charlie's silence with her own words. "Not to be able to see what was happening must have made it more frightening, I think. Do you not think so?"

Again there was no response.

"Charlie?"

"I am trying to understand, Alice, but I cannot for the life of me make out what you thought you were about, rushing to the stage and putting yourself in that kind of danger."

"They needed to be defended!"

"You are but a girl. How did you think you could defend them?"

"I *didn't* think. I knew only that I could not abandon them. I was not alone. Others came to their aid, and not only men."

"It helped Mr. and Mrs. Fawcett not at all for you to be violated by a blackguard."

"I was not *violated*."

"Are you saying I mistook that man's hands?"

"I am unhurt," she said.

Chivalry prevented his calling attention to the fact that, though she might not be, he himself had been injured in saving her from further harm, but that he was favoring his wounded arm was unmistakable.

"Is your arm very bad?" she asked.

Because he would neither lie nor complain, he said nothing.

She assessed it. "Your shoulder is dislocated, I think," she said. "It happened once to my brother. The doctor pulled it back in place. It hurt Pete awfully, but once it was done he was better right away. Does Lord Wynstowe have a doctor who might attend you?"

"Lord Wynstowe has a fleet of doctors, physicians, apothecaries, and surgeons, all of whom cost the earth."

"It was I who insisted you join me, so I will pay for the doctor."

"You are generous, Alice, but you know I wouldn't take money from you. Anyway, it's already feeling better."

He tried to lift his arm to prove his claim, but gasped.

"Oh, Charlie," Alice said, anguished at having caused him injury.

Charlie said, "No matter. It will feel better soon, I'm sure. But, Alice, we must never go to another of those meetings. It's too dangerous. For me I don't care, but I can't tolerate the idea of you being hurt."

His tone was gentle but brooked no disagreement. It reminded her of his attempt to prevent Mary from accompanying them to London. By what authority did he seek to impose such a restriction on her? As soon as she asked herself the question, she knew the answer. The law would give Mr. Wells precisely such authority over Mrs. Wells. Charlie might not be able to make such dictates now, but when they married he would, just as he would have the right to decide where and how they lived, what they did, how their children were raised. Charlie was kind and loving, and she trusted that he would make such decisions in concert with her, but he would not be *required* to. Such consideration as he granted would be always a gift, a generosity, and she a grateful recipient.

She determined to put such disloyal thoughts out of her mind. Charlie was injured. Once he was no longer in pain, he would have a better perspective and would reconsider his words.

Fortunately, Lord Wynstowe accepted Charlie's tale of being set upon by ruffians, a story that had the virtue of being true, if incomplete. The viscount insisted on calling for the doctor and paying the fee himself, and would have had the police round, had Charlie not made light of the incident, saying that he would be himself again after a night's rest. Indeed, this was the case, for, like Alice's brother, he found his pain ended the instant his shoulder was returned to its rightful place, though that process was so agonizing that he could not help but shout. Although he was cured in the moment, the lingering effects of the injury would plague him for the rest of his days. His shoulder, having been loosened once, would be forever inclined to pop out of alignment. It would happen so often that he would grow adept at jamming it back into place himself, to the endless fascination of his children, who took a bloodthirsty delight in Papa's "wobbly arm."

THIRTY-FIVE

I esteem you too well, dear Reader, to drag out the events that followed. You have both imagination and experience sufficient to anticipate what next occurred. Mr. Smythe-Roberts, unceasing in attention to his self-interest and ever indulgent of his weakness of character, failed even to pay a last call on the young lady to whom he had made love for so long. In lieu of his presence, a small package arrived. Lady Jemima tossed it aside with disdain, instructing Alice to dispose of it. As Alice had received no specific instruction not to open the package, she did not deem it necessary to resist her curiosity. Inside was a twist of white tissue paper, and in that a lock of Lady Jemima's hair tied with a pink velvet ribbon. Alice had been searching for that very ribbon for weeks. She pulled out the hair, tossed it into the fire, and pressed the ribbon back into shape with a hot iron.

Though Mr. Smythe-Roberts's fate is not of great interest, those who are curious might like to know that the young man took as his wife Miss Caroline Mountjoy, who brought with her a great deal of money and a surprisingly iron will. She put her husband on a strict allowance, barred him from gambling, and kept him so close to her side that other debaucheries were no longer part of his life. Though he might have strained at the leash, his mistress kept it short and him at heel for the rest of his days.

One suitor thus disposed of, Lady Jemima turned to the second. In the final analysis, the young lady decided that the viscount's appearance and his wealth outweighed whatever minor flaws he might have, and certainly he could be cured of those by a determined and authoritative wife. Moreover, she had been on the marriage market quite long enough. Younger girls were being presented at Court every season, and it was necessary to settle on a husband while she still possessed the freshness of youth, if not its first blush. She set about attracting Lord Wynstowe's attentions with all her considerable wiles. If the interest she evinced in his experiments and explorations was feigned, it was a feint of such competence that the young viscount was easily convinced of its veracity and suitably flattered. Within two weeks of Lady Jemima's having taken up residence in his mother's bedchamber, and after receiving Lord Alderwick's enthusiastic consent, Lord Wynstowe proposed marriage and was happily accepted.

The wedding was what a wedding should be. The bride's dress was a confection of Spitalfields silk satin and Honiton lace, the groom's frock coat an elegant dark gray, his brocade waistcoat a daring periwinkle to match the bride's crown of gentians. These flowers had made the journey to Marlecombe Park from the hothouses on the groom's estate in a padded basket on the lap of Mrs. Sweet in what was to be among the last duties the housekeeper would carry out on behalf of the Wynstowes of Wynstowe Manor. The new Lady Wynstowe would spend but a single week in residence before pensioning off both Mrs. Sweet and Cook. The butler would survive another six months before succumbing to his liver and saving her the trouble of showing him the door.

As for the couple about whom we care most, the two whose machinations brought about the happy union? Their story, like their lady and gentleman's, reached its climax the day of the wedding that united the Wynstowe and Alderwick names. Alice was by then exhausted. The previous two months had been busier than ever she had experienced. Readying Lady Jemima's wedding clothes and dressing her for the ceremony was work enough, but in addition she had spent weeks preparing and packing the young lady's trousseau, as well as all the new matron would need for her honeymoon voyage to the Continent, the very voyage Alice had imagined when she first was raised to the position of lady's maid.

Much to the consternation of the bride, the morning of the wedding threatened rain, though by the time the guests arrived at the church, the sun had broken through the clouds. Alice and Charlie watched the bridal procession from the back of the church with the other senior servants. In addition to her sister, Lady Jemima was escorted by a bevy of female cousins in white gowns and flower-trimmed bonnets, the two tiniest sprinkling petals from their baskets as they tripped ahead of the bride. Lord Alderwick's usual mien of boredom was absent; he looked proud and pleased, which countenance lasted until the ceremony began, at which point he resumed his typical aspect of staring out the nearest window, looking as if he wished he could be anywhere else in the world than in this place with these people.

Tears pricked Alice's eyes as she watched the ceremony, even as she smiled when the couple plighted their troth. The prospect of the new Lady Wynstowe's obeying anyone other than herself was amusing to contemplate. Once the beaming groom had escorted his lady down the aisle and out of the church, she and Charlie slipped away. The servants of Marlecombe Park had been granted a half-day in honor of the nuptials, and Alice and Charlie were due at her family home, where he would meet for the first time the couple whom he dreamed would step into the shoes left empty by the deaths of his parents, one beloved and newly passed, the other long gone and little missed.

When they walked up the path to the small farmhouse, Alice and Charlie were greeted by the faces of her sisters pressed up against the glass of the window, waving their hands in welcome. Janet pushed open the window, stuck out her head, and shouted, "Ma's made a roly-poly and a Queen of Puddings, both!"

"Two puddings?" Charlie said. "You can't possibly want two puddings. We'll tell your ma to feed one to the pigs, won't we?"

The little girls screamed and slammed the window shut.

"Not once in my memory has my mother made a second pudding," Alice said. "You must promise not to listen to a word she says, for I am sure she's lost her senses."

Charlie shook Mr. Lockey's hand solemnly, presented Mrs. Lockey with a small bag of sugared almonds, and the children with a larger bag of sherbet lemons. The handshake was returned with suitable sobriety, and the candies were received with murmurs of appreciation and squeals of delight, depending on the recipient. Mr. Lockey pressed upon Charlie a small glass of bitters—brewed, he told the young man, by Mrs. Lockey herself with herbs from the garden.

"Aids the digestion and keeps a man regular," he said,

causing Alice to groan and remove to the kitchen to help her mother with the meal.

Mrs. Lockey served as fine a dinner as Alice had ever seen on her mother's table, and Janet and Susan insisted that Charlie sit between them.

"Will you say grace, Mr. Wells?" Mrs. Lockey said.

"Only if you call me Charlie," he said.

"You mustn't say a long grace, Charlie," Janet said. "We don't like long graces, do we, Alice?"

"Hush," Alice said.

"A short grace it'll be, then," Charlie said. He bowed his head in mock piety and recited, "Double the puddings, double the pleasure. Bless this feast beyond all measure!" This elicited loud peals of laughter from the girls, chortles from the boys and Mr. Lockey, and an "Ain't you a naughty boy," from Mrs. Lockey. Alice rolled her eyes—Charlie was working hard to charm the lot of them—but she could not help but smile.

As Mr. Lockey carved the roast and passed the platter round the table, Mrs. Lockey said, "Help yourself, Charlie."

"Oh, I couldn't, ma'am," Charlie said. "Not until Lady Janet and Lady Susan have been served."

This elicited another round of giggles. He speared a generous slice and placed it on Janet's plate with a flourish, and another on Susan's. Then he passed the platter to Mrs. Lockey. On its way across the table, Pete tried to grab a slice of beef, but Charlie stopped him with an expression of mock astonishment. Pete laughed even as he laid his fork down to wait until his sister and mother had been served.

Conversation at the table was cheerful, all the more so when the two puddings were laid out and served.

Charlie deemed the puddings delicious and would not, despite the insistence of the children, name a favorite.

When last they laid down their spoons, Mr. Lockey adopted a serious expression. "What are your plans, young man?"

"Plans, sir?"

"For your future."

"Dad!" Alice said, but he silenced her with a look.

"I am settled well for the time being," Charlie said. "Lord Wynstowe is generous, and I generally manage to put aside some money each half-year. I've had to use my savings for my mother's burial, but there will be more. Someday I hope to have enough to open a shop."

"You'll not want to farm, then?"

"I wasn't born to it, sir, and I've not the experience or the know-how. But I know clothes and the like from working for Lord Wynstowe, and I believe I could make a go of it as a draper or haberdasher."

"Is London to your liking?" Mrs. Lockey asked. "Is it there you'll want to live?"

"I don't think so, ma'am. I'd rather a market town like Horsham, big enough to support a shopkeeper but not so large as to overwhelm."

Alice had not heard of Charlie's plans in such detail, but thought it no accident that he named a town not much more than an hour's distance from the village.

"Horsham!" Mrs. Lockey said. "I've a cousin there. Alice, we visited once or twice when you were a girl. It's the loveliest place, isn't it?"

"I was small, Ma. How could I remember it?"

"Isn't it the loveliest place, Charlie?" Mrs. Lockey said. "I think you'll do very well in Horsham."

"Horsham it is, then," Charlie said.

As they walked back to the Park, Alice told Charlie that the evening went off even better than she could have hoped.

"You've made of Pete a friend for life, and both Susan and Janet have set their caps for you."

"A shame I'll have to disappoint them," he said. He helped her over the stile into the meadow that had been the scene of their first private conversation. It was carpeted with bluebells and lady's-smock, and the evening air was redolent of their delicate fragrance. The sky was pinked by the setting sun, sending over the couple a warm glow. Charlie stopped and took Alice's delicate hands in both of his.

"My love," he said.

This was the moment Alice had dreamed of for months, one that she knew would be her greatest happiness.

"Dearest Charlie," she said. But her tone was not joyful. It had a quality of poignancy, of sadness. She could see her future with Charlie so clearly. They would work side by side, sharing the bliss of nights like the ones that had been the most wonderful feature of the previous two months. Eventually, they would open a draper's shop in a pretty country town, and make a cozy home above it. They would have children with his gray-blue eyes, whom they would provide with an education beyond what she and Charlie had been lucky to receive. Their children would go on not to be servants or tenants on an estate, but freeholders or merchants. She and Charlie would grow old, content in the lives they had built in their homey rooms in their pleasant village. A good life. A happy life. But not, she realized in that moment, the life she wanted.

The life she sought was bigger than that. She had aspirations that were neither domestic nor romantic. She wanted a life that had meaning beyond the walls of a home, no matter how agreeable. Satisfaction for her, she realized, could come only from service to a cause greater than herself, greater even than the man whom she held so dear.

She lifted a hand to his cheek. "I will always love you," she said gently.

But once Lady Jemima and Lord Wynstowe were away, she told her lover in a tone compassionate yet firm, she would be moving to Manchester to join the struggle for women's suffrage.

Charlie pleaded with her. He told her he would leave his employment, would follow her to Manchester, would even take up her cause as his own if that would change her mind. Alice allowed herself to imagine such a possibility: Charlie working alongside her, the two of them united in purpose, like Mr. and Mrs. Mill or Mr. and Mrs. Fawcett. But she knew that the future she was choosing was hard, and the challenges would be many. For Charlie to commit to such a life not out of principle but out of love would be a doomed enterprise, one that would inevitably lead to resentment and dissatisfaction.

The tears Alice shed that evening were as genuine as his own, but her resolution was fast. She would not marry him.

By now my reader has realized that the young heroine of these pages is none other than the good lady whose fame has spread throughout our nation and beyond. Our Miss Alice Lockey is the very one who, alongside her friend Emmeline Pankhurst, went on in 1903 to become a founding member of the Women's Social and Political Union, and one of its most uplifting leaders. Alice became a noted speaker and lecturer, traveling throughout the country and, as she had once dreamed, throughout the Continent and even across the sea to the Americas, lending her considerable oratorical skills to the cause.

It was at one of her lectures that she saw Charlie again. Over a decade had passed since their final goodbye, and

Alice had grown from a pretty girl into a strong, dignified, and handsome woman, at home on the soapbox in Hyde Park from which she exhorted the assembly to rise up and demand votes for women. So intent was she on speaking in a manner inspiring and convincing that it was a little while before she realized that the man in the derby hat holding the hand of a flaxen-haired child was none other than Charlie Wells. He winked at her, which caused her to stumble over her words. She was far too accomplished, however, to flounder more than momentarily, and resumed her passionate speech.

Afterward, Charlie waited patiently on the edge of the crowd.

"I am so glad to see you," Alice said when, finally, the others had dispersed and she was attended only by her aides and colleagues. She crouched down to the girl's eye level. "And who is this?"

"This is Phoebe," he said.

"It is very nice to meet you, Phoebe." She shook the girl's tiny paw. "You are the image of your papa. Especially around the eyes."

Alice stood up. "And you, Charlie? Are you well?"

"I am. We came to town to visit with Phoebe's cousins—didn't we, my girl? Mary told us you might be here."

"Mary! How is she?"

"She is well. Expecting again." Mary had surprised no one more than herself when she fell in love and married a fellow trade-union activist and immediately set about producing a passel of children. "This'll be her fourth."

"My goodness. And you have three of your own, do you not?" Alice said, revealing that she followed the affairs of her former lover, as he did hers.

"And another on the way." But this fourth daughter would,

alas, be taken in her second year by a pneumonia, breaking her father's heart.

"That's lovely, Charlie. You're happy? Your life is as you hoped it would be?"

What was happiness? Charlie thought. He loved his children, and his work was satisfying. His wife was intelligent and kind, and if he wished sometimes that she were more expressive in her affections, that was a small thing. He was content. That was more than most could say of the lives they led.

He lifted his daughter into his arms and kissed her on her plump cheek. "I am," he said.

They parted that day, and did not see each other but one more time. Alice continued for the rest of her days to inspire the masses and influence the powerful, though eventually she would resort to tactics beyond the power of her oratory. Always a quick learner and good with her hands, she became an expert in the art of arson and the construction of small bombs, and was responsible for no small number of the fires and postbox explosions that disrupted the workings of the nation and convinced the leaders of government that peace would not reign until suffrage was granted. As a result of her steadfast militancy, Alice was arrested no fewer than half a dozen times, culminating in her final arrest in 1910, at the ripe age of fifty-five. During the months of her incarceration in the notorious Holloway Prison, Alice and her friend Mrs. Mary Clarke, the younger sister of Emmeline, undertook a hunger strike. Alice's fortitude was impressive. She turned away all but a small cup of water each day, refusing to consume a crust or crumb voluntarily, and resisted even when a wooden gag was forced into her mouth, a tube brutally shoved down her nose, and a vile slurry of raw egg, porridge, and broth poured into her belly.

Alice's will was stronger than that of her tormentors, and eventually, weak, starved, and suffering from the brutalities of force-feeding, she was released from prison. Many desired to take her in, but it was I who was granted the honor of nursing her. I ensconced her in the best bedroom at Wynstowe Manor, and brought in the finest physicians and apothecaries. I could not bear to allow anyone else to care for her, not even my dear Lizzie, once chambermaid at Marlecombe Park, whom so long ago Miss Lockey had trained to be her replacement. I myself brewed the beef tea that was the only sustenance Alice's traumatized belly could tolerate.

From the day Alice was removed to my home, suffragettes desperate for news of their idol's health began appearing at my door and filling my drawing room with anxious conversation. My darling husband grew ever more disconcerted by the invasion of women in sensible shoes, until finally I suggested that, as neither he nor they seemed able to find a way to be useful, he might consider dusting off his calipers and measuring everyone's heads and hands. "You can lay to rest once and for all the urgent question of who have longer thumbs and more protrudent noses, the women of the National Union of Women's Suffrage Societies or those of the Women's Social and Political Union."

This my adorable Lord Wynstowe set about doing with zeal, aided in the endeavor by two "ladies in trousers" who had hitherto been tormenting him by smoking his cigars and monopolizing his billiard table.

By now, dear Reader, you must realize that your authoress is none other than Lady Jemima Wynstowe, née Alderwick, wife of Lord Wynstowe of Wynstowe Manor.

You are wondering, I know, how I, once so rigid in my notions of class and station, came to embrace my former abigail as my equal, nay, my superior in all things. The transformation of our association happened fifteen years after she left my service, when the youngest of my sons left for school. William, only seven years old, was the dearest to my heart of the three, and I found myself quite bereft when off he went. To cheer me, my sister, Grace, by then the Marchioness Lady de Grey and herself the mother of children so numerous (and poorly behaved) that I had long stopped troubling myself to count them, let alone learn their names, insisted that I accompany her and our Aunt Bennett to a lecture given by a noted suffragist, one whom Grace coyly told me I might recognize. I was acquainted with no suffragists, I told her, nor desired such association. Grace could not be dissuaded, however, and with nothing else to distract me from my loneliness and lassitude, I allowed myself to be persuaded to attend.

I am ashamed to say that it was some moments before I recognized the lady at the podium. In my defense, Alice was by then a woman of confidence and presence, not a young girl wearing a servant's mask of subservience. Though, in retrospect, I think that mask had always been ill-fitting, for Alice's worth was impossible to miss, which perhaps explains why, as a young lady, I so often tried to put her in her place. I believe I knew even then that of the two of us she was by far the more impressive person.

She spoke that day with an eloquence that astonished me, though not those who knew her and her works. I marveled at the way she held the crowd mesmerized, their near-silent absorption disturbed only by the occasional "Hear, hear!" or "Well said!" Soon enough, however, I, too, was swept up in her oratory. A woman, Alice exhorted us, could be an agent of change, capable of shaping not only her own destiny but the destiny of nations.

"Courage calls to courage everywhere, and its voice cannot be denied. It is this courage that will see us through to victory. The enfranchisement of women is the crowning glory of democracy, and it is a glory that must and will be shared by all!"

The applause and foot-stomping shook the room, mine as vigorous and ebullient as any. Gazing over her audience, the great Miss Lockey noticed me, startled for a moment, and then graced me with a wide and generous smile. From that moment on, I was her acolyte, and eventually was proud to call her my friend.

After her release from prison, Alice lay sapped of her customary vigor, desperately ill, her face gray against the fresh-bleached linen. I knelt by the side of her bed, and laid a hand on her sweating brow.

"What can I do for you, my dearest friend?" I asked. "Is it time for another injection?" Because Alice could not tolerate tincture of laudanum, the doctor had instructed me in how to inject her with morphine.

"Not yet," she said. The drug put her to sleep, and she resisted unconsciousness, as if trying to grasp whatever shards of life were left to her.

I picked up one of the silver-backed hairbrushes I had had Lizzie provide for Alice and set about trying to smooth away the tangles in her hair. "A Eugénie coiffure, this evening, ma'am?" I asked. "Or perhaps a Grecian plait?"

Ill as she was, she allowed me a smile.

"Ribbons or bows?" I continued. "Both, I think."

"You were never one for moderation," she whispered hoarsely.

"Says the woman who was force-fed near one hundred times."

"One hundred and six."

The horror of this number exhausted my capacity for contrived levity, and I dropped the brush and embraced my friend.

There was a delicate tapping at the door, and Lizzie walked in. She bent to me and whispered in my ear. I nodded and picked up Alice's hand.

"Charlie Wells is here, dear one. Would you see him admitted, or are you too tired?"

Alice, who had not yet had the strength to see anyone, now nodded her permission. I sent Lizzie to fetch Mr. Wells.

At sixty, Charlie Wells was still a fine-looking man, his hair threaded with only the smallest amount of gray. His bearing was dignified, as befits the steward of an estate as grand and prosperous as Wynstowe Manor. He had risen to this trusted position despite no specific experience because of his loyalty to Nigel and to our family, and because his judgment was unimpeachable. When he petitioned for the job, Nigel had hesitated for only a moment before acquiescing. The most important quality in a steward was honesty and trustworthiness, Nigel said. Anything else could be learned. And, of course, it did not harm his application that his features were unusually refined for a man of his station.

Under Mr. Wells's supervision, our farms and coal works produced vast sums, much of which, to my husband's tolerant bemusement, I poured into the coffers of various suffrage organizations.

Now Charlie stood in the doorway—horrified, I knew, at Alice's appearance, for she was emaciated and in a state of complete incapacitation. In a voice cracked with pain, she said his name. He came to her, sat down on the bed, and kissed her gently on the forehead. For the first time since she had arrived in my home, I saw on her face an expression of ease, and I left them to each other's embrace.

Miss Alice Lockey, once my maid, forever my friend and comrade in the struggle for women's suffrage, was laid to rest on Christmas Day, 1910, eight years before the right for which she battled so valiantly was finally granted to some of the women of the United Kingdom, and eighteen before full suffrage became the law of the land. Mrs. Emmeline Pankhurst was meant to give the eulogy at her funeral, but as her own sister had died that very day, of injuries similar to Alice's, it was I who stood on the pulpit and described the accomplishments of this most influential leader of our movement and most loyal of friends. The church was filled with women from all over the country who had made the journey to honor her.

Charlie Wells sat in his customary pew alongside his wife, their daughters, and his sister, Mary, and her family. He made no attempt to hide his tear-streaked face, but I saw in the expression of his wife no hint of condemnation, only of compassion, concern, and perhaps even pride that her husband knew the lady so well as to so grieve her loss.

When suffrage for women finally became law, this fine man, a gentleman by nature if not by birth, escorted his wife to the Wynstowe community hall to cast her first vote. It became a tradition in the Wells family to lay a posy of purple pansies on Alice's grave on each election day, a custom eventually adopted by all the voting women of the village of Wynstowe, including myself.

I bid you, dear Reader, to take inspiration from the narrative of the early life of the esteemed Miss Alice Lockey. Circumstances of birth limit the realizations of our ambitions and the nature of our commitments only if we allow them to. As Alice led a most unusual and unexpected life, and as I overcame the limits of my class and, though it pains me to admit it, my character, so, too, can you and your daughters become anything you desire. May you go forth, your aspirations limited only by your imagination.

ACKNOWLEDGMENTS

The line in Alice's speech that begins with "Courage calls to courage everywhere, and its voice cannot be denied" is taken from a famous speech delivered by Millicent Fawcett in 1913. Fawcett was a leading figure in the British women's suffrage movement and the president of the National Union of Women's Suffrage Societies (NUWSS).

Miss Sarah Bennett's analogy of marriage to an electric battery or a toboggan ride comes from an 1889 issue of the British magazine *Tit-Bits,* in which unmarried women were invited to explain why they remained single. The particularly memorable response, which I attribute to Miss Bennett, actually came from Miss Laura Bax of Wood Green, London: "Because matrimony is like an electric battery, when you once join hands you can't let go, however much it hurts; and, as when embarked on a toboggan slide, you must go to the bitter end, however much it bumps."

My dear friends and critically important readers Ann

Packer, J. Courtney Sullivan, and Andrew Sean Greer helped me at crucial moments. Ann provided endless editorial consultations, and Courtney came up with the perfect title.

Thanks to the 7 Minute crew, without whom I would not have made it through COVID and the ensuing years: Amy Barrett, Lisa Brown, Semi Chellas, Deb Copaken, Pamela Druckerman, Monique El-Faizy, Jenji Kohan, Maile Meloy, Peggy Orenstein, Jen Pahlka, Suzi Parrasch, Esta Spaulding, Lindsey Strasberg, Desi Van Til, and Johanna Weinstein.

Thank you to MacDowell and Civitella Ranieri for giving me the space and time to write.

I cannot express how grateful I am to Dr. Phyllis Weliver. Without her generosity in sharing her expertise in the Victorian era as well as the early feminist movement, this book would have been replete with embarrassing errors. Thank you to Zadie Smith for suggesting I reach out to her. Thank you to the VICTORIA discussion group of the Victoria Research Web, which spent untold hours debating terms of address for me.

Thanks to Meleena Leon and Charlotte Wilson for research assistance.

Thanks to my wonderful editor Jennifer Jackson. Her editorial guidance is always spot-on, which makes sense given that she herself is a wonderful novelist. What is even more remarkable is her patience.

Thanks to Tiara Sharma, Terry Zaroff-Evans, and Anna Carson.

Emily Mahon came up with a cover that makes me smile every time I see it. Thanks to Lisa Brown for her notes.

Thanks to the rest of the Knopf team: Jordan Rodman, Anna Noone, Emily Murphy, Anne Achenbaum, Arianna Abdul, Beth Meister, and Tyler Goodson.

Dan Kirschen waited year after year for me to find an idea that sparked my interest, always supportive, imperturbable, and generous with his time and attention.

Thanks to Adam Shulman, who keeps me both financially and emotionally stable, not always an easy task.

Thanks to my team at CAA: Brooke Ehrlich, Tiffany Ward, Leah Terushalaim, and Jiah Shin.

Gratitude and love to Zeke, Ida-Rose, Abraham, Mike, and Nadia.

Most of all I must thank Sophie Chabon, who made the ultimate literary sacrifice and gave the idea of this book to me rather than claiming it for herself.

Love to Michael Chabon, always and forever. *In our long, sweet, tempestuous tale we unfold.*

A NOTE ABOUT THE AUTHOR

Ayelet Waldman is the author of *A Really Good Day: How Microdosing Made a Mega Difference in My Mood, My Marriage, and My Life;* the novels *Love and Treasure*, *Red Hook Road*, *Love and Other Impossible Pursuits*, and *Daughter's Keeper;* the essay collection *Bad Mother: A Chronicle of Maternal Crimes, Minor Calamities, and Occasional Moments of Grace;* and the Mommy-Track Mystery series. She is the co-editor of *Fight of the Century: Writers Reflect on 100 Years of Landmark ACLU Cases,* of *Kingdom of Olives and Ash: Writers Confront the Occupation,* and of *Inside This Place, Not of It: Narratives from Women's Prisons.* She won a Peabody Award and an AFI award and was nominated for the WGA, PGA, Critics Choice, Golden Globe, and Primetime Emmy Awards for the Netflix Limited Series *Unbelievable.* She lives in Berkeley, California, with her husband, Michael Chabon.

A NOTE ON THE TYPE

This book was set in Adobe Garamond. Designed for the Adobe Corporation by Robert Slimbach, the fonts are based on types first cut by Claude Garamond (ca. 1480–1561). Garamond was a pupil of Geoffroy Tory and is believed to have followed the Venetian models, although he introduced a number of important differences, and it is to him that we owe the letter we now know as "old style." He gave to his letters a certain elegance and feeling of movement that won their creator an immediate reputation and the patronage of Francis I of France.

Typeset by Scribe,
Philadelphia, Pennsylvania

Designed by Casey Hampton